AURORA'S
BETRAYAL

THE LOST COVEN | BOOK TWO

K.A KNIGHT

AURORA'S BETRAYAL

COVEY PUBLISHING, LLC

Published by Covey Publishing, LLC

PO Box 550219, Gastonia, NC 28055-0219

Copyright © 2019 by K.A Knight

Cover Design Copyright © 2019 Covey Publishing, LLC

Book Design by Covey Publishing, www.coveypublishing.com

Copy Editing by Covey Publishing, LLC

Printed in the United States of America.

ISBN: 978-1-948185-90-5

First Printing, 2019

ALSO BY K. A KNIGHT

THE LOST COVEN

Aurora's Coven

Aurora's Betrayal

THEIR CHAMPION

The Wasteland

The Summit

Circus Save Me

1

AURORA

The bed I lay on is pure white and probably the comfiest fucking bed ever. With a groan, I sit up. The room resembles something out of a dream. Marble floor, white and gray walls. Massive white sofas.

But the best bit? Two French doors open out onto a balcony covered in every flower imaginable.

The only problem? The locked door.

Oh, and I think I might be dead.

I don't know how long I've been in this room, but I memorized the layout and how many steps it takes to walk between the bed and the door. Forty-five, if you're curious. Thirty steps from the door to the balcony.

Now, I stare at the ceiling. If this is death, it sure is boring.

What are my guys doing now? Have they moved

on? Disappeared as quickly as they appeared? Is Lane looking after Nev? Hmm. She better take care of him after they bury me.

Sighing, I run my hands along the silky bed sheets.

I miss them. Jason's sweet smile. Ben's laugh. Ezra's kiss. Alex's confidence. I even miss Mikael. I miss our nightly talks and games. The way his eyes lit up when I told him something embarrassing. The way his lips twitched when I begged him not to laugh.

I close my eyes and imagine I'm in the guys' living room.

We cuddle on the sofa watching films. Their warmth and smells surround me like the best blanket. Oh, look. There are cookies. Damn. I miss cookies. Do they have them in the afterlife?

Like, *"Oh, yes, you're dead, but this here's a cookie bag which never runs out and changes flavor at will."* I wipe the drool away.

I know I should be worried, but for once, I'm calm.

Lost in my thoughts, the door banging open makes me jump upright. The long, white, swirly dress I wear moves as I do. One shoulder slips down to reveal my pale skin. The bodice, with a tight sweetheart neckline that tucks in at the waist, gives way to a skirt that flares out down to my feet.

When I see the person framed at the doorway, I gasp and stand.

Okay, Toto, I have a feeling we're not in Kansas anymore. Yes, that's a Wizard of Oz quote, but I think it fits the current situation, so leave me alone.

2

ALEXANDER

*I*t's been two weeks of no change. Her body is alive, yet her eyes don't even twitch. I can barely feel her. I stroke the hand I hold. Mikael coughs behind me, and with one last squeeze of her hand, I turn to my brother.

Mikael woke up two days ago, confused at first. The healer didn't expect him to wake up at all, but whatever Aurora did to him allowed him to heal. The healer suggested Aurora might have sparked his magic, allowing it to recharge, and he awoke once it did.

He's still weak, and his sore throat sports a killer scar. Other than that, he's fine.

However, he's as worried as the rest of us. Running footsteps sound outside the room, and I move to stand in front of her body before Mikael sits up.

Ben runs into the room. His once longish hair is

dull and greasy, and he's lost weight, but for the first time in two weeks, something akin to emotion fills his face. He stares at me, excitement and hope lighting up his blue eyes. His chest heaves, and as I knew he would, he glances at Aurora before swallowing and looking away. He rubs his hair, not bothered by the disarray. Stains cover his shirt, and I'm pretty sure he hasn't showered in days. It's a total contrast to our usual smooth-talking lady's man. The worry is doing a number on him.

Just another thing I need to add to my list to sort out.

"I think we've found someone who can help," Ben rushes out, excitement and desperation clear in his voice.

At his words, I stand up straight and hope blossoms in my chest. I show nothing on the outside, though, not wanting them to know how much I need someone to help. I need our witch back, or I fear my family might fall apart for good.

3

AURORA

I sit cross-legged on one of the white sofas, my dress spread around me like a princess. "I'm not dead?"

The being opposite me laughs. "No, sweet Aurora."

At the reminder of the reaper, I flinch, the endearment bringing up a memory I'd rather forget.

Moments ago, I stood in disbelief at who filled the doorway, but hell, I decided to roll with the crazy. The foggy memory of me healing this being flits through my mind.

The reaper was right. He's almost too much to look at. Too formidable. The power rolls off him in waves, and I don't think he even knows.

His body looks like the gods made it, and his face is perfect. Too perfect. I debate what he could be. The list is endless, but I'm eager to hear what he has to say. To find out how I know him and why I can only remember that day.

Did I mention he only wears pants?

Yikes.

His wide thighs are encased in—I shit you not— leather pants. Not the cheap kind, either. They look hand-stitched and coat his legs like a second skin. His well-defined chest practically glows golden. My eyes run over the black patterns on his skin, unable to see them clearly. I'm sure one just moved, though.

"So, where am I?" I try to keep eye contact, but find it hard. And not because of the body that fulfills wet dreams everywhere.

No, because looking at him is like looking into an abyss: stare too hard and you might fall in and never come out. Every time I glance at him, his eyes change, and I give up trying to figure out their color.

His pants creak as he crosses a leg at the knee. "In-between, of sorts."

What the hell does that mean?

"Okay, dude, all this mystery stuff is getting boring. The last thing I remember is healing Mikael, and then I woke up inside a giant cloud. I could really use some answers. Is Mikael okay?" Tone sharp, I manage to hold eye contact as I speak.

Yay, point for me.

He sighs, then nods. Standing, he offers me his hand, his fingers lean and smooth.

I debate my options but finally heave myself up and grab it lightly.

He pulls my hand to the crook of his arm, then turns to the door to leave.

He walks slowly, probably for my benefit. We walk along marble corridors arm in hand, so to speak. The white colors continue throughout, with gold decorations every now and again. My dress sweeps behind me and twirls around our legs with every step.

We pass a gold, decorative mirror with leaves and trees carved into the wood. I can't help but notice the difference between us. Where I'm moonlight with pale skin and dark hair, he's the sun. Golden and almost too much to look at.

He leads me down a curved, ornate staircase, the golden banister curving with us.

The bottom opens into a foyer with marble—shock —flooring, and doors that lead off of it. I can't see much else, but I stretch my neck trying to. I glance back to where he waits patiently as I peruse his house.

He smiles down at me and leads the way to the front door, if that's what they could be called. Carvings cover every inch of the two large, wooden doors. I run my eyes over women and men in robes wielding swords. It looks like a battle scene. At the top of one door is a carving of the moon; the sun on the other. Before we reach them, they open smoothly.

Okay, officially starting to get creeped out.

When I get a look at where we are, though, that all disappears.

I forget everything and let go of his arm to step out onto the grass. Flowers reach toward me, their petals opening. The sun shines down, warming my skin. Trees blow in happiness, and water trickles from a stream somewhere. I lift my head to the sky and let myself breathe deeply.

Peace settles in me, calming all my worries.

The earth calls to me, and I spin with its murmurs and laugh freely. I look back toward the house—well, more of a mansion—and there on the steps stands the creature who brought me here.

He observes me with a knowing smile on his face. "Welcome home, απόγονος μου."

4

ALEXANDER

*T*he dance music pulses in time with the gyrating bodies, and I look at them with indifference. The club is a supernatural one. Shifters, witches, and more clog the dance floor. I scan them whilst sipping whiskey from the tumbler in my hand. I don't plan on getting drunk, but if there was a time I could use a drink to steady me, this would be it. The music beats get louder and the grinding increases.

"He's here," Jason offers.

With those two words, I drain my drink and place the tumbler next to the rail I lean on. I turn to the table where my brothers patiently wait.

Ben managed to shower and looks a little better. Currently, he's ripping the label from his beer bottle and not talking. I really need to corner him, but not now. Ezra sits rigid in his seat; the only one not drinking. His hair, the longest I've ever seen it, almost covers his ears and his beard is wild. Jason stands next to me, and I follow his eyes to the man Ben found.

He's wiry and doesn't look old enough to be here. His black-rimmed glasses keep falling down his crooked nose, even after he pushes them back up. He yanks on his loose-fitting shirt, pulling it away from his skinny body. With amusement, I notice what it says. 'I like big books and I can't lie' He glances around nervously as he approaches us.

"Are you Alexander?" His voice warbles with nerves.

It stretches an unpleasant smile across my face. I watch his discomfort and do nothing to lessen it. "Indeed."

I walk over to the table where I sit next to Ezra and gesture for the man to follow. Jason waits until he slides into the booth. He sits on the edge of the seat, still not making eye contact with us. Only then does Jason sit, caging him in.

From his gulp, he knows it.

"So, you're the guy everyone goes to when they need knowledge?" I ask casually.

He meets my eyes for a second before they flit away again.

I frown.

"I erm—I," he stutters out.

Ezra leans forward, every word laced with anger as he growls, "Spit it out, kid."

The poor kid looks like ready to piss his pants, but as amusing as that would be, we need to know what he does.

I put my hand on Ezra's shoulder. He shakes it off but leans back. His fists clench. I frown at him but switch my attention to the person we came here to meet.

"We need information. This information may not be passed on to anyone else. If you tell anyone that you spoke to us and what about…" I trail off, and he looks at Ezra in fear.

The poor kid has a right to be scared. The way Ezra looks right now would terrify anyone. My lips quirk. Well, maybe not everyone. Our Aurora would probably smile sweetly at him and tease him.

I come back to the moment when he mutters a reply.

"I didn't hear that." I cross one leg over the other and wait.

"Okay," he whispers.

I clap and he jumps. "Brilliant. Now that that's out of the way, what do you know about souls?"

I lean forward, eager to find out everything.

"Fascinating." The kid keeps saying that over and over again.

He stands next to Aurora, examining her. As soon as we hesitantly described why we needed to know about souls, he came out of his nervous shell, fully in his element. And, apparently, he needed to see her in person, so we brought him back to the house.

When the kid said 'fascinating' for the tenth time, I kicked Ezra out of the room before he punched the guy. I now lean against the wall, watching him study my kitten, my anger at breaking point.

"Well?" I growl.

He turns to me and pushes his glasses up his nose. "I don't have a clue."

I step away from the wall, my power unfurling like a beast inside me.

"But," he hurries to carry on, "this is an anomaly. She should be dead. No one can exist without their full soul. However, there might be something." He rubs his glasses as he glances away with a distant, thoughtful expression.

When he snaps his fingers, and I jump.

"Yes, I think there might be something in the books!" His eyes widen with excitement.

"What books and how long will it take?" I ask, looking back at my kitten.

"I don't know."

I growl and step closer.

He holds up his hands and squeaks a response. "I

don't! It depends how deep in the books and if it's in English…"

I nod, clenching my fist with the need to destroy something, and grit out, "Go."

He runs from the room like the hounds of hell are on his tail.

I let my anger deflate with one look at her. A whimper comes from the door, and I open it to find Nev with his tail between his legs. As I step aside, he sprints to her bed and sits at the bottom of it, his head on her lap.

I rub his head. "I know how you feel buddy."

Poor dog was inconsolable when he first saw her. He only stopped crying when he laid next to her, and he hasn't left her side since. When the kid approached, he didn't like the stranger being near her, so we took him outside. He'll only listen to Ezra, so he went with him, just another excuse to get him out of the room.

With a sigh, I sit next to her. "I'm working on it, kitten. I'll get you back. I promise. Don't give up on us, okay?"

I lean forward and kiss her forehead gently.

Regret pulls at me for not kissing her properly that night I was with her and Ezra. She had looked so beautiful stretched out beneath me, her eyes dilated with lust, her shirt ridden up to expose her creamy flesh. I had stroked it and marveled at its softness.

I knew then and there that if I kissed her, I wouldn't have stopped until she was moaning beneath me.

Had I known that might be my only chance, I wouldn't have back off. When we have her back, I won't hesitate again.

5

AURORA

I walk along a stone path, with flowers of every color on each side. The man whose name I still don't know walks next to me, silently letting me enjoy this. It feels like a fairy-tale here, too perfect to be true. I plan on enjoying it while it lasts, but I can't wait to return home, even if it's raining.

He stops and bends down, tilting my head, and I watch him curiously. He plucks a flower and silently shows it to me.

The outer petals are violet, but toward the middle, they turn black. It's beautiful. I touch the petals and feel their silkiness between my fingers.

He reaches out and adds it to my hair, making me smile.

We turn in unison and carry on our walk.

He leads me to a fountain. It's huge, spanning the

clearing it sits in; so large I could probably swim in its water. A statue of a beautiful woman stands in the middle. Her long hair wraps around her waist and robe, and she holds two torches in her hands.

Unable to help myself, I step closer.

"She's beautiful." Awe softens my voice as I turn to the being.

He faces the statue, sadness carved into his face. "That she was."

His voice holds a melody to itself that brings tears to my eyes. They well and fall down my face slowly at his pain and heartbreak. It hits my heart as if the pain is my own.

He turns to me in surprise, and seeing my tears, he approaches me. He cups my face and wipes them away. His face closes down, the pain cutting off as quickly as it started, leaving me gasping from the onslaught.

"I'm sorry, Aurora. I'm not used to being around people anymore." Soft regret fills his voice, and I simply nod.

He steps away and gives me a minute to compose myself.

I gently sit on the rim of the fountain and run my hands through the water. The water is cool, and I have the insane urge to jump in, to disrupt the perfect in this place. Out of the corner of my eye, I see him sit next to me.

"So, what's your name? I don't think I can keep

calling you 'being' or 'creature' in my head," I joke, needing to break the silence.

As he laughs, the world lights up and laughs with him. A smile comes to my lips without thought, and happiness blossoms in my chest.

"Sorry, απόγονος μου. I am rusty at this. My name is Perses." He toned his voice down, and I'm grateful. All the emotions were giving me whiplash.

"Like the god?" Hey, I'm not a complete idiot.

He smiles at me and it's like the sun shining down. I swallow hard and try to control my reaction to his emotions.

"Yes, απόγονος μου." He watches me. His eyes have settled into one color each, one blue and the other green. Much better than their ever-changing state, which gave me a headache.

"Makes sense." I look back at the water, loving the feel of it running through my fingers.

"You believe me? And you're not running?" Disbelief fills his voice, and a small smile graces my lips.

"Yes." I keep my reply short and watch the sun's rays play on the water.

"Just like that?"

When I look at him, he catches my hand. "Yes, just like that. It's obvious you're not human, and I've never met a supernatural like you. Granted, I haven't met many, but I've read about a lot. That, and I'm stuck in some in-between place. And, well, I decided I might as well start believing in the impossible."

He smiles at me, flashing perfect straight white teeth. "Truly you are απόγονος μου."

I tilt my head again. "What does that mean?"

"It is Greek. It roughly translates to 'my descendant'." He speaks slowly, fearing my reaction.

I breathe in and digest his words. I'm no fool. I know there's a reason I'm here, a reason why I can see this man. "Am I? Is that who I am?" My voice mirrors my mixed emotions.

"Yes, λουλούδι της νύχτας μου." His voice softens again.

As birds from a nearby tree take flight, I look up. "Why am I here, Perses?" I stumble over his name, foreign to my tongue.

He doesn't comment or correct me. "Did you get the book I left for you?"

I snap my head to him. "That was you?"

"Yes. It's important you know our history." He reaches for my hand again and squeezes it.

"Okay. So why am I here?" I ask again, getting a little impatient.

"You are here so I can help you," he replies unwaveringly.

I can't hide my frustration. "Help me with *what*?"

"That's a long conversation, my dear Aurora. I know you're impatient, but you must understand I've been waiting a long time for you. I must do this right." With that bomb, he stands and offers me his hand. He waits, not moving or saying anything else.

This right now is a choice. I could go back to my life and my men. Maybe I would be happy and forget all of this. But would I always wonder, what if? I'm sick of being in the dark.

So, I grab the god's hand and allow him to lead me back to the mansion and hopefully some answers.

6

AURORA

"Why aren't I hungry?" My question echoes in the massive living room.

When we entered the mansion again, he simply walked to one of the closed doors in the foyer and opened it to reveal a cozy living room.

Unlike the rest of the house, this looks like somewhere I can relax.

Velvet sofas face each other and in the corner of the room is a bar, like a real bar with, yes, a marble countertop. Large, floor-to-ceiling windows let the sun stream in, giving everything a dreamy quality. A huge, golden fireplace sits in the center of the wall near the sofa, and I imagine curling up there with a book. He folds himself into one sofa so I perch on the other and ask all the questions which are crammed into my head.

"Your body isn't really here; therefore, you don't

have need for natural bodily functions. You will feel ghost hunger pangs, so you can eat if you want. That will satisfy them; however, it won't nourish your body." He answers question after question but avoids any serious talk.

I look toward the fire burning next to me and think of my guys. Where are they? Are they worried about me now that they have Mikael back?

Now that their family's whole, the thought that they don't need—no, don't *want*—me anymore sends a shooting pain into my heart. I rub it absentmindedly and stare at the flickering flames.

"Come." With that, he rises.

When I simply watch his retreating form without following, he stops at the door and turns back to me.

Really? Why can't we stay in one spot? I mean, give a girl a break. I did nearly die and transport to wherever the hell I am now. Bloody hell, I could use a nap right about now. Wait, do I even need to sleep?

"It's time to show you something," he says.

With that, I jump up and follow him, my worries and fears left behind in the flames.

7

BENJAMIN

I watch as the scrawny kid searches through book after book, muttering to himself.

Rubbing my tired eyes, I lean my head back. I should probably learn his name, but honestly, I don't care. If he can save Aurora, I might make the effort. Until then…

I keep thinking about that night, the one where Aurora promised me she'd save Mikael. Maybe if I didn't ask her to, maybe if she didn't promise, she might still be here.

My chest tightens, my emotions all over the place. I see the same in my brother's eyes, and that hurts more. Doubts run through my mind.

The kid suddenly shouts something, and I leap up. "What? Did you find a way to help her?"

He glances up with a guilty look and smiles

sheepishly. "No, sorry. I found my other pair of glasses I lost in a book years ago."

With a growl, I step toward him, ready to smack some sense in him.

A hand lands on my shoulder, and I tense, then breathe through my nose and let it out slowly.

"Why don't you take a walk, brother? Or better yet, a shower? You stink." Despite the words, caring fills Jason's soft voice.

I use that as the excuse as to why I don't slap him. With one last growl at the kid, I stomp out of the library and down the hallway with no destination in mind.

When I stop in front of a doorway and realize where I stand, I snort. Of course.

I gently open the door even though that won't make a difference. Stepping into the darkened room, the moonlight streams through a window, its curtains billowing in the wind. I glance at the figure, so still and perfect in her bed.

Mikael is nowhere in sight, and for that, I'm grateful.

No one needs to see me in this state. I'm not good company to be around, but it's not like she'll mind. I stop when I stand beside her, and with a pained noise, I drop to my knees next to the bed.

"Please come back," I whisper brokenly.

Nev lifts his head and crawls toward me. When I

ignore him, he nudges my hand. I gently palm his head and he stays there with me.

"I was right. You're sunshine. Without you right now, it's like being trapped in darkness." I stroke Nev's head and watch over my princess.

The night she kissed me burns in my head, and I wish it had been under different circumstances. It was the day in the car when we were singing. She was so beautiful. The usual guards were nowhere to be seen. Her eyes were open and free, her smile full of joy.

Looking at her, I knew then and there she would be my downfall. With one word, this little witch could break me, yet she comforted me and held me when I needed someone. She saw my pain and didn't run because it mirrored hers.

Now, as I look at her, my determination returns. I won't lose her, and when I get her back, I'm holding on to her as tight as I can.

8

AURORA

*L*eaning back, I rub my head in exhaustion. I yawn and stretch my tired muscles from being cramped over the book in front of me. My eyes squint from reading too long, and I decide to take a break.

When Perses led me from the room, he took me to a library. He sat me down and deposited a book in front of me with the directive to learn. Then he disappeared. That was hours ago, and I'm still only halfway through. It's not a book but more like a never-ending history lesson.

I know why it's important, but my brain protests all the knowledge being shoved in it. From the birth of the Titans to the wars, it tells the story of how we came to be. My mother told me some of it, but not all. I haven't even gotten to the birth of the witches yet.

With a sigh, I stand and walk to the window.

The moon is huge, so close I can almost touch it. I stare at its beauty. I rub the condensation on the window pane. I miss my guys. That's all there is to it.

I turn away from my depressing thoughts and look to the room. The library stretches as far as I can see with floor to ceiling, mahogany bookcases and a table. Sofas and chairs dot throughout.

I wander around the bookcases, running my fingers lovingly over book spines. So much knowledge held between these pages. When I spot a painting on the wall, I stop and cock my head before moving closer to examine it.

It's an exact, spitting image of Perses, only he's smiling, love evident on his face. Next to him stands a woman who looks familiar. With her head thrown back, she appears to be laughing, her cheeks flushed rose. They appear happy. I study her closer and recognize her as the woman from the fountain.

I peer down at the inscription on the bottom left: Perses and Hekate.

Hekate. I frown as I search my memory for the name. Wasn't that the name of one of the ten council seats? I rush back to the tome I was reading and skim through, searching for her name.

When I find it, I gasp. "She's his daughter."

"Was."

Jumping, I look at Perses who leans against the doorway.

"Was?" I ask.

He nods and steps into the room, bringing his power with him. "Was," he confirms and stops at the painting. His fingers gently hover above her face.

I step up next to him and study his profile. "What happened?"

"She was killed." His face tenses, becoming like the statue of her outside.

Losing a child? No one should go through that. It's obvious he loved her greatly.

I grab his hand and squeeze. "I am so sorry."

He glances down at me, surprised like he just remembered I'm here. "You remind me of her so much, Aurora." His voice cracks over the words.

"I do?" My astonishment is clear. How can I remind him of the goddess?

He nods. "She was brave. One of the bravest. And her beauty was untold. But for me, it was her laughter. No matter how the darkness of this world tried to taint her, she still had this knowing smile on her face." He looks back at the painting. "So do you."

I examine the woman. A black dog lays at her feet. I tilt my head. His bright blue eyes look far too intellectual for a dog. In fact, it's like he's looking right at me.

"Have you finished the book?" Perses asks gently.

I shake my head and walk back over to it, folding myself back into my chair.

He grabs a book at random, sits in the chair opposite me, and without a word, opens it.

I open mine again with renewed determination. I cannot blemish the memory of his daughter with my lack of knowledge.

"So, let me get this straight." I pace as I talk, trying to make sense of everything I learned. "There are ten council seats, and each is descended from a god or goddess. Hekate was the first to bless a being who saved her life, and that's how the first witch came to be? Other gods and goddesses marveled at her creation and traveled to the human world to bless their own. Thus, the witches were born. The strongest of each house became its leader and automatically gained the chair on the council, which was created to rule our people and help navigate this world."

I stop for a breath and face Perses.

He sits watching me with a proud smile on his face. "What else?"

"We worshiped those who gave us these powers. But over the years, the legacies and truth of our existence washed away until we thought we were born with this power. We grew entitled and the witches' power started to dwindle with our respect for those who created us." I glance at him, and he nods for me to continue. "Now, only four houses remain, and they do so because they have distorted and blackened their powers."

"They are corrupt," he interrupts.

I nod. "Hekate, Selene, Astraea, Circe, Morpheus, and Gaia are all houses that have been forsaken. Hekate was the last to die out. Now, there is only Athena, Themis, Asclepius, and Krastos. The gods have forgotten about them; therefore, their houses and powers still remain within them." I glance at him before continuing. "Now we follow these houses who rule over the witches, but our power is dying, and new witches are being born with less and less power."

I turn to him, finished with my summary.

He smiles at me. "Correct."

"Where do I come into this?" I ask the question I still don't understand.

"You, my Aurora, are pure. You will save them all... you and your men."

I fall back a step. "What?"

He stands and stops before me. "I told you I have waited a long time for you. Each time a descendant of my daughter was born, I approached her."

"My mother," I gasp.

He nods. "To see if they are the one. Your mother was close, but she wasn't strong enough. When I saw you, Aurora, I knew you were the one. That day in the field, when you saved me, I knew you would be the one my daughter spoke of. You would save us all." His voice is gentle, unaware of the bomb he dropped on me.

"Us? You as well?" I ask, trying to work through his declaration.

"When the witches stopped praying to us, so did the other supernaturals. That weakened us and now we're barely more than ghosts," he says.

"Why can't I remember that day I saw you? Sometimes I can, but then it's like trying to grasp air."

He leans forward and drops his palm against my forehead. "I took it away from you because you weren't ready. But now you are."

With that, pain stabs into my brain, and I scream, and only his hand prevents me from falling. It's like I'm locked in my own body as my mind is flayed.

Eventually, it stops, and I fall to my knees as my mind is thrown back to that day.

I walk through a field, the long grass tickling my bare legs. I glance down at the flowing white dress that swirls around me with every step I take. The bright sun warms my skin as I slowly make my way across the field. The soft ground beneath my bare feet welcomes me. I allow my fingers to trail through the grass and plants, and they sigh with happiness.

When I spot a hunched over figure, I try to stop, but my feet keep walking against my orders until I halt before the creature.

He looks up at me, and I gasp. His face is too perfect to look at, like staring at the sun for too long. I focus on one feature at a time, trying to get my poor, young mind to focus. His lips are red, like he's been sucking on a strawberry. I follow the curve of his mouth up to a straight nose. His skin, golden and flawless, holds an unnatural glow to it.

But it's his eyes I find myself staring at. Surrounded by long, black lashes, his eyes change color. As I watch in fascination, they shift from emerald green to lighting silver. It almost makes me nauseous, so I look away.

His bare chest shows off the expanse of his glowing skin. Black symbols mar his skin, marking him as other. Leather pants encase his long, thick legs, and his feet are as bare as mine.

"με βοηθήστε, απόγονος μου." His voice flows out to surround me, and as he speaks, I hear swords clashing together and men chanting.

It's too much. My mind blackens from the obvious power coming from the man, the god before me. I gasp through it and when I come to, I'm on my knees before him.

"Πως?" The foreign words flow out of my mouth in response.

I gaze up to find him smiling down at me. He tones down his power and glow so I can look at him without squinting.

"Will you save me?" he asks again, this time in English.

I nod automatically. I would."Yes."

My knees shake, and my power rises in me - called by his. I try to push it down like mum showed me, but it won't have it. When I next look up at him, I know my eyes glow violet.

He kneels down in front of me.

"Be you." He caresses my cheek, and I lean into his warmth, feeling starved like I've been caught in the desert. "One day, you will have a choice to make."

Curious now, I stare in his eyes. "What kind of choice?"

"Between saving yourself and saving those you care about."

I cock my head. "Like my mum?" Confused, I nibble on my bottom lip.

"No, my little flower. They who need you. For now, all I need is your trust." He waits patiently for my answer, allowing me to choose.

The earth trembles beneath me, eager for my answer. The winds brush me hesitantly, and the sun falters in its shining as if nervous.

I look back at his brilliance and nod. "I trust you."

And I do. Something in me recognizes him and a feeling of trust and importance rips through my little body. I know, whoever this creature is, he's important, and this decision will impact more than just myself.

This is bigger than me.

"Close your eyes."

I immediately do, trusting this god. His lips touch my forehead in a gentle whisper of a kiss.

"Trust me, απόγονος μου." His whispered words offer comfort and determination.

I nod once again, and I feel him move away.

A whistle sounds through the air, then pain hits me. My eyes pop open, and I stare down at the knife protruding from my stomach. Blood seeps around it, staining my once white dress. I watch in fascination as the carvings and runes light up on the blade's handle as my blood touches it.

I look back up at the god.

"I am sorry, απόγονος μου. It was the only way. The pain will fade." His words offer me the determination I need.

I slowly nod, then look back at the knife, which now glows almost as bright as him. My body weakens and sways like the grass I sit in. The field quiets, no more wind, no more animals.

I don't cry as I fall. He's there to catch me like I knew he would. He lays me gently on the floor. I stare at the sky, and the sun weeps for me and the earth welcomes me home.

My blood pumps around the blade, and I stare at the sky as I die, feeling at peace.

If this is what it takes, so be it.

My body cools and my eyes flutter. I try to keep them open to catch a last glimpse of the sky, but it's useless.

Everything fades to darkness, and I'm reborn; no longer the little witch, but now a descendant of the gods. The chosen. The blood pumping through my veins holds power and purpose.

When my eyes snap open and lock with the god kneels next to me, I see mine reflected in his. Swirling with violet and black.

I stumble away from Perses, ripping myself out of the memory. I cry out in pain and my breath heaves out of me. "You killed me!"

Silence meets my accusation, and I stare up at the god before me.

"No, my Aurora, απόγονος μου. I saved you. I brought your power to awakening. Only death and suffering will awaken a reaper." His voice is sure and without inflection.

"So, I'm dead?" I ask.

Fear laces my words with a quiet acceptance for whatever this god did to me.

"No, my Aurora, you are alive more than any supernatural before you. You are truly a descendant of the gods, and the power of all of us runs in your blood."

9

JASON

*B*en still sits by Aurora's bed, and I guide Mikael back to bed after finding him in the library watching over Sheldon, the kid Ben found to help us. It seems I'm the only one who bothered to learn his name. Not only his name, but where he lives, his family, and everything else I need to destroy him if he betrays us.

I adjust Mikael's pillows and ignore his grumbling as he steals glances at Ben to see if's he's asleep.

"Hush, let him rest," I admonish.

Mikael glances at him and then at Aurora, and his face softens.

I tilt my head; seems she managed to thaw our Mikael.

"Let me know when we find anything," he whispers.

I nod, and with one last look at my family, I gently close the door.

We decided to stay here at the healers in case moving her had an adverse effect, and at least we have a healer on hand, although I have no clue where the healer is right now. My mind turns to Ezra, I know he is down in the healer's gym. I'm not sure why the healer has a gym, but it's pretty state of the art even after Ezra got a hold of it.

Ever since we took up residence, Ezra's been spending his time down there when not checking on Aurora. Alex sparred with him for a little but left him to it when it became clear it wasn't helping.

Knowing Ezra hasn't eaten all day, I head to the kitchen.

I might not be able to smile and get him to do anything like Aurora, I think to myself and laugh as I make sandwiches for everyone. *Like the time she did his makeup. That smile, so sweet and full of mischief, could make any of us say yes. But at least I can make him eat.*

I make a couple of extras sandwiches for my brothers and even one for Sheldon. Like my mother used to tell me, keep your enemies close. I might be nice, but only because it serves my purpose right now. My own panic and desperation hide under a carefully veiled smile.

Every step down to the gym holds determination to keep this family alive and well for when Aurora comes back. I have to believe she will; she's too stubborn not to.

I hear Ezra's music blaring from the top of the stairs, and heavy metal pulses through every step I take. I head down, treading carefully.

When I push the door out, I allow myself to take a look at how he's doing.

Sweat covers him, his face red either from anger or his workout. His chest heaves as he pounds into the bag. I head over to the music and turn it down. He turns with a snarl, ready to rip the shit out of someone.

When he spots me, he falters for a second.

I smile in victory.

"Fuck off," he snarls and turns to continue punching the bag.

I head over and stand there waiting for him to stop.

He does so with a growl, anger and fear clear on his face. "What?"

"You need to eat." I make my voice soft but steel coats every word.

He doesn't answer and turns back to the bag.

"If you don't eat, you're no good to anyone," I chastise.

His chest heaves a reply.

"If you don't eat, you'll lose your strength. What if you need to protect Aurora or Mikael and you can't?" I ask softly, hoping to soften the blow.

He leans his head against the bag and nods.

Progress.

I hold the plate out to him, waiting.

He turns, and without looking at me, takes the plate and stomps over to his stuff. Grabbing his towel and top, he storms off upstairs.

One down. I head back upstairs and grab another sandwich, this one for our fearless leader.

He might think he's fooling everyone, but the tightness around his eyes and mouth scream his emotions more than anything. Alex's usually cool mask is starting to slip, and we can't afford that if we're to get Aurora back.

I walk to the library where I know he's watching Sheldon. None of us are willing to leave him alone. The kid in question bends over two old looking books, muttering to himself.

"Sheldon, there's some food on the kitchen counter for you," I say with a fake smile.

He glances up, but it takes him a few seconds to register what I said. When he does, he jumps to his feet and races out of the room, only stopping to thank me.

I walk slowly to Alex where he stands staring out the window.

"Here." I push the plate at him.

He blinks and looks down at it before frowning at me. "I'm fine. Give it to Ezra. He needs to eat."

Even his voice sounds tired.

I smile smugly. "Already done." I push the plate.

He turns back to the window, his tone curt. "Then give it to Jason."

"He's asleep. And before you say, Mikael has eaten, and I told Sheldon his food's in the kitchen."

Confused, he stares at me; a testament to how shaken he is by everything.

I soften my voice and try again. "The kid is eating right now."

He glances over his shoulder, obviously not hearing Sheldon's and my conversation earlier.

"Oh." That's all he says.

I put the plate down on the side table next to him. "We need you, they need you… she needs you. So eat." Mothering him won't work, so I tell him the truth.

Not waiting for his response, I turn and head out.

I stop at the door when he clears his throat. "Thanks, brother."

I nod and head toward Aurora's room. It's my turn to spend some time with her and Ben needs to eat. I'll keep this family together even if it kills me.

For her; always for her.

"No night sky can be complete with only the moon; it needs stars. Just like you are not complete, Aurora. You need your men." With that statement, Perses spins and leaves me confused in the room I started the day off in.

Brilliant, silly gods and their riddles. He can't say, 'Oh, by the way, Aurora, this is what needs to be done and while we're at it, here's a cheat sheet.'

Damn, what I wouldn't do for some cookies right now.

A creature pops into existence right in front of me.

With a high-pitched scream, I run and jump on the bed. I'm woman enough to admit the scream was indeed screechy in quality. Mother fucker scared me, though.

It looks like one of the goblins from Harry Potter.

Large pointy ears, small pinched face. Oh, and it's only as big as my legs. I tilt my head and it copies. I tilt my head the other way and it copies.

I'm pretty sure Perses wouldn't let random evil creatures pop into his house.

Still standing on the bed, I part my legs in a defensive stance and prop my hands on my hips. "What do you want, gremlin?"

"You're gremlin." Its voice is high and annoying.

"No, you," I taunt.

Okay, so I'm standing on a bed in a god's house arguing with a gremlin. When the hell did my life get so weird?

"You," it says and matches my stance.

I throw my hands in the air and fall backward so I'm spread out on the bed.

Something wet swipes my forehead. I jump up again and point at the creature where it stands in the same spot. It looks innocent, but it's hard to tell.

My eyes narrow. "Did. You. Just. Lick. Me?"

"Did you just lick me?" it mocks.

Fuck this, I'm going to kick some gremlin ass. I jump off the bed and go to do… what, I don't know. I approach it, and when I go to kick the little fucker, he vanishes, and I end up sprawled on the floor.

"Slimy bastard," I mutter.

His head pops over mine upside down. "You going kick me!" it screeches, making me cover my ears.

"Dude, tone it down, and you so deserved it," I moan, sitting up as it paces in front of me.

"Ignorant witch. I lick to taste strength of magic as compliment and greeting. I act polite and it goes to kick me!" it rants.

At the ignorant witch comment, I shout, "Hey!"

It ignores me. The more it rants, the bigger it puffs up, like, well, a puffer fish. Its little body continues to grow. Shit.

"Hey, erm, little gremlin," I coo.

"No gremlin!" it screams and gets even bigger.

"Okay, not gremlin. We got off on the wrong foot." I keep my voice soft. "Where I'm from, you don't lick someone to say hi, so sorry. I freaked."

It stops ranting and stands in front of me, somewhere around my height now. It narrows its beady eyes. "Yous sorry?"

"Yes." I nod.

It stares at me before nodding. Then, like letting the air out of a balloon, it shrinks back to its normal size.

I slump, sitting crossed legged on the floor in front of the creature. "I'm Aurora."

I hold out my hand. Might as well be nice; don't want it going hulk smash again.

It looks at my hand, then leans forward and licks it again. "Bob."

I pull my hand back and try not to wipe it on my

dress. Holding in my laugh, my voice comes out tight. "Bob?"

"Yes, Bob." It nods.

"Bob?" I repeat. Come on.

It narrows its eyes again.

I hold my hands up in defeat. "Sorry, thought you would have a more... mystical name."

It props its hands on its hips. "My names is Borbus Ornetials Bookus," it says proudly.

"So, Bob," I conclude.

"Silly witch," he chastises.

"Hey," I warn.

"Sorryss sorrys." He doesn't look it.

With a huff, I watch him as he watches me.

When he sits crossed legged in front of me, I ask, "So, Bob, not to be rude but what do you want?"

"Master said I to be your, how you say it? Friend." He nods, happy to find the word.

"Friend," I repeat slowly.

"Yess."

Okay, sure. "Master?"

"Perses, silly witch."

"Sure, sure." I nod like this all makes sense.

"If witch needs anything, I help."

Oh, I can get on board with that. I sit up excitedly. "Do you have cookies?"

It nods and jumps up. "Follow me, silly witch."

With a happy squeal, I jump up and follow the

gremlin on the search of cookies. Never thought I'd say that.

"What. Is. That?" I gawk in horror.

"Cookie, silly witch." Bob holds the object out to me.

"That is *not* a cookie." I sulk, dejected.

"Oh." It looks at the brown lump. "My bad."

Throwing the lump behind him, he looks back at me.

It's going to be a long night.

Four hours later, I'm starfishing on the giant cloud bed when the tell-tale pop echoes around the room, announcing Bob's return. I groan.

Since I asked for cookies, he's been appearing at random times with objects.

He holds up his latest find for my approval, saying only one word: "Cookies."

I stopped describing what cookies were hours ago and now I just say yes or no. It's a good thing my body isn't actually here, and I don't need to sleep.

I look over and there he is, an object cupped in his

hands held toward me like a prize, expectation on his face.

"Cookies," he announces.

I sigh.

He opens his hands to reveal a bird. I shit you not. A live bird.

"No," I groan.

Without another word, he pops out again, and I lay back, throwing my arm across my face.

Long night indeed.

11

AURORA

I lounge in the bath, soaking in happiness.

While wandering around the hallway, I found this bathroom. It's the size of my whole living room and the large, copper, claw-foot tub in the middle called my name. It's been an hour since Bob last appeared, and I figured I was safe.

My eyes are closed when the pop sound echoes around the room. Tell me he did not just—

I screech and cover my bare breasts. "Bob!"

He stands next to the copper bath with his hands outstretched toward me. He cocks his head. "What?"

"I'm naked! Get out!" I shout.

"Silly witch, I seen naked before. Here." He drops something in the bath, and I scream when it moves.

Thrashing to escape, I fall out of the tub and land on the floor, a soapy, naked mess.

"Cookie," he announces happily.

I moan at the word. "No!"

I look up in time to see him turn, grumbling to himself as he leaves through the door.

"Bloody gremlin," I mutter.

Drying off, I dress and head downstairs in search of Perses.

I find him in the living room reading, so I wearily plop onto the couch next to him. "Mornin'."

"Morning." He places the book face down and turns to me with a smile. At least he's not one of those sick people who folds the corner of the page over. I shiver in horror.

I lean back and stare at the ceiling. "So, what are we learning today, master Jedi?"

"I would make a good Yoda."

Shocked, I stare at the laughing god. "You've seen Star Wars?"

"I'm a god, Aurora; not a hermit."

I feel silly and mutter to myself.

The pop sounds again, and I groan loudly.

"Cookie!"

Shaking my head, I turn to Bob. He holds a smaller goblin in his hands.

"No!" I say in disbelief.

He drops the goblin, who walks around muttering about stupid people.

"Erm, Aurora?" Perses hedges.

Cautiously, I turn to him. "Yes?"

"What's Bob doing?"

"I asked for cookies, and he clearly doesn't know what they are, so we're playing a lovely game where he pops in unannounced all the time, even when I'm bathing." Sarcasm laces my words.

Perses tries to contain his laughter. "You want cookies?"

I nod in defeat.

He does something with his hands, and two seconds later, a plate of what looks like double-chocolate cookies appears.

"Now *that* you have to teach me!" I yank the plate from him and start on my first one, moaning at the heavenly taste.

I glance at Bob who looks desolate. Shit. I sigh, then hold out a cookie to him.

His eyes light up, but he grabs it hesitantly, watching as I take a bite of mine. He copies and smiles at me. He devours it in seconds and stares at the crumbs left behind in sadness.

"Can I have one?" Perses asks.

When I nod, he grabs two, giving one to Bob.

If only the boys could see me now, sharing cookies.

I sit and watch as the cookies dwindle. My life has become so weird. Sharing cookies with a god and a gremlin in a god's house in the in-between.

Oh, and did I mention a god killed me? Weird.

49

12

ALEXANDER

I hold in a moan as Aurora's phone rings again. The little human has been ringing her nonstop since we picked up Nev, informing her Aurora asked us to.

I lean over and swipe to answer the call, my voice calm and collected. "Yes?"

"You fucking prick. I've been ringing for two days with no answer!" the human screams down the line.

I hold the phone away from my ear and let her rant. She's such an angry human, but I can understand. When I can't hear her scream anymore, I put the phone back to my ear. She's panting.

"Lane, I apologize. We were out looking for ways to help her," I say softly.

We told Lane that Aurora was in an accident on a trip with us and is in a coma in a private hospital. It was a hard sell, but when we sent her a video, she broke down in sobs and demanded to be told where Aurora was so she could come. We ignored her request and told her we'd keep her updated on Aurora's condition every day.

It was the only way we could keep her from hunting us down.

When I called Tom, the grouchy bear and Aurora's boss, I told him the truth. Fair enough to say they are both pissed.

"How is she?" Lane's voice breaks and my coolness falters. This little human truly does love Aurora, and I remember how much Aurora cares for her.

"The same," I allow, despair coloring my words.

"Please tell me where you are. I need to see her," she begs.

She sniffles, and I stop myself from giving in, instead rattling off the excuses. "It wouldn't make a difference, Lane. Please, she would hate for you to see her like this. Plus, we need you to keep an eye on her house and Tom."

"She's my family," Lane whispers, making me swallow hard.

"I know. I promise I'll call if anything changes." I take a breath. "I'll make sure she comes back to you."

With that, I end the call. It rings again right away, but this time, I don't answer.

I grab Aurora's hand again.

"You shouldn't lie to the human," a voice says from the adjoining bed, stronger than it was last week.

I look over at Mikael. When he woke, we asked him if he would like to be moved. He point blank refused and hasn't left Aurora's side. Seems our little witch thawed the heart of our cool brother.

"What else would I say to her?" I lean back, keeping hold of Aurora's hand.

"The truth." Propped up against the single bed's headboard, he swallows hard, his voice already sore from talking. He's gained some weight back, and he's not as pale anymore. It's good to see.

"That's not mine to tell. That's up to Aurora."

He nods and gazes at her, his expression softening. "She's special."

When his voice cracks, I lean over to pass him a glass of water.

He nods his thanks, and I look down at the little witch, my lips twitching. "That she is."

We caught Mikael up on what happened while he was gone, and he told us everything, too. Seems our Aurora kept him company.

"I don't think she had a good life," he mutters, his voice stronger after his drink.

I turn back to him and tilt my head in question, genuinely curious. She'd been tight-lipped about her past. "Why do you say that?"

"She told me she didn't have any family, anymore.

She didn't celebrate Christmas and never had a birthday…" He trails off, and a stab of jealousy hits me.

She told him all this?

He looks at me and smiles. "No need to be jealous, brother. I think the only reason she told me was because she thought I wasn't real."

Am I that easy to read? It does make me feel better, though. "She flinched the first time I touched her, and when we came at her too fast, she moved away without even realizing it. I heard her scream in her sleep a couple of times as well."

He nods. "They all seem to like her."

I snort at his understatement. "I think they all like her more than they're willing to admit." I keep my voice soft as if not to wake her. "She has Ezra's heart already, and even our Ben falls at her feet."

"And Jason?" he asks.

I nod. "Him, too, although he doesn't show it as much. You know him. By the time she became one of us, he'd stopped hiding behind his books."

I smile, thinking about how she helped my family.

"That's good," he trails off, hesitating. "And you?"

I look down at her again.

"I would die for her," I say, meaning every word.

Other words bubble to the surface, but I'm not ready for that, yet. They're words I'd only say to her, but I think if I do, she'll run the other way.

Yes, our Aurora certainly isn't the normal witch, and

I love it.

13

AURORA

"So, what did you mean about me needing my guys?" I try to sound casual.

Perses has been teaching me more about the gods, Hekate in particular, for hours. I'm in dire need of a change of subject, and that question has been bugging me.

He sighs and runs his hand through his hair. It reminds me of Alex, and a pang runs through me. "Your powers will continue to grow, Aurora. I unblocked them that day, and now that you're around your men, and when you go back—"

I interrupt. "I'm going back?"

I can't hide my excitement. I must admit, I worried I was trapped here forever. This place is lovely, but I miss my home and my family.

He smiles. "Of course. Now, as I was saying, your

powers will continue to grow, but not even Hekate herself could hazard a guess on what will manifest. You need help, people to ground you, to stop your darkness from overtaking your light. You are both the sun and the moon, Aurora."

"What if I don't want to be?" Voice quiet, I look down at the floor, remembering the capacity for darkness I hold.

He leans forward and gently lifts my chin. "One cannot exist without the other. The sun is nothing without the moon. Darkness is not evil, my sweet Aurora, like the light is not wholly good. Both have the capacity to be evil; it is the way you use it. Think of it like this: the wanderer in the desert begs for the night where those in everlasting night beg for the sun."

His explanation settles me a little, but I roll my eyes. "Fine." Then, I shake my head. "Is a man evil because he holds a gun?"

"The gun itself is not evil; it is the way it is used. It could be used to protect or to kill. Either way, the power is there to do its master's bidding. It's you who decides how."

I nod slowly, thinking his logic through. "So, I need people to ground me?"

"Yes, and you already have them," he says smugly, making me tilt my head. "You do not fool me. I see your heart. They hold it."

I swallow hard, my eyes widening in panic.

He reads my fear. "It's a good thing."

"Why?" I seem to be asking that a lot.

"Those witches are destined to be at your side, to guide and support you as you save the houses."

"But there's only five of them and ten houses?" I ask, confused.

"Six. There are six of them, so far," he replies, ignoring my other question.

"Who is the sixth?" I'm more confused than ever, a constant state recently.

"There was another of them, a brother. He was killed in an accident. Too early, his life ended. He was destined to be with them and meet you."

I think back to the photograph.

"You've seen him," Perses says softly.

"Yes, once in a photo," I reply.

"At birth, nine boys and one girl were blessed. Three of the boys were lost—hidden in the human world. You must find them."

The flip in conversation throws me. "Me?"

"Yes, you were the blessed girl," he says helpfully.

"Blessed by who?" Voice quiet, I take in all this new information.

"Hekate herself. She gave her life for you." No blame fills his expression.

"What?" I exclaim.

"She was weaker than the others. You see, she watched over her descendants when all the others turned away. She intervened when needed and offered guidance, which is why your house not only survived, but thrived; why you were pure, unlike the others who turned to the darkness. But when this decision to save them was made using a new generation, she was weak. She gave her remaining power to you, and so did her watch. And with it, her house died out with only you left to survive."

Tears stream down my face and thicken my voice. "I'm sorry."

"Don't be sorry. What is gone is never truly lost. She lives on in you, and you must save them, Aurora. You must become what she predicted."

"How?"

"You must first save the lost one," he helpfully states.

Bloody god riddles. "But he's dead."

Perses smiles. "Indeed."

"Then, how do I save him?" I ask slowly. I must be missing something.

"By the power you were born with. Your parentage was not a mistake. You were always destined to be a hybrid. You freely use your witch powers, and now you must master and accept the other half of you."

"Then, we're fucked," I grumble.

I sit holding a glass of scotch. Not really my drink of choice, but I needed something while the god and I continue our conversation.

"So, let me get this straight," I say. "I've got to master my darkness, save a dead man, go back to my guys, find three lost witches in the human world, and save the rest of the witches?"

He thinks his answer through. But seriously, I hope he doesn't mean I have to, you know, connect with all nine men, because holy hell. That's a lot of dick, even if I do like it. That's more than one a day, so they couldn't have a schedule…

"Less elegantly put, but essentially yes." He sips his scotch.

I down mine in one shot. The burn helps me wake up a bit. "Okay, so let's say I master my other side and manage to save the dead man. How are they supposed to help me?"

"You bind them to you; their power increases yours and vice versus. It evens out the load. As yours grows, you can share it when it becomes too much." He pours me another drink and with a nod of thanks, I take a sip. "Don't worry so much about the other three at the moment. You'll find them when you need them."

"How do I bind them?" I'm curious about that, even though it's not something I plan on doing. Yet, anyway. And I'm going to ignore the other three comments. One crazy thing at a time.

"You have already started to."

Great. Well done, Aurora.

I stand and pace again. I seem to be doing that a lot recently. "What if they don't want to? They should have a choice in this; not because some gods said they had to."

The thought makes me mad, and yes, a little insecure that they might reject me.

"They're blessed, Aurora, but that does not mean it's not a choice. They can choose not to, and the power will pass to someone else eventually."

The fact they have a choice makes me happy but anxious.

"The relationship does not need to be sexual, either. It could be friendship or closer to a family. But I don't think that will happen," he says smugly.

"Wait, what?" I turn to him, stilling my movements.

"I've watched you and them, Aurora. They knew deep down what they were getting into, yet they carried on because they care for you."

At this, I down my drink, and again, the burn gives me a bit more confidence.

"You're uncomfortable with the thought of love or someone caring for you?" Perses asks.

Wow, okay. I'm going to need more scotch. I pour myself a glass full and tumble onto the sofa, the scotch loosening my tongue. "Yes. I'm broken, Perses, by this darkness and my fucked-up history."

"That's exactly why you deserve it; because you think you do not. You do not see yourself, Aurora. But they do. You should give them a chance. You're dying for love, Aurora, to be held and supported. Let go of your fear that they'll leave you like your mother did. Trust me, απόγονος μου." With that advice, he leaves the room.

I remain sitting, drinking, and staring at nothing while I try to work through my issues. I have so many that, by the time I'm done listing them all to myself, I'm drunk.

Great. Some savior I am.

14

EZRA

I've stood outside her door for hours, unable to sleep. When I try, her eyes are there when I close mine. But I can't bring myself to go in. Her stillness horrifies me. Usually, her attitude and laughter fills the room. Its absence now sends pangs through my heart.

My brothers all cope in their own way, but me? I sit outside her bedroom door like the stalker she accused me of being. My lips quirk at the memory. She can call me whatever she likes as long as she opens her gorgeous eyes again. I bang my head back against the wall.

Someone sits down next to me, but I don't bother to look. I know who it will be.

"You get any sleep?" Alex's calm and collected voice makes me want to scream not be so perfect.

I glance over, ready to growl at him, then really look at him for the first time in days.

Without anger and worry clouding my vision, I realize my brother is broken, too. Huge bags hang underneath his dark and wild eyes. His usual mask is gone from his pale face. His hair sticks up at all angles like he ran his hands through it. He stares at me, his suffering on full display.

"No, I can't. Every time I try, I see her," I admit.

He nods and focuses on the door. "Do you love her?"

Despite his even voice, I sense his hesitation.

I look at the door, too, and think about my answer. I like spending time with Aurora. She makes me smile and feel young for the first time in a long while, and holding her in my arms is like heaven. I would do anything to see that smile on her face; let her dress me up or make fun of me… Anything.

When I kissed her for the first time, I knew there would be no other woman for me. God help someone if they hurt her. I honestly don't know what I'd do. I let myself feel pain at the idea of losing her.

I turn back to him with the answer on my tongue.

Ben comes sliding around the corner. His eyes twitch between us with excitement. "He's found something."

We spring up and jog to the library.

The kid smiles hugely when we get there. Jason

already sits on the sofa, a tense expression on his face. I lean against the wall and cross my arms to hide my trembling hands. Alex stands in front of the kid and Ben sits down.

"Ben said you found something?" The vulnerability is wiped from him, our fearless leader back in his place.

I think not being able to do anything wounded him more than anything. He's a man of thinking and action, and not even he knows what to do.

"So, I was reading this book— I mean, it's not really a book, you know, because it's so big... Why do we even call it a book?" He babbles on, his glasses shifting repeatedly.

"Your point?" Alex asks, calmer than I feel.

Ben smiles at us with glee. "She's not dead!"

"Come again?" I growl.

"She'll wake up. If her soul had left her body, she would be dead already. So, I believe she's still there, just not here."

Like that makes sense?

"Explain," Alex snaps, his emotion getting the better of him.

"It's like dream walking. Have you heard of it?"

We look around at each other with guarded glances and don't say anything. We all researched it after the incident with Aurora.

"So basically, your soul and body are still here, but it's like being asleep. Your consciousness, the thing that makes you… you, alive and functioning with charming personalities, isn't here. I think her conscious is dream walking, and she's trapped wherever she is. That's why she isn't waking up. She's asleep."

Jason twists his hands in his lap. "So, what do we do?"

"Well, erm, nothing." The kid winces at our reaction.

"Nothing?" Ben repeats. The anger on his face rivals even mine.

"There's nothing we can do. She needs to find whatever is trapping her and stop it, and then make her way back to her body. It's all up to her."

Alex starts pacing. Jason and Ben remain silent and stare at the floor. I turn and punch the wall, then lean my head against it.

"How long can she be trapped there? Won't her body deteriorate?" Jason asks, ever the knowledge seeker.

"I'm unsure. There are no cases of anyone being trapped in their dream walk for extended periods of time. I would say her body won't deteriorate, as her magic will keep it alive. But I could be wrong." The kid sounds worried.

Good.

"So, there's nothing we can do?" Alex sounds lost.

"I mean, I guess…"

I turn back around and step toward Ben with a

growl. "What?"

My snarl makes even Ben and Jason look up, but no one makes a move to stop me.

"In theory, another dream walker could track her and maybe help her back. But it's all theory. Dream walking is extremely rare, and I haven't heard of anyone who can do it." He sounds sorry, and it's the only reason I don't smack him.

I turn to Alex. He nods, obviously on my wavelength. He stands straighter and strides to me with purpose.

"Ben, you're to guard and watch her and Mikael. He'll need to be informed about what's happening. You're to eat and stay healthy, and when you need to rest Ezra, will swap. Jason, you're going to contact everyone we know and poke around for dream walkers. There has to be someone out there. Kid, you're to do the same, as will I."

I turn to the kid with my eyebrow arched.

Alex continues. "You'll swap with Ben and help Jason if he needs to track anyone down. You're our center. Everyone clear?"

Everyone nods and jogs off, happy to have something to do.

"We need to find a dream walker," I state.

"We will. Finding people is what we do." Alex's confidence is infectious, and I nod at him before heading off.

"*T*his isn't working." I sprawl back on the marble floor.

We're in some kind of observatory where I've been trying to meditate for hours. Perses thinks it will help me control my power. I think he's full of shit.

"Try again."

I lean up and look at his eyes. They're doing their ever-changing thing again. "It's not working. I'm not saying it to be stubborn or childish. My power comes from my emotion, not peace. The only time I can use my powers is when my mind is clear enough to sink inside and focus on those emotions."

Perses nods and rubs his chin in thought. He sits in a chair with another book in his hand. It looks like a first edition, and I'm jealous.

He gently places the book down, stands, and walks

over to sit opposite me on the floor. "If your power comes from emotions, how do you control it?"

I cock my head as I try to think of how to describe it. "It's like a cage or a wall. I trap it inside. It's hard when the power wants to come out, but I think I'm so used to it..." I trail off with a shrug.

"Then you need to break that cage," he says, like it's simple.

"But—"

"No buts. Your magic will be wild if you cage it. It's like an animal; treat it with respect and it will respect you. Your magic is part of you. The more you pull away from it, the more you remove your humanity from it. You are it and it is you," he says in a lecturing voice.

I consider his logic and understand his reasoning, but worry about what will happen. "So, you think letting my magic out will help me control it?"

"Yes, but it won't be easy. It will fight for control, and your body is so starved from magic, that it might hurt," he warns.

"I'm used to pain." I wave away his concerns as I consider how to go about this.

New determination settles in my bones. The sooner I get this done, the sooner I can return to my fur baby, Lane, and, well, of course the guys.

I nod at Perses and close my eyes, this time allowing myself to embrace my emotions: worry for the guys, fear of their rejection, determination not to let Perses down. I let it all run through me. Once I'm calm, I reach down deep inside myself and look at my power. *Really* look at it.

My power swirls in a steel-barred cage; violet on the outside and black in the center. It slowly spins. I reach through the bars and let it wash over my fingers. A tingling begins in my fingers, and the deeper I poke, the stronger it grows. When I reach the center, I gasp in pain. It feels like a stabbing in my hand. My eyes water, but I grit my teeth.

As I try to pull the power back through the bars, it doesn't budge.

I retract my fingers, then coo and whisper to my power, reaching for it like I usually do. Only a small amount escapes to stretch between me and the cage. I frown. What did I do that day in the pub? I know I let it out; not all, but some. I was angry.

Maybe that's the key? Anger breaks inhibitions, so it makes sense it would weaken my cage walls.

I think of the father from the pub, and my anger rises like a slow mist. It's not enough. I focus on the reaper who tried to kill us.

Ah, there we go.

Anger burns through my body. I carry on, allowing the memory of my mother's death to run through my mind, knowing now who killed her. The cage creaks. I need more. I dig deeper than ever, allowing memories I would rather forget come to the surface—the ones I hid so deep, even from myself. Some I purposely blocked out, and others my mind blocked to save me from them.

With a deep breath, I dive in.

My father stands above me like an avenging angel. His black, feathered wings spread out behind him. The evil sneer on his face only adds to the image. His hands hang by his sides, knuckles coated in blood, both his and mine.

Eyes tearing, I gaze up at the man I once sought shelter in, who I now seek shelter from. My heart rests cold in my chest, now used to the abuse. He kicks me in the side, one of my ribs cracking, and I curl up to avoid the pain, knowing it will hurt tomorrow.

"It's your fault!" He kicks me again. "Your fault she's dead."

He kicks me harder, and I bite my tongue to hold in my whimper.

I drag myself out of the memory. My rage remains a small flame, not the wildfire I need.

I flick through the memories of my suffering, not stopping to watch too intently, just stopping so snapshot images fan the flames of my anger higher. With each one, the bars around my power creak and bend under the weight of my fury.

My father stands above where I lay at the bottom of the stairs where he threw me. As he comes toward me, the knife he holds glints from my bedroom light. His belt buckle is undone. The glass whiskey bottle shatters over my head …

It goes on and on until, with a roar, my power bursts from the cage and the bars explode.

The pain explodes like a bomb going off in my body. My bones break, my muscles snap, and my organs stutter.

I come around slowly, feeling groggy. My head rests on something cool, and my body feels like it's been through a battle. I gasp in horror when I check my cage only to realize it's not there. The conversation with Perses comes back to me.

With my eyes still closed, I search for my power, finding it settled in every bone and muscle, finally a part of me. Like it was always supposed to be there.

I smile in happiness. Feeling it there offers me a confidence I didn't know was missing.

My eyes flutter open and meet Perses's.

A smile stretches across his face. "Well done, Aurora. There you finally are."

The pride in his voice puts me on cloud nine, and my power hums in response.

16

AURORA

"What now?" I ask.

We returned to the living room, where I stretch out on the sofa, still a little sore from unlocking my power. Perses sits opposite me while Bob makes a fire next to us. I kind of missed the little gremlin, not I'll tell him that.

"You need to practice with your powers, and when you're ready, you need to find your man." His voice sounds tired, and I tilt my head at him in question. He smiles says as he leans back to observe me. "I'm fine, απόγονος μου."

I prop myself on my elbows and lean up. "I didn't say anything."

He laughs. "I saw it in your eyes. You really are an open book."

I look at him seriously, for once I feel the age gap between us. "Is that a bad thing?"

"No, sweet Aurora. It's refreshing." Gentleness fills his voice.

I smile and lay back down. Comfortable silence stretches between us, both lost in our thoughts.

"My— I mean, the guys. Do you know if they're okay?" I've been too scared to ask before now.

When Perses doesn't respond, I look to him.

He studies me with a closed expression. "Would you like to see them?"

Hope flares in me but tapers down when I think about it. Do I? What if they moved on because they have Mikael back?

I nibble on my lip and hesitantly nod.

Perses stands gracefully and offers his hand. This has become a ritual now, but I actually need it to help steady myself. He waits until I stand straight, then leads me from the room.

We head upstairs, my legs protesting the movement, but I don't moan. Excitement and nerves settle in my stomach at seeing the guys.

Perses leads me down the corridor opposite my room, through twists and turns until I'm lost. He stops in front of a door at the end of the corridor. With a wave of his hand, it unlocks.

He pushes the door open and leads me in, gently

tugging on my hand when I stop and stare, my mouth hanging open like a fish. Opening and closing.

The room is one giant mirror. Two small walls lead away from the door and then curve into a mirror that spans the opposite wall. A chair rests next to the door.

I stare in awe. "What is this?"

"This is how you see, απόγονος μου. Did you think I would just pop you home?" He laughs.

Honestly, I didn't really think about it. I walk up to a section of the mirror and hover my finger over it. Nerves and tension roll over me in waves.

I turn back to Perses.

He takes one look at me, then steps up to my side. "Why are you worried?"

I stare at him, my eyes filled with all my questions, before I whisper brokenly, "What if they've moved on?"

He doesn't respond except to grab my hand and tug me so my back faces his front. He doesn't touch me, but leans over and whispers to the mirror. The heat of him on my back is the only thing stopping me from running from the room.

The mirror fogs.

I hold my breath and wait to see my boys.

When the mirror clears fully, it reveals Mikael laying next to me on a single bed. It's strange seeing my own body, but I'm more interested in the guys. Ben sits next to me, holding one of my hands. Nev lays at my feet.

My eyes fill. "They didn't leave."

I don't realize I said it out loud until Perses squeezes my shoulder. "I never doubted them."

Perses's touch drops away, and a moment later, the door softly closes, but I don't glance away from the mirror.

Ben doesn't look good. I move closer and touch his face. It appears haggard, and his beautiful hair isn't brushed.

I frown and turn my attention at Mikael. His hair is washed, and he looks better than when I last saw him. A scar stands out along his neck. Will he hate me for that?

Nev lifts his head, and I step back, waiting to see who caught his attention.

Ezra walks into the room, and my heart nearly stops. I grab my chest as I stare at my giant. His long hair nearly covers his ears, and the unruly curls make me smile. His beard is untamed and scraggly like he can't be bothered with it. His clothes are dirty and ill-fitting. But it's his eyes that hold my attention. They look so lost.

"Ezra," I whisper.

He looks up.

Did he hear me? But that's not possible, right?

He glances back at Ben and says something. Ben nods and leans over to kiss my forehead. He whispers something, then walks away.

Ezra takes his spot. He leans his forehead against my hand, and my heart nearly breaks for my giant.

I don't know how long I watch, waiting to see Jason and Alex. I need to know they're all okay. Ezra is by my side, and my heart warms. Mikael still shares my bed and reads to me.

My smile turns full blown.

"Where are you, Alex?" I ask.

The mirror fogs again, and I jump up in panic.

"No, wait, please!" I shout, reaching for it.

Ezra and Mikael vanish, and dejected, I step back.

About to leave, the mirror clears again.

There they are. Alex and Jason. I tilt my head. They both sit at a table in some sort of library.

I run my eyes over them lovingly, memorizing their features. Alex's hair is in disarray, and he appears upset. I frown and glance at Jason. His usual smile is nowhere to be seen.

I step back.

"What's wrong with them?" I ask, not expecting a response.

"They miss you."

Spinning, I find Perses, he must have snuck back in while I was distracted. He holds my gaze, and I'm the one to break it.

I turn back to my guys, watching their every move. "I miss them too. Can it show me anyone?"

At the question, he steps up next to me. "Yes, why?"

I sense his confusion and look at him. "Can you show me my best friend, Lane?"

"The human?" he asks.

"Yes." I turn back to the mirror.

He does the whisper thing again. As it fogs over my guys' faces, I promise myself I'll soon see them for real soon.

17

ALEXANDER

I hold on to the seat as Jason goes around another corner. Driving isn't his strong suit, but he looked so lost that I let him. We're on our way to meet a contact of ours. He usually tips us off on locations of missing witches or keeps us up to date with what's happening in the supernatural world. I reached out to him in hopes he might know something about dream walkers or know someone who would.

When we arrive at the restaurant he requested to meet, we find it empty at this time of morning. The sign outside proudly declares breakfast until eleven a.m. When I check the clock, it reads six a.m.

I roll my eyes and climb out of the car. Meeting our paranoid contact at this run-down restaurant in the middle of nowhere is just the beginning.

We make our way through the door, which chimes a bell at our entry. I look around for him. He's late. Great.

I make my way to a booth in the back corner with Jason on my heels. We both sit on the same side facing the door and wait.

A tired-looking waitress wanders over.

"Order?" she asks around a yawn.

I don't even bother reading the menu, attention focused on the parking lot. "Black coffee, strong."

"Tea, please," Jason says kindly.

She huffs and walks away.

A black BMW pulls up and parks at the back of the lot.

I lean back in the booth and lay my arm across the back as our contact walks up to the door, shades on. I roll my eyes again.

He swaggers in, yelling as he does, "Alexander, my friend! How good to see you!"

I stand when he reaches our table, and he kisses me on both cheeks. He leans over and does the same to Jason before he sits down opposite us with a sly smile.

I wait for the waitress to return before talking. She sets our drinks down, and I nod in thanks.

Our contact gives her a wide smile. "I'll have a coffee, doll."

The waitress doesn't respond; she just walks away.

He leans back, imitating my position.

"Henry, the reason—" I begin.

"Not yet, mate. I haven't had coffee. How you bastards been?"

I grind my teeth and Jason answers for us. "Good, and you?"

His hard voice is the opposite of his smiling face. Looks like our sweet Jason isn't up for small talk today.

"Good. I heard you lost one of you fuckers. Like, couldn't find him." Henry belly laughs and slaps his leg like it's the funniest thing ever. Like we lost Mikael in a supermarket, not because a reaper who went bad kidnapped him.

"You heard wrong," I say.

Henry stops laughing and raises his eyebrow at me.

"That's right. The grapevine does tend to be wrong, mate," I sneer at him.

"Well, it is this time."

The waitress returns and plonks his coffee down in front of him, spilling it in the process.

"Ah, there we go." He grabs the mug and sips it.

"Let me cut to the chase, Henry. We need to find someone. I need you to put out some feelers. Discreetly." I sip my coffee and hide my grimace at it.

"Don't you always. It's gon' cost you." He slurps his coffee.

I place my mug down gently. "As you said, 'don't you always.' Now, we need you to find a dream walker."

Henry whistles. "Whatcha want with one of them?"

He's nosey.

"Not of consequence." I look at Jason with a nod.

"Do you know any?" Jason asks.

Henry looks between us. "Nah. Fuckers are almost extinct. I'll put some feelers out tho'."

I nod, ready to be done with this and home to Kitten. I glance at my watch in frustration at being away from her. "What's your price?"

"I want a favor."

Looking up at this, I raise both eyebrows. "You're requesting a favor from the Witch Council's hunters?"

We don't hand out unspecified favors. Henry could ask for anything, and it could come back to bite us. In the position we're in, we don't barter.

But the idiot doesn't heed my threatening tone. "Yep. I might need your help. So, it's a favor or nothing."

"I don't—" Jason begins.

I cut him off. "Done. Now, if you'll excuse us? I expect to hear from you tomorrow." Without waiting for Henry's reply, I stand and stride out of the restaurant.

I don't bother looking at Jason. I know my agreement confused him. It's always been my rule after all: we don't barter. We set the rules, but if it helps Kitten, I'll do anything, even barter with the devil.

18

AURORA

"Again!" Perses shouts from his spectator spot on the edge of the flat field.

He brought me out here at the crack of dawn to train.

Really, I think it's that and a distraction from my emotions yesterday. I'll admit, burning the shit out of stuff helps.

When I first saw the field, I was in awe. Trees made an archway for entry, and wildflowers surround the border.

For the first hour, Perses made me draw my power as quickly as possible, then cleanly merge it back into myself. I did this on his command, and every time I was too slow, Bob hit me with a tree branch.

Bloody gremlin. I'll be covered in bruises.

Perses spent the second hour testing what kind of

reaper powers I possess. We know I can touch a soul. He tried to test my wings, but I only managed to make them from smoke, so we gave up. Perses claims more powers will appear, and I need to be ready.

I don't know how to do that, but okay.

Now? He moves a target for me with his magic, shouting defensive options. Apparently, I need to work on defending myself. Saving the witch world won't be easy, and he wants me to have the best options.

"Fire!" he shouts as the wooden target springs up in front of me.

I call my magic, I'll admit a lot faster than I was ever able to before, and form a ball of fire. I fling it at the target. The first couple of times, my aim is off, but I get better as we practice.

Another target pops up and makes its way to me.

"Flame!" Perses shouts.

In the process of making the ball, another target appears to the right of the first.

"Explode!" he orders.

I stare at him in horror, but the targets draw closer.

Quickly, I throw the fireball, and the target catches fire. I focus on the second target and imagine it exploding as I fling my magic out. Wood splinters fly everywhere.

I stand there in shock. Holy shit, I'm a badass.

Perses laughs and claps from the sideline.

I collapse on the grass in a sweaty lump.

Bob comes to stand over me.

"Don't you dare lick me," I warn him.

He smiles and nods to himself. "Silly witch is fast."

As I move to stand, Bob uses his stick to sweep my feet from under me. I tumble back down again and stare at him in shock.

"Hmm, not fast enough." He hits my leg with the stick. "Silly witch."

Satisfied with that, he waddles off.

"Gremlin!" I shout after him.

"Silly, slow witch!" he shouts back.

I lay in the grass, contemplating throwing a fireball at him. He'd probably catch it or something crazy. I allow my eyes to close, trying to rest my magic a little from all its use.

Perses claimed it's like skinny jeans, I need to wear them in or they'll stay tight. Him and his metaphors. I guess he means the more I use my magic the more access I'll have to it.

Also, gods wear skinny jeans?

My magic buzzes through me. It's become a comfort knowing I can protect myself if needed. A bit filters out of my fingers, and I watch as the violet power plays over them.

When the ground reacts under my hand, I scramble up. I watch where I had lain, mystified. Perses's shadow falls over me, but I don't pay him any mind.

A green bud shoots up through the soil, and a

second follows. I tilt my head as they grow rapidly until they reach my ankles. They stop and blossom. I can't look away from the first flower. It's violet. Like, actually violet. The second one is black. Four more appear around the violet one, creating an incomplete circle. They each bloom a different color: green, gold, white, yellow, and blue.

"What the—" My voice fills with awe.

"The earth is welcoming you. Your power called to something in it." Perses watches as the flowers continue to grow.

They now reach to my knee. "What do the colors stand for?"

"One for each of your bonds," he says with a serious expression.

I look to him, more confused than ever. "The earth knows what my bonds are?"

"The earth is a sentient being, Aurora. This is a prophecy ring. They see what you do not." He begins to walk away.

Okay, too much information for today.

I turn away from the weird flowers, but whisper a thanks to the ground because, hey I don't want it to trip me or something for being ungrateful.

As I walk away, a rumble sounds, and I glance back. Three more flowers joined the six already there and complete the ring around the violet one.

I hurry after Perses.

"You know, I never asked where we are. I know you said in the in-between, but is it real? Is this house real?" We sit in the library again.

Perses, stretched out across from me, quirks an eyebrow.

Why can everyone do that? I try, and when he throws me a strange look, I let my face relax. They always make it seem so easy. If I can master two powers, surely mastering my eyebrow shouldn't be hard. Dammit.

"Are we real?" I ask again.

Bloody gods. Why can't they be like yes or no?

Obviously reading my face, he says, "This is my house. You're here, so yes, this is real. You, however, are not. You're like a ghost here."

I nod. Makes sense if my body is back with my guys. "So where is here?"

"This is where the gods live," he replies cryptically.

Okkkaayy.

"So, when do I start looking for the dead witch?" Not to sound impatient, but I want to go home.

"You're not ready yet. You need to hone your abilities. I need to know you have the skills you might need when bringing him back."

I guess I never thought that through. I'll be bringing someone back from the dead. "How will it work?"

Perses sits up and takes on a serious edge. "He has not passed to the other yet. So he's stuck in—how do you humans say it—Purgatory?"

I nod and drop my legs from under me to sit up. Yikes.

"You'll need to travel there. Then, when you find him, you must lock his soul with yours. This will complete the binding process and effectively give life to his spirit. When you return to your body, you'll bring him back with you."

Okay, makes sense. Ignore that. It's crazy.

"But he'll have a body?" I worry I'll have a spirit stuck in my body. It's enough with me in here.

"He will."

I know I look confused.

Perses sighs. "Magic, Aurora. You're born of magic. You're in a realm in your mind, and you're questioning if bringing him back to your world will bring all of him back?"

Okay, when he put it like that, it sounds stupid. "Will his body be rotten?"

I have a weird image of a zombie witch in my head.

"No," he says through a chuckle.

"Wait." My voice rises. "Did you say I have to complete the binding with him?"

"Yes," he answers carefully.

Smart.

I stand and pace, trying to form my thoughts into a

cohesive sentence. "You said he had a choice. That's not much of a choice. Plus, I don't know him!" I throw my hands in the air. "How can I bind to someone I don't know?"

Trying to control my panic, I stare at Perses. I mean, what if this guy is a total asshat?

Perses is quiet for a while, taking it all in.

I twiddle my fingers.

"I have a plan," he finally replies.

Relieved, I nod.

"We'll train every day, work on everything," Perses continues. "Every night, you'll review the lost witch's memories. If you find yourself not completely horrified and are willing, I will guide you through the binding process, and you may bring him back."

I sit back. Okay. There's a choice. My panic lessens.

"His memories?" I ask for clarification.

"The mirror can do more than see into the now."

Wow, that's some mirror.

Perses looks worried. "Is that okay?"

"If I decide I can't—" I look away and pause. "If I can't bind him, is there another way without me going all dark and crazy?"

"There are always other options, Aurora. But they chose these men for a reason, and each strengthens you in a way. When your men were blessed, every aspect of them was checked."

"What does that mean?" I really need to stop asking questions.

"It means, Aurora, each man is selected because of their strength, heart, and loyalty. I think, if you give him a chance, you'll be surprised." His voice is neutral.

"Okay," I grumble.

He smiles and stands. "Good, now get some rest. Tomorrow will be a big day." With that, he walks toward the door.

I twist to stare at his retreating form. "Wait. What's his name?"

The guys never told me.

"Darius," he says over his shoulder, then sweeps out of the room.

I turn back to the fire. Darius. It's a nice name.

Let's hope he matches it.

19

AURORA

The boy, no, the *man* in front of me is, in one word, stunning. His skin reminds me of moonlight, and his smile lights up the room, yet there's a softness to him. His coiled muscles, though, point to a dangerous side.

Does he still have that softness? Is he awake like me in Purgatory, or does he sleep?

I can't imagine being awake all that time, trapped. It would twist even the best of men.

Perses brought me to the mirror room last night and showed me how to use it. He kept his promise and offered me the chance to watch the memories of the man who I'm supposed to save.

I hesitated at the time, feeling like I was invading his privacy, and went to bed to think on it.

This morning, I trained in a daze. Sometime during

the night, I got over my uncertainty and decided to watch a few memories to learn more about the witch I would bind myself to.

If this binding is forever, I deserve to look.

That's what I tell myself, anyway, when the guilt arises. It helps, as well, that I get to see my men. They're nearly always present in Darius's memories. Their bond and brotherhood are more obvious than ever. I knew they were a family, but their closeness in his memories is a reminder.

Seeing them now compared to in Darius's memories, I notice a difference in them. The sadness, the hardness, but it's the distance that shocks me. Like they're avoiding getting to this family state again in case it only leads to heartache. I also notice how they started to open up when I was there, but I'm not too big headed to think it was only because of me.

"Fine," Ben grumbles in the mirror in front of me, throwing me back into what I was doing.

Watching the first memory or so made me uncomfortable. Now, a sudden thought hits me. What if I see Darius with another woman? That would be weird. What if I see my guys with other women?

Irrational jealousy runs through me. Logically, I know they have a past like I do, but there's a difference between acknowledging it and seeing it firsthand. Nerves make me sit up straighter, and new tension runs through me.

I can't believe I didn't think of this before.

As Ben makes his way through the restaurant to a man in the corner, Darius throws his head back in laughter. I don't know what they're doing, but it's obvious by Ben's displeasure it was a dare.

I watch Darius. He's an attractive man, I'll give him that. Okay, not attractive, but rather, hot as hell. His face is chiseled and handsome, his body muscular and trim, his lips full and lush. An ever-present twinkle fills his eyes, like he knows something no one else does. From the memories I've seen so far, it's obvious he and Ben find trouble when they're together. It sheds light on Ben's heartbreak. I knew they were close, but losing this type of friendship, brother-bond, would break any lesser man.

I watch in disbelief and amusement as Ben tries to flirt with the man in the corner, his back to Darius. From his tight eyes and stiff body, he's not comfortable.

Eventually, he walks back over to Darius.

"So, need a condom?" Darius says through laughter.

Ben grimaces and slumps in his seat. "Shut up. Like you could do better."

Darius laughs again, flashing that same smile from the photograph. "Wanna bet, princess?"

Ben sits up with new determination. "Wager?"

Darius nods. "If I can get his number, I want you to perform a song for all the guys while wearing a pretty dress."

His smile is infectious, and I find myself smiling with his mischievous mind.

Ben's excitement falters but he replies anyway. "Fine, and if you lose, you have to."

Both men smile at the challenge, then lean and shake on it.

"Watch and learn." Darius downs his drink and struts to the man.

It's like I'm a camera in the room. It's strange, because sometimes I'm in Darius's head, sometimes I'm in one of the other guys' heads, focusing on Darius, and sometimes it's like I'm a statue in the room. I did ask Perses about it and he smiled at me. Sneaky gods and their secrets.

I can't hear their conversation, but the guy slips a napkin over to Darius, who winks at him. He slowly walks back to Ben, fanning himself with the napkin.

Incredulous, Ben's mouth hangs open as he watches Darius sit back down. "No way."

Darius nods smoothly, throwing the napkin at his stunned friend. "What will you sing, twinkle toes? Oh, how about *Barbie Girl?*"

Darius is almost giddy with excitement, and I find myself shaking my head with a smile at their banter. It makes me miss my guys, and a pang of longing hits me.

The mirror knows what I want, don't ask how, and fogs over.

Seconds later, I burst out in laughter. There, in

nothing but his trousers and a pink feather boa is Ben belting his heart out to 'I Will Always Love You.'

In the corner, Darius cries with laughter. Jason laughs, too. Ezra looks stunned, and Alex wears his usual blank mask, but his lips twitch. Ben shimmies around them and uses the boa to wrap it around Ezra's neck.

I find myself laughing along as I watch the performance.

Ben gyrates his hips at Alex, then turns and sits on Jason's knee. He carries on singing and leans back, wrapping his arm around Jason's neck as his sings.

Near the end of the song, he jumps up and belts out the last few words.

"Thank you, thank you very much." He bows and I can't help but laugh.

I miss my Benny. I miss his teasing, his laughter, but this will do for now.

The mirror fogs again, and another memory pops up.

I'm in Darius this time, and I giggle to myself because that sounds filthy.

He's in what looks like a library, sprawled on a chair reading a book.

I sit with him for hours as he reads. It's another side I didn't expect from him. To be honest, he's not what I expected at all. It's clear he's loyal and kind of a joker, but there's also this seriousness, like he might be laughing at the world underneath a thousand plans and thoughts that run through his head. He faces the world with happiness and wonder.

I tingle as nerves run through me, then sadness. Will he still be like that?

"Again."

Perses and I sit on the sofa in the living room facing each other.

Our knees touch, and he smiles patiently at me.

I close my eyes. Apparently, to bond to someone fully, everything must be laid bare. Perses hesitantly told me Darius might not be completely sane, so I might have to force the bond.

The idea makes me sick, but I nod.

He's trying to teach me to pass someone's barriers. It's important that our magic and minds touch at the same time. Then, we must share blood. Seems easy enough, right? I've pushed into someone's mind before, but he was human, and I sort of fumbled my way through it.

Perses doesn't make this easy. He built a steel wall around his mind, and his magic attacks me as I struggle to pry it open. I've tried nearly everything: climbing it, searching for a way around it, looking for cracks.

"If he's not completely himself, he won't make it easy," Perses says.

I open my eyes to look at him again. "What if this isn't what he wants? What if I bind myself to him, and he comes back and hates me for it? What if everyone else hates me for it?"

Perses gently grabs my hand and pries open the fist I didn't realize I made. "It's not so black and white, little Aurora. He might be mad at first, but he'll be happy to be alive, as will his brothers. The connection doesn't have to be sexual. You could make it a friendship. If there was any other way, I would tell you." He squeezes my hand. "Could you really leave him there, stuck in that place, knowing you could have tried to save him, but were too scared?"

I shake my head immediately.

He squeezes my hand again and let's go.

I look away in thought. "How did he die?"

Perses leans back, obviously sensing my need to talk. "Do you really want to know?"

I face him once more and let him read the answer in my eyes.

"It was an accident, like I said. The fates control the threads of life. Everyone is destined for something. Him more than most, as you know. But with so many lives hanging in the balance, sometimes mistakes happen. This was one of them. He died protecting his brothers like he would have wanted. The only reason he stayed in Purgatory is because of his destiny, his blessing."

I think it through. "Did— Was it painful? Protecting them from what?" I tilt my head in thought. "You said the fates controlled everything. Does that mean we have no free will, no choice?" My voice rises in anger at the end.

"They do not control everything. You have choice and free will, which can change your path. However, there are those with destinies, like you. You still have choice, but fate has mapped out your life and see the choices you might make." His expression holds no regret. He's just telling me the truth.

I stand and pace, annoyed that everything I'm doing is on the whim of some random women playing with me.

"Do not be angry, Aurora. You still have your free will. You can choose to cut the threads to the prophecy and destroy the last hope for witches. It's all on your shoulders. They just watch over it."

The use of my name with no endearments makes me take his words seriously. The anger drains from me, and I sit facing him again. "So, I could walk away?"

The question's bugged me since he told me what the gods want from me. I watch his eyes. They offer the truth.

He doesn't hide anything from me, and I love that. "Yes. But tell me this, απόγονός μου. Could you really walk away from them? That's what it boils down to."

I look down in thought. Could I?

They're under my skin and something in me rebels at the idea. Everything I learned here I want to share with them. I want to go home and cuddle and watch movies. I want to sing duets with Ben and talk for hours with Jason. I want Alex to challenge me, and I want to see that soft smile Ezra offers me as we walk through the world together.

No, I don't think I could walk away from them. They've slowly wormed their way into my cold, protected heart with every look, touch, and smile. I don't think I could ever get them out.

I keep my thoughts to myself but ready myself. "Let's go again."

Perses smiles and I move back into position.

This time, I let my instincts guide me. I drop my shield and allow my magic to reach for him. His greets mine, curious but dormant for the moment. His steel wall appears in my mind's eye, and instead of relying on brute strength, I place my hand on it and imagine it opening, allowing me to slip through.

I stay there with my hand on it and wait.

Slowly, it turns soft in my hand, then nothing. I'm through. Not wanting to look in his memories, I pull back to myself, and a huge, triumphant smile crosses my lips.

Startled, Perses stares at me like he's never seen me before.

My smile slowly fades, and I stare back, now afraid. "What?"

"In all my years, none have penetrated my barriers," he admits.

Confusion swirls in me. "But I thought you said I was practicing and that's what you wanted me to do…"

"Yes, απόγονος μου. I expected to have to let you in. Instead, you waltzed into my head with a smile." His voice is careful, his face blank.

Hesitant, I ask, "What does that mean?"

"It means, Aurora, you are more than we could have ever expected."

I gulp at that.

Later that evening, I stand at my spot in the mirror room.

After our training, Perses departed without a word, leaving me more confused than ever. Today was full of ups and downs. I don't even know where to start, so the mirror remains fogged.

With a defeated sigh, I lean forward and gently place my hand on its slick surface.

It clears around my hand, and I pull it back.

Darius appears, smiling at someone I can't see.

I imagine it's me. Lame, I know.

Over the last couple nights, something in me shifted, and a soft spot appeared for the gentle man. It's obvious why he fits in with the others so well and that he genuinely cares for them.

I've learned a lot.

He likes country music, although he'll never admit it. He loves to read, he's mischievous, he finds joy in life, and he cuts all the guys' hair. I thought, watching the big man trimming their hair would make my heart explode. This giant delicately holding scissors and softly cutting their hair weakened my resolve to not force a bond.

His voice could lull me to sleep, and I imagine him singing to me.

Would he?

As I fall asleep in that room, watching the man the gods deemed mine, my heart flutters in anticipation.

Over the next week, I spend my days with Perses, testing my boundaries and pushing my power. I'm still hesitant, but I slowly start to accept both sides of me. When it feels so natural, it's hard to fight it.

I spend every night learning everything I can about Darius, and watching his and my mens' happiness before he died.

Slowly, I fall for them further. It feels like I've known them my whole life. I guess I've seen pretty much all of their lives.

I smirk. I can't wait to tease them about it. Just have to save a witch from Purgatory and bring him back from the dead first.

Easy peasy lemon squeezy.

20

AURORA

"You're ready?" Confidence fills Perses's loud voice.

I'm glad one of us is. "I think maybe I should…"

He places his hands on my shoulders and towers above me. "I wouldn't send you there lightly, απόγονος μου. You're ready."

I take a deep breath and smile at him.

He grabs my arm, and we go for a walk in the gardens. It's become somewhat of a ritual, and a little bit of me will miss this. Lost in my thoughts, I let my hands trail through the flowers as we stroll.

We stop at the fountain and the irony isn't lost on me. We came here on my first day and now on my last.

"What will it be like?" I ask tensely.

I've tried not to think about it, but now that it's happening, the idea of Purgatory terrifies me.

"Honestly, I don't know." Perses sits but I chose to stand, too wound up. "I've never been there. I've heard the stories. They say it's different for everyone. It's not one place."

"So, it's like an individual thing?" I ask.

He shrugs. "Maybe, but who really knows?"

I laugh bitterly. "I figured a god would."

He smiles at me to masks a flash of hurt in his eyes. "I'm not all-seeing, Aurora. I know a lot, have seen a lot, but Purgatory isn't one of them."

I grab his hand. "I'm sorry. I shouldn't expect you to hold my hand through this."

"It's okay, απόγονος μου. I know you'll handle whatever is there. But know this, Aurora. Nothing there can hurt you. You're the living whilst they're the dead. But they'll be drawn to you, drawn to your life."

I look over the garden and spot Bob chasing a bird. I smile in spite of the dark conversation.

"But they can't hurt me?" I ask, needing to be sure.

"Again, I'm going off stories. This is new territory. But, I don't think so."

I nod. I trust him, but I'll only have myself to trust in there. I plan to get in and get out as soon as possible. In the distance, the bird turns and pecks Bob, and he shouts then buffs up to twice his size.

"What is he?" I point to Bob. I never asked before.

With everything going on, his arrival was just one more weird thing in this strange place.

"He's magic. He doesn't originate from here, but I saved him when he was younger. He sticks by my side and now yours. He's grown attached to you."

I snort but hold in my smile. I've grown strangely attached to the gremlin, too.

We're quiet for a while, and I enjoy the peace before the storm.

"When do I go?" I ask, finally breaking the silence.

"Tomorrow morning."

I nod. Okay, one night to prepare. Staring at the ground, I consider everything I need to do when Bob pops up in front of me.

"Cookie!" he shouts, scaring the shit out of me.

With a scream, I leap back as he lets the bird cupped in his hands go.

I fall backward into the fountain. My head submerges, and I sputter water from my mouth. When I try to stand, I fall back again.

Eventually, I get up and stand there soaking wet as I glare at the laughing gremlin.

A smile stretches across my face. "Run little gremlin."

He stops laughing and backs away. "Silly witch waits."

I fling a fireball at him.

He yelps and breaks into a run.

I chase after him, throwing more fireballs. What a sight I must be. A witch, no, a hybrid in a soaking wet red dress chasing a gremlin around.

When night comes, I can't sleep.

Instead, I stare at the ceiling and go over everything that can go wrong.

With a grumpy sigh, I get up, knowing I won't sleep.

I make my way by moonlight to my sanctuary and place my hand on the mirror.

When it slowly clears of fog, my men sit before me.

I smile and the tension leaves my body.

I'll see you soon, I promise silently.

21

ALEXANDER

*A*pparently finding a dream walker isn't as easy as we first thought. Henry contacted me the day after our meeting and informed me he would need more time. I haven't heard from him since.

It feels like we've reached a dead end. All our hopes are dwindling.

Ezra is more volatile than normal, Ben mopes around, and even Jason seems to have lost hope. Yet I know with certainty we won't lose her. No matter where she is or how long it takes, I will get Aurora back.

I sit by her bed as I vow it. We haven't been this lost since Darius's death. Even thinking about that sends me into a spiral. I couldn't protect him, but I will protect her. I shove memories of my lost brother away, not ready to deal with the pain. I know one day it will bite me on the ass, but I can't afford to be weak while my team, my family, falls apart.

We healed from his death, but it was like putting a band-aid on a bullet wound. The pain, the guilt, lessened with Aurora around. Now though, it swims back to the surface, and it's only going to be so long before it takes over.

22

AURORA

"Are you ready, απόγονος μου?" Perses stands before me, we are back downstairs in the room with the fire, ready for me to head to Purgatory.

I nod, mutely aware that my nerves make me feel sick. Can I even be sick when I haven't eaten?

I force my voice to be strong. "How do I get there?"

"You're already separated from your body, which is the hard part, so essentially it should be easy." Despite the words, he sounds unsure.

My eyes narrow on him. "*Should* be?"

"Like I said, Aurora, I've never known anyone to go."

I sigh. "Okay, so how do I get there?"

"You mentioned when I asked you what happened the day the reaper captured your men, in the cave, that there were six threads, and one was black?"

I nod, not seeing where he's going with it.

"I don't think the black thread was the reaper. I think it was Darius."

I start to pace. How would I have connected to a dead guy? I ask him as much.

"Honestly, I'm not sure. You might have reached out to him subconsciously, or it could be due to your connection with the guys."

I stop and stand before him. "So, you think I follow the black thread like I did with Mikael?"

He nods, a smile on his face.

"Okay." I get ready to lay down, then glare at the gremlin who stands in the doorway. "Don't you dare lick me while I'm out or I'll turn you into a frog."

Laying down on the sofa, I think through how I found the threads.

"This is some inception shit right here," I mutter, stalling. As I close my eyes, a thought hits me, making me bolt upright. "Wait! How do I get back?"

Honestly, it should have occurred to me before now, but it really didn't.

Perses crouches next to me, reaching forward to brush a stray hair out of my face. "Follow your other threads back."

"So, I'm not coming back here? I won't see you again?" My voice echoes his softness and sadness rolls through me.

In the time I spent here, my attachment to the

ancient god has grown. He feels like a brother to me. I'll even miss the little gremlin.

"This isn't goodbye forever, Aurora; just for now."

I stare at him, memorizing his face. "See you soon."

He takes a deep breath and allows me to feel his emotions, all the ones he hides.

I gasp with their intensity. He's sad, proud, and... lonely? On impulse, I lean forward and wrap my arms around his neck. He remains stiff for a moment before relaxing and wrapping his arms around me.

"I've lived a long life, απόγονος μου, yet I've rarely met any who shine as bright as you, who love as deep as you, and who care as deeply as you. You are truly pure." I lie back and smile at him, his words spreading warmth through me.

He leans forward and kisses my cheek. "See you soon, my little Aurora."

With an ancient destruction god and a gremlin watching over me, I follow a thread to Purgatory. Fun.

23

AURORA

I don't know how long I lay there, lost deep within myself, hunting for the threads.

My magic pulses through me, a comforting warmth. I go to where I used to cage my magic only to find nothing.

With an internal frown, I think about binding as Perses described. It's about the head—magic—but most importantly, it's about the heart.

I make my way through my body with my magic open, allowing me to see.

When I focus on my men and the feelings they induce, I notice the threads instantly. I ignore all the others, no matter how much I want to stop and marvel at them. There, in the shadow of the others, hides a black, frayed thread. It's weak, but there.

I wrap my magic around it, surrounding the black

with my violet. It intertwines and pulses. I gasp. It feels like its tugging on my magic, feeding on it.

I follow the thread.

It's hard to describe, but it's like feeling around a room in the dark with nothing to guide you but a light at the other end. I walk toward that light, the thread, my anchor. I don't know how long I walk. My feet hurt and my chest is tight. My magic twists and turns in me.

My steps slow, like I wade through deep mud that tries to pull me down. I struggle with each step, but somehow, I know if I stop now, there's no going back. I push through, my breathing the only noise in the void.

When I see a light ahead, I squint and pick up my pace, gritting my teeth through the exhaustion and pain.

I stumble and fall through the light with a scream.

My body aches like it was torn apart and put back together again. I lay on the floor, panting.

Slowly the pain recedes, allowing me to think. I drag myself to my feet, spinning to look around. I feel like I'm in a forest, with light streaming through fog where it can. Fog as thick as my magic spreads through the clearing, working its way around me. There's something off about the clearing, though, and it's not the fog.

Everything is too dull, too dark, like a nightmare version. Okay, so I'm guessing this is Purgatory. It isn't too bad, but which way do I go?

As I debate my options, a crashing noise comes from behind me. The noise grows louder, and the sound of trees crunch under the weight of whatever heads toward me.

It gets closer and closer.

Stepping back, I keep my eyes on the tree line and try to keep my footsteps as quiet as possible. I feel the other trees moving at my back, but I don't turn as a shadow moves at the other end of the clearing. I blend into the fog and trees, using the trunk of one as a shield. I peek around it as the thing appears in the clearing.

Thing indeed.

Shaped like a human, with two arms and two legs, it stands hunched over. But like the forest, it's warped, corrupted, and dark. The thing wears no clothes, revealing dull gray skin. Its arms bend at impossible angles, so too long that they almost drag on the floor. Its legs, splayed and bent, end in feet bigger than any human's.

It lifts its head and sniffs.

I watch in horror and fascination as it turns to where I hide. Where its eyes would be, there are none, just wrinkles, gray skin, with holes for a nose and a slit for a mouth. With a start, I realize it only has holes for ears, too.

What the hell is this thing?

I step back behind the trunk. A good guess is it can't

see me, but I bet it can hear and smell me. I turn to look back, trying to think my way through this.

Suddenly, it vanishes.

I look around wildly. Where it stood is only empty earth and fog.

A breath moves the hair on the back of my neck and sends a shiver down my spine. I don't move, too afraid that whatever it is will attack. It stays there, breathing down my neck, and I hold my breath.

At last, it moves away, and I slowly turn to look. I let my breath out in a low whoosh as the creature creeps away through the trees.

Lifting my feet, I watch where I walk, trying not to make any noise as I sneak away from the creature. I have no idea if I'm going in the right direction, but I want space between me and that thing.

The forest thins out eventually, and a field greets me at the other end.

Great, an open plain where anything can attack me. I have no idea what awaits me, but I'm guessing it won't be good. I debate my options. If I go back, it means facing that creature. When I open my magic to see the thread, it leads through the field.

Of course, it does. Decision made.

Looks like I'm going through the creepy field.

As I step out into the field, I stay low to the long grass. With a start, I realize it's black. I stare down at the earth. It, too, is black. Is everything dead here? No sun shines down, and even the moon seems muted, only offering enough light to see by.

Halfway through the field, it changes. The grass becomes plants that reach my hip. I stop for a moment before pushing on. My hand brushes one as I walk, and I hold in my yelp of pain. Breathing through it, I hold my hand up.

There, on the outside, blood oozes from a cut. I stare at the plant in horror. Barbs jut out from it, like rose thorns only bigger, at least the size of nails. I peer around and notice the same barbs on all the plants.

Ready to head back and find another way across, I turn and freeze. At the other end of the field, the creature paces at its edges.

Okay, so, no turning back.

I look back at the plants. Not only do I need to be nearly silent, I also have to try to avoid the barbs as much as possible. I nearly laugh. The dense plants stretch as far as I can see.

It's just pain; I've handled worse. Perses said nothing could hurt me here, right? What if he meant I can only feel pain while I'm here, but the pain can't physically hurt my body?

Enough stalling.

Sucking in a deep breath, I slowly start walking again.

Every plant that cuts me adds to the pain, and bloody lines cover my hand and arms. The plants slice through my jeans, the fabric tearing with every step. I bite my tongue to hold in the screams I want to let out.

Pain turns my mind fuzzy, but I stumble on.

When the plants thin, I throw myself across the last few. I fall to my knees on the earth, breathing through the pain. I don't examine the cuts, knowing that will make it worse. Have you ever cut yourself and not felt it until you saw the blood? Yeah, well, I'm going to roll with that idea.

Pushing myself up, I look at where I am. A broken stone path lays in front of me, more trees at its edges. I glance back, but fog obscures my vision of the field.

This place gets creepier and creepier.

I step lightly on the first stone, in case it stabs me or something crazy. When nothing happens, I walk forward. My magic rises again, the soothing warmth burning away some of the pain as it shows me the thread stretched into the distance.

I don't know what I expected for Purgatory, but this isn't it. Every little noise has me nearly jumping out of my skin, so I sing in my head to keep myself calm.

As I reach the chorus of TLC's "No Scrubs", a growl sounds behind me.

Oh, for fuck's sake, what now?

I cut off mid-rap and turn to look. A couple of steps behind me sits a two-headed dog. I shit you not, this mother fucker has two heads. It's all black with red eyes. I try to hold in my snort. Someone's been really unimaginative. I must not hold my snort in because the dog steps closer and growls.

Okay, not imaginative, but it sure as hell does the trick.

"Nice, two-headed doggy," I whisper, holding my hands up. "I'm passing through. Would you like me to throw you a bone? A branch? Maybe two?" A laugh bursts out of my chest at the images of its two heads fighting for a stick.

The one on the left opens its mouth, and I yelp. Large, gleaming, white fangs are revealed, but it's the noise it makes that stops me cold. A human scream comes out of its mouth.

I am officially freaked out.

It opens its mouth wider with human screams for help.

Nope, not today, Satan.

I begin to back away. It advances with every step I take, following me but not getting closer.

"Help me!" it screams. The moans of pain carry on as it opens and closes its mouth.

I nearly fall on a loose rock behind me and it uses this opportunity. It jumps at me, and I react immediately by throwing a fireball at the still screaming head.

It yelps and drops to the floor, screaming as it catches on fire. The smell of burning flesh wafts to me.

I watch as the two-headed dog burns, my violet

flames licking over its nightmare body. The screams of the human only grow louder, and I feel blood trickle out of my ears. Yet, I watch.

When it stops moving, I call my flame back and the body disintegrates. It lays on the path, a pile of unmoving ash. Huh, guess there's no wind, after all.

Ignoring the nauseous bubbles in me, I turn back to the stone path. I need at least ten showers to get rid of the smell of its burning flesh. With renewed determination, I stride down the path.

I want this nightmare over with.

24

AURORA

A freaking castle, like the ones from old films, stands before me. It stretches to the left and right as far as I can see. One lone path leads to its open door.

I so don't want to go in there, but I have to, don't I? Why can't it be like a nice little cottage? Well, I guess that didn't work out too well for Hansel and Gretel.

Darius owes me a lifetime of cookies for this.

Walking through the large stone door sends a chill down my spine. The inside looks like something out of a horror movie set. Darkness casts shadows all around the room, making it difficult to see beyond the stone and the two curved staircases leading up from the foyer.

Okay, so, where to now? I watch the thread, which of course leads upstairs.

Grumbling to myself, I walk up the stairs, listening for any freaky ass monster waiting around the corner. All I hear is the creaking of the steps beneath my feet.

When I reach the top, a corridor runs to the left and to the right.

The thread leads down the one to the right. I follow it as the hallway darkens until, eventually, I walk in pitch black. Usually, I'm okay in the dark, but this one? It feels oppressive, like I can actually feel the weight of it pressing on me, closing in on all sides.

The only sound is my breathing, and I can't see anything. At this point, my eyes glow, the reflection from them barely lighting up the dark, but not even that breaks the void in front of me. My magic pulses in me as a reminder I have easy access to it now.

I smile happily, which feels wrong in this place.

"Light," I whisper, gathering my power in my palm.

I throw it gently in the air and a floating orb of violet light bobs near my head. I look back down the hallway and freeze as the light casts shadows across the thing in front of me.

It stands mere inches away from my face. I don't know how I didn't feel it breathing, then realize its chest stays still. Oh, that's because it's not.

I swallow and look around it. It leans with me, and I stop. Okay, then.

Not going to freak out. When it steps closer, I stop myself from stepping back.

It looks like it was once a woman. Long, bedraggled, greasy hair hangs in clumps on its head. Clouds film its eyes, its skin gray and mottled. As its skeleton-like body moves, and I can see the bones moving, too.

The more it stares at me, the more hated and desperation crash through me in waves. Unwilling to close my eyes with this creature so near, I concentrate on the negative feelings while watching it. With a start, I realize they come from the creature. Its mouth opens slightly, showing sharp, pointed teeth. As it does, all happiness is sucked from me, and all my fears doubled.

I take a deep breath, then blow it out, moving the thing's hair, and push the bone-deep fear back.

When it stands there not attacking me, I try something.

I step to the left, and it mirrors me. I step to the right, and it mirrors me again. I put my back to the wall, and it copies on the other side. Slowly, I step away, so I stand in the spot it previously stood, and it moves to my abandoned place. I walk backward, my light bobbing along with me. The creature copies, and soon, all I see are its eyes, then eventually nothing.

Turning, I slowly make my way down the corridor.

A shuffling noise comes from up ahead, and I freeze again. To my left, I see a doorway, and when the shuffling grows louder, I dart behind the door, leaving it open a crack.

A man, similar to the skeleton lady, shuffles down

the corridor. His head leans to the left and when he passes, I see why. His head hangs on by only inches.

"What are you doing here?" The soft growl brings me spinning to face the room, the door at my back.

My light only penetrates so far into the room, and I can't see anything. I step in farther, the light following, until I see who spoke. His stands with his back to the wall, as far away from me as he can get.

I recognize him. "Darius?"

He tilts his head like an animal and stares at me.

When he doesn't speak, I step closer. "You're Darius?"

He nods slowly, his voice disjoined. "You are?"

I stop and study at him. His clothes lay in tatters, and he's skinny—a lot more than in his memories. Not as bad as the skeletons, but getting there. If I leave him longer, will he become like them?

"Aurora. I came here for you," I whisper softly.

"Then, you're dead." His face loses his humanity, and for a minute, a distinctive, animalistic quality taking its edge.

I'm aware he can step forward and attack me at any minute. Remembering the advice I received once about what to do when facing a wild animal, I try it now.

Eyes downcast, I stay still, my hands out to the side of me, my palms facing inward. I don't let my fear show. I watch as he seems to struggle against whatever's taken over him. Eventually, the snarl recedes, and humanity slowly ebbs back into his eyes.

I decide to carry on the conversation like nothing happened. "I'm not dead. I'm a witch. Well, a hybrid, actually. I came here to bring you back."

As I step closer, he growls like a feral dog.

I stop instantly.

His growl dies down. "How are you here?"

I watch his eyes carefully. "I'm bound to your brothers, which somehow bound me to you."

A flash of something lights up his eyes, but I don't have time to consider what. "You're the one."

It's my turn to look confused. I stay where I am, not risking him sliding back into his primal state. "The one?"

A noise comes from the door, and before I can move, Darius grabs me.

I start to struggle, power filling my hands, when I realize he's not hurting me. I stop and let my body go pliant.

He slams my back against the wall where he previously stood, shifts in front of me, and lifts a finger to his lips, which are full and plump. Probably not the best time to notice that.

I nod to tell him I understand.

The door slowly opens, and we stay silent. He stares into my eyes, and I stare back. I know something came into the room, but it's like we're in our own little bubble, assessing each other.

I spot something out of the corner of my eye and freeze.

When the thing comes to stand behind Darius, I nearly scream. It looks like the skeletons I passed in the hallway but so much worse. The thing twitches from side to side and growls. I can't tell if it used to be a man or a woman. It has no hair and its eyes are cloudy.

As it begins sniffing around the room, I swallow nervously.

I stare into Darius's dark-brown eyes, unable to hide the fear in my wide ones.

He lowers his finger from his lips and cups my cheek before he lays his forehead on mine, blocking my view of the creature.

I still hear the thing sniffing, but my world now exists of the darkest brown eyes I've ever seen. I would describe them as soulful. There's something about his emotions and the way he moves. He might be human, but there's a wild quality to it like he can slide back into that feral primal state at any given minute.

I should be terrified, but a shiver of excitement slides through me at all that power and wildness gazing at me like I'm his savior. I hope he mistakes my shiver for fear.

Something peeks out in his eyes, and they dully

light up with his power, but I can tell it's not as strong as it should be.

We stare at each other as the thing sniffs around us, now next to our faces. I don't even breath as it growls and twitches against me. Its bones scrape as they slide underneath its paper-thin skin. As it hunches over, something hits my feet.

I still don't move, and neither does Darius.

Slowly, it walks away. As I let my breath out, it mixes with Darius's.

Only when we hear the door shut do I allow myself a deep breath. "What was that thing?"

Darius doesn't move, and I become aware we're pressed up against each other tightly.

His head is tilted down to meet mine. He must be over a head and a half taller than me. "Souls that are trapped here. If you're here too long, that's what you descend to."

So the man and the woman I saw outside, I'm guessing, haven't been here as long as the one who came into the room. Fun place.

"The castle is full of them," he whispers.

"How come you aren't one?" I whisper back.

His eyes shutter, and I miss their depth. "You."

I snap my head back away from him as far as the wall at my back will allow. "What do you mean?" I ask, no longer whispering.

"I don't know how you did it, or how long ago it was. Time moves differently here. I was trying to exist, but my emotions and humanity had nearly left me when this light surrounded me. It made me human again."

My voice gentles. "What does that have to do with me?"

"It's the same power calling to me from you now. If you stretched out, you'd feel it," he says, still so soft.

Doing as he instructs, I gasp when I feel him. My power is deep in him, almost animating him.

"They hunt your light, your humanity. Your liveliness."

I look at him again. "What do you mean?"

"When I came back to myself, all the creatures and lost souls were drawn to me like a beacon. I keep moving, yet they always find me. Now they'll be drawn to you."

Great. So that's why I've had so many encounters. "We need to get out of here."

"No shit, angel face. So, you're here to save me?" His question holds a growl at the end.

I nod again.

"So, you can get us back?" he asks, his voice even.

"I think so."

He moves away finally, and I'll admit, I miss his heat.

"Then, we need to get somewhere safe for now, so you can try." He flicks his head at me. "Come on, angel face. We don't want to be here when the rest of the lost ones in the castle realize we're here."

I step forward with a frown. "Why were you here, then?"

"I felt something pulling me across the lands. I'm guessing that was you. I didn't know where, so I came to check here."

I follow him to the door.

He sticks his head out, then waits a moment before he opens the door fully and heads into the hallway.

I follow him, my light still above me. Silently, I walk by his side, on alert for another lost one, as he calls them. We make it to the front door of the castle without any more run-ins, and once we're outside, I wordlessly follow him through the trees.

We walk for a while before I decide to speak. I didn't want to risk anything overhearing us in the castle, but I figure we're far enough away now.

"Where are we headed?" I look through the trees for any other creatures this place has to offer.

"Somewhere deep in the lands. It will give you a place to get us out of here without your magic drawing everything in a five-mile radius." He looks over at me and I nod.

As we continue forward, I study him out of the

corner of my eye. He's not what I expected. I knew being in this place would change him, but there's nothing of the teasing, laughing man I saw in the mirror. Will he change back once we're back home?

"So, you're bound to my brothers?" His quiet voice moves through the trees like a magic of its own.

"Sort of. It's not completed yet. You don't sound like you're questioning it?" I carry on my search of the trees as we walk and talk.

"Dying and living here changes the way you see things," he mutters.

Yeah, I can imagine.

"So, they're okay?" His question is so quiet I almost don't hear him.

"Yes. The last time I saw them, they were."

We fall silent for some time. I don't know what to say to this man. I know the him from the past, not this one who appears half dead and animalistic.

He stops at the edge of the tree line. I peek around him and see a lake of some sort. He scans the edge of the land before it.

"Is this safe?" I whisper.

He flashes me a smile that stops me cold. It's bitter and nothing like the one I'm used to seeing on his handsome face. "Nothing here is. Come on, angel face."

As he walks over to the water, I follow. "My name is Aurora."

He turns with a flourish, revealing a little boat that's

seen better days. He bows mockingly to me. "Well then, angel Aurora, your chariot awaits."

At the challenge in his eyes, I grit my teeth and clamber onto the rickety wooden boat, sitting on one of the slats. After pushing us off, he jumps in and sits opposite me.

"I didn't expect it to look like this." I don't realize I spoke out loud until he responds.

"It's a reflection of the world. Just a distorted one."

I tilt my head in consideration. "I've never seen a place like this."

With a growl, his face closes down. "I have."

I stare at him. "Where?"

"My home," he grunts.

I look out across the water. Where did he grow up? I thought the boys knew each other since they were little? I lean over the water and watch as it gently laps against the boat.

"Don't fall in, angel face." He's back to mocking again, making the word angel sound dirty.

I bite my tongue from reminding him of my name again and don't even look at him.

"Why?" I ask, my curiosity getting the better of me.

He sticks his hand in, and I watch as he brings it out again. Red, thick liquid covers his hand.

"Blood," I whisper in shock.

"Blood, angel face," he confirms.

I sit back in disgust, trying to get as far away from the water as I can.

He laughs mockingly at me, and I scowl at him. What the hell is this problem?

"Welcome to Purgatory, Angel Aurora."

25

AURORA

*H*e rowed until a small island appears, made out of sharp rock, then led us to a cave inside the island where we sit now.

"Are we safe here—as much as we can be?" I look around like the walls might jump out and attack me.

He leans back opposite me, the lethal grace clear in his body. "For now. The things here don't like to cross the water and the things in the water will leave us alone."

I nod okay.

"So, Aurora," he sneers my name, "how do we get out of here?"

Since our conversation in the woods, he became an asshole. I get being moody. He's dead after all. But I'm trying to save his life, and with every sneer or rude remark he makes, I want to smack him.

I manage to hold back my frustration at his attitude. "I have to bind us first. Then I follow my bindings to your brothers out of here."

"That will work?" His scorn is palpable.

I stand in a rage and point at him, all my fear and worries over the binding exploding in one rant. "Look here, asshole. I came a long fucking way to find you. The only reason I'm not leaving your ungrateful ass here is because I care for your brothers and they would never forgive me."

I pace in front of him, muttering about how much of an asshole he is. His laugh makes me stop, and I turn to face him, my fists clenched. It doesn't seem mocking this time, but you never know.

"At least you're honest, angel." He leans forward. "So, you have to bind to me? Is that permanent?"

At his questions, the fight goes out of me and I plop back down in front of him, rubbing my head wearily. "Yes."

I could explain what Perses said to me, but honestly, I'm too exhausted from my journey through these harsh lands.

"Okay." He nods.

I stare at him in disbelief, the shock evident in my voice. "Just like that?"

He sneers at me again. "Unless I'm not pretty enough for you, angel."

Mother fucker.

"You won't be when I cut off your dick and feed it to you!" I scream.

Something about him pisses me off. It's hard because, in my head, I keep remembering the old Darius with the soft smiles and mischievous twinkle in his eye, but here I'm faced with a major asshole with attitude problems.

"Ah, so you've been thinking about my dick?"

Un-fucking-believable. I glare at him silently.

"So, how do we do this binding?" He leaves the attitude off for once.

"I need to breach your mind and magic, and then we finish using blood," I mutter, still angry over his attitude.

"Awesome, your highness. Let's do it." He stands, and I stare at him in surprise.

I guess I would be eager, too, if I was dead.

"You deaf, angel? I said come on." He smirks down at me.

"Cum guzzler," I mutter, getting to my feet. Reigning in my anger, I step toward him and stretch out my hands. "It's easier if we're touching."

"If you wanted to touch me, all you had to do was ask."

I grit my teeth and wait for him to put his hands in mine.

A spark instantly runs through me to him, and he makes a noise.

Ignoring him, I close my eyes and get ready to bind this giant asshole to me forever. Who says I'm not selfless? Alex and the guys owe me a bloody house made of cookies at this rate.

My power stretches toward him, and his eagerly rushes up to meet mine. Violet and black twirl together, and I almost sag with the euphoria it creates.

When I reach the barrier into his mind, it's like a stone wall.

Let me in, I whisper in his head.

He answers out loud, "How, your highness?"

I think I prefer angel.

I consider his question. *Drop the wall.*

The whisper floats into his mind, and he struggles with my suggestion, which is understandable. Letting someone into your mind voluntarily is not high on anyone's to-do list. It leaves you vulnerable, and this man is acutely aware of that. Eventually, the wall drops, and I rush in before he reconsiders.

I don't look at his memories or thoughts. I don't want to see them.

Instead, I allow my mind and magic to merge together as one with his.

We fall to our knees in pain and pleasure as our bodies are ripped apart and put back together again. I don't know where he ends and I begin.

I imagine a cut on my palm and feel the blood ooze from it. I imagine one appearing on his hand, and slowly, I push my bleeding palm to his. Our blood mingles and falls to the stone floor beneath us, every drop loud like a thunder.

My ears fill with noise and it becomes too much. My blood pulls from my body and into his. I scream silently in my mind; his growl of pain echoing mine.

Then, it cuts off like a switch.

I float back to my body and fall to my side on the stone floor. He does the same, our hands still clasped together, only now I feel him inside me. If I wanted to, I bet I could read his thoughts and emotions and even talk inside his head. I don't do any of that, though. Instead, I allow my eyes to flick open.

His dark-brown eyes meet my violet ones. Gaze soft, his eyes run over me with a strange expression. I am way too tired for that.

"Sleep, angel. I'll watch over you," he whispers, the term no longer holding scorn but instead tenderness.

I don't know if he spoke in my mind or out loud. All I know is it's the trigger needed to get me to pass out.

When I wake, I feel Darius beside me. I'll be able to find him anywhere now. I take the time to search through my body with my magic and find no damaged. Darius's consciousness hovers at the edge of mine, and I don't like it. I build a wall between us, blocking out his mind from mine.

He gasps out loud, and I open my eyes.

He sways where he sits, gripping his head. "What did you do?"

I drag myself into an upright position. "Sorry. I don't want you inside my head, and I figured you would feel the same."

My voice comes out rough, and I wait for him to acknowledge me.

He doesn't.

I glance around and see we're still in the cave.

Eventually, the pain must ebb because he releases the vise around his head and looks at me with a growl. "Warn me next time, angel."

I nod. "Sorry, I didn't realize it would hurt."

Despite my soft apology, he snorts and turns away from me. "Whatever. Now that you've finished napping, let's get the fuck out of here."

I grit my teeth and stand. "Fine, asswipe."

"Good one." He rolls his eyes at me.

"Jackass," I mutter.

He narrows his eyes at me, but I smile innocently at him.

"So, how does this work?" he asks.

"I don't really know. I was told I could follow the threads back."

"Bloody brilliant. Well, come on then."

Jesus, he's a prick. I can't believe I'm bound to him. I definitely prefer angel over princess as well.

He must hear my thoughts because he flinches before he covers it with a smirk, and his response floats in my mind. *Back at you, princess.*

I ignore him, choosing instead to close my eyes. The sooner we get out of here, the sooner I can be home. I concentrate on where I know the threads reside now. It's hard with him so close so I push him away.

The threads of my men flash in my mind, their colors bright. I smile. I can't wait to see them.

I wonder if they missed me like I did them.

With a start, I realize the thought isn't mine. This bonding will take some time to get used to, and the wall doesn't seem to block everything. I grab on to the closest thread and think it through. I don't think I can hold onto Darius as well.

Give me your hand.

So needy, princess. He does as I say, though.

I grab the threads again and yank. We fall into the void from which I came through. The pain returns, and so does the bone-weary exhaustion, double this time as I bring someone else with me. Like carrying someone on my back.

My knees weaken and almost give out. My head

spins and roaring fills my ears. I grit my teeth and push through. Pain lances through me with every step. It almost becomes too much.

You can do it, angel.

I gather strength from his voice and pull us through the void and out the other side.

26

ALEXANDER

"*H*ello, brother."

Spinning as fast as I can to stand guard in front of Aurora's sleeping body, my mouth drops open in shock. Maybe I've finally gone mad from lack of sleep because my dead brother stands in front of me.

"Darius?" I ask. He doesn't smile. Despite his blank face and slimmer his body, I recognize him. "Are you real?"

He nods and gazes down at Aurora with a little smile. "Why don't you get the others and I'll explain everything."

His voice isn't as strong, nor as cocky, as normal, but it's him.

Everything is a blur after that until we are all sitting around the table in the kitchen in shock.

Ben nearly fainted when he saw Darius. After he hesitantly hugged him, he burst into tears.

Ezra breaks the silence. "How?"

"Aurora." That little smile comes again, and my jealousy rises.

Then I register what he said, and I stare at him. "Explain."

He laughs, a bitter sound nothing like his usual carefree laugh.

Jason lays a hand on my arm, his voice soft and soothing. "What Alex means is, will you tell us how?"

Darius looks at us, marginally warmer. "Nothing changes, eh?"

"Not everything is the same," Ezra mutters.

Ben's been silent since he sat down, and I cast him a worried look.

Darius begins, "Aurora saved my life. I don't know all the details, so you'll have to ask her."

"How can we?" Mikael moans.

Darius smiles wide at this. "She'll wake up soon. The binding and bringing me back took a lot out of her."

I rub my head. I don't want to get my hopes up, and I feel the others doing the same.

Binding? I need answers.

"I think you better start from the top." I lean back, my face expressionless.

Darius nods and launches into his story.

27

AURORA

*U*gh, my head is killing me. I try to blink my eyes open but pain shoots through me, so I scrunch them close.

Take it easy, angel.

Jackass?

I feel laughter echo in my head.

That's me. Just go slow.

I allow my head time to stop throbbing, then slowly blink my eyes open. They're fuzzy at first but soon clear.

Everyone hovers around where I lay in the bed I first saw in the mirror. A giant exhale goes through the room, and I take in their grave expressions and tired eyes. Darius stands behind them, offering me a rare, supportive smile. I return the smile, glad I managed to bring him back. That definitely means he owes me cookies.

My attention shifts to my guys once more, and when the silence stretches, my sarcastic side comes out to play. "Who died?"

"You're really awake." Ben throws himself at me, burrowing his head against my neck, and tears hit my skin. His voice comes out low, and I feel his lips move against my skin as he talks. "Goddammit, sunshine, don't do anything like that again."

"Sorry, Benny."

Ezra strides to my side and, in front of everyone, kisses my lips, quick and desperate. I look into his panicked eyes as his strokes my cheek gently like I'm made of glass. "Jesus, baby, I thought you weren't coming back."

I untangle my hand from the bed and cup his cheek. His eyes close in bliss, and he leans into me. He kisses my hand tenderly and steps back.

Alex takes his place. He kisses my forehead lovingly. "Never doubted you, kitten."

I smile at him in thanks.

Jason tries to nudge Ben out of the way, but he clings to me like a monkey.

Alex sighs and steps back to let Jason come around and take his spot.

Jason leans down, his usual soft smile nowhere to be seen as he whispers in my ear, "You ever do anything like that again and I'll tie you to my bed. Understand?"

Despite my tired body, his words and the low growl

in his voice spreads warmth through me. "I understand."

He squeezes my hand and steps back.

I turn to Mikael, who hesitates like he's unsure of his welcome. I notice the scar on his throat, and without saying a word, I hold my one free arm out to him. That's all the encouragement he needs, and he rushes to my side. He sits on the bed and holds my hand, his usual stormy eyes muted.

"Thank you, Aurora." His eyes drop to the bed. "You saved my life."

I squeeze his hand and wait for him to look back at me. "Who else is going to sit playing Never Have I Ever all night with me?"

At my soft smile, he answers with one of his own.

"Well, this is touching, it really is, but do you think someone can show me where I can shower and then eat? It's only been, like, five years." Darius sneers, and Ben flinches against me.

"Stop being an asswipe for one second," I growl at him.

His laughter brushes my mind.

Mikael glances between us and stands with a sigh. "I'll show you."

I go to protest, but he leans over. "I'll come back. We have some catching up to do."

He gently kisses my cheek, then leads Darius out of the room, who throws me a wink on the way.

"Can't believe I'm bound to that asshat," I groan.

Ben laughs against my neck. Jason takes Mikael's place, and Alex and Ezra stand at the foot of the bed.

My gentle giant won't look at me, and I don't like it.

Alex crosses his arms, his blank mask in place. "You have some explaining to do, kitten."

My nickname rolling out of his mouth soothes any worries. God, I missed them. I nod my understanding.

"Can I have a cookie first?" I ask sweetly.

Ben and Jason laugh, and Alex's lips twitch. Ezra doesn't even move from glaring at the comforter. I watch him, then flick my eyes to Alex.

He nods. "Okay. Jason and Ben with me. We'll sort out food for everyone, and Ezra can help Aurora."

His smiles gently at me and I smile my thanks. My green giant needs me.

Both Jason and Ben protest, but one look from Alex silences them.

Ben mutters something on his way out.

Jason offers me a smile and follows.

Alex kisses my forehead again and whispers, "Go easy with him, kitten."

He follows his brothers out.

I stare at Ezra, but he doesn't look at me.

"Cupcake?" I whisper.

He swallows but doesn't move.

Okay. If he won't come to me, I'll go to him.

When I try to sit up, he comes to my side in a second. "What are you doing?"

"You needed me, so I was coming to you," I say, annoyed.

He helps me sit up so my legs hang off the bed, then kneels in front of me. Before I know it, his head rests in my lap. "I thought I'd lost you."

His broken whisper tugs at something in me.

I run my hands through his hair. It's longer than last time I saw him, with the natural wave more pronounced. "Nah, I'm not that easy to get rid of."

He doesn't laugh, just sits with his arms wrapped around me like a teddy bear.

"I missed you," I say softly.

He moans and lifts his head, tears swimming in his eyes. "I missed you, too."

I lean forward and tenderly kiss him. He doesn't respond, but I don't stop. I kiss each eyelid, his forehead, his cheeks, then back down to his lips.

This time, he pulls me to him like he's starving and devours me. I let him, knowing he needs this.

Eventually, he pulls away, breathing me in. "Don't ever do that to me again."

I nod. I would agree to anything for him.

"And don't think you're not in trouble for going to Purgatory." His usual growl returns, but he could never scare me.

I lean forward and quickly kiss him happily. "I can't

wait."

He moans and leans back on his heels. He gazes at me, emotion swirling in his eyes. "You'll be the death of me."

I pretend not to hear.

He sighs. "Come on before they all come back looking for you."

He jumps up and scoops me into his arms. I wrap mine around his neck and cuddle into him. I really did miss my teddy bear.

"Where are we?" I ask as he strides down the hallway.

He looks down at me, his lips twitching. "It's a long story."

I nod. They'll tell me when they're ready.

He carries me to the kitchen where all conversation dies when we walk in. Ezra gently sets me in a chair at the wooden table and they all sit down around me.

"Tea is cooking," Jason offers helpfully.

He then sets a bag of cookies in down front of me. I look at them in wonder, my eyes filling with tears because of the thoughtfulness.

"Is she crying?" Ben whispers.

They all laugh.

"Doesn't cry when she nearly dies or comes back from Purgatory, but cries at cookies." Ben chokes.

I ignore him, snatch them off the table, and bite into the chocolate deliciousness.

28

AURORA

*O*nly wanting to do this conversation once, I wait for Darius to come back.

I sort through my thoughts as I go. It's hard knowing where to begin. My time with Perses and Purgatory made me realize I need to trust and open up more, and I'm really going to try. I'll start by telling them everything.

When Darius slides into the room and the seat opposite me, I have to stop my jaw from dropping. He cleaned up, his hair now shaved close to his head. His clothes are tight but fit him. I'm guessing they're Ben's. Overall, he looks good.

Blaming the binding for the need pulsing through me, I glance away before I do something stupid.

A snort sounds in my head, but I ignore it.

I focus on Alex who sits at the head of the table and wait for him to lead.

As he sees this, happiness and lust enter his eyes, darkening his usual amber color. "Okay, kitten, why don't you begin with what happened with Mikael and go from there? We will try to not interrupt."

I nod and lean back, getting ready for a long conversation.

Ezra, who sits to my right, lands his large palm on my knee, warming it. He rubs it in soothing circles, and I draw strength from him.

"I'm guessing you all know what I am now." I glance around, running my eyes over them.

It's so good to see them for real. The mirror helped, but it wasn't like being in the same room.

Alex gives me a small encouraging smile. "Let's say we don't."

I steel my spine. "I'm a hybrid. My mother was a witch and my father was a reaper—"

Jason goes to interrupt, probably with a question, but Alex shakes his head at him, and I carry on.

"I don't know how it's possible, but I inherited both of their powers. My mother and father realized what I was and hid me from the world. They continued with their lives in the coven and his duties while they taught me to control my witch powers and hide my reaper ones. But when one rises so does the other. So, I had to hide it all. They never really told me why." I look down at the table. "Expect, one night, I overheard them talking. My mum was worried, she was shouting at my dad, saying we couldn't trust anyone. If they knew what I was, they would…"

I stop and take a deep breath as the memory fills my head. Another hand lands on my other thigh, offering me warmth and support. I nod to myself and look up. "They would kill me. So, I hid my powers well. One day, I managed to slip away from my mum and dad, and I went into the woods behind my house. I was young. There was a being there and I saved him, he offered me a choice."

Perses's eyes run through my head, and a pang of sadness for the god hits me.

"A choice?" Mikael's soft voice prompts me.

"To save the witches. I didn't understand what he wanted, but it felt right. Every word he spoke, the earth whispered to me the truth and destiny behind his tale. I accepted it, and he killed me." They gasp, so I quickly carry on. "Well, not really. He stabbed me with a spelled blade to bring my powers out. I don't remember much after that. Like the reaper said, he must have seen it. I went back home, but my mum knew, so she and my father took me and ran. I don't know how the reaper found us again, but he did. He killed my mum while I hid. He was looking for me. When they left, I went to her, but it was too late. After her death, my father changed. He let the darkness consume him."

I stop for a second, and two hands squeeze my thighs. I decide to gloss over the details.

"Eventually, I knew I couldn't stay there anymore, so I ran…" I look up with a small smile "…right into you."

Apart from Darius, they all smile at me. I choose to skip what they already know, jumping to my recent absence. "After I saved Mikael, I awoke in a strange place to the man I had saved that day."

"Who was he?" Ezra asks, his voice deep and rumbly.

At his hint of jealousy, I control my laugh. "He's a god. His name is Perses."

I let that bombshell drop.

"The gods are myths," Jason protests.

I look at him. "No, they're not. They didn't fade, and they aren't myths. We took the power they offered us, and we corrupted it, so they turned their backs on us; all but one. When our lines started dying out, the gods decided they needed a solution. The one, Hekate, who didn't turn her back on us, decided to bless a group of children."

I look up to see if they are following.

Questions fill their eyes, but I decide to go on. "I am the descendant of her line that she blessed. You are the others."

"Run that by me again," Alex says.

I nod. "It's hard to explain. Basically, I'm supposed

to save the lines and return the power to our people. Hekate died to bless me with her power. She knew I would be too powerful and unbalanced because of it, so the gods blessed a child of each line. That's the pull you feel to me." I watch their faces. "You're supposed to help me contain and even out my power."

"Makes some things clearer," Ben mutters.

Alex nods at me to carry on.

I decide to spit it all out. "Perses trained me to control both sides of my powers. He helped me release it from its cage. He also told me I could bring Darius back. I agreed to try, and he informed me I would have to bind him to me to do so."

Alex holds his hand up. "Bind?"

I nod. "It's a connection. I have partial ones with you all, but I completed his. It's supposed to help me and will also help you."

Ben frowns. "So, you're, like, together?"

"Not really. Perses explained it can be like a sibling bond, and I offered him a choice." I look to Darius.

He nods.

"So, we're all going to bind to you?" Jason asks quietly.

"I, err— Perses mentioned it, but I don't want to bind anyone who isn't willing, and to be honest, the whole thing is still a bit weird for me." I fall silent and allow them time to digest.

"We can deal with that later. Now, what happened

after?" Alex asks, obviously feeling my anxiety on the matter.

I offer him a grateful smile. "That's when I went to Purgatory, bound Darius, and came back here."

"So, you're supposed to save the witches, and we're, like, your helpers?" Jason says, trying to sort through my disjointed story.

"Like your brother-wives." Ben snorts.

I giggle, and before I can help myself, I slap my hand over my mouth.

Embarrassed, I look down and finally notice my clothes. It's been a whirlwind since I woke up.

I hold out the bright pink nighty I'm in before looking around at them in horror. "What the fuck am I wearing?"

They all burst out laughing.

Even Darius's lips twitch.

29

AURORA

"So, what was Purgatory like? Sunny?" Ben asks.

We switched locations to a massive living room, and I now sprawl across the sofa, my head in Ezra's lap and my feet in Alex's. Ben sits next to me on the floor. Jason and Mikael sit on another sofa, while Darius prowls around the room. I alternate between watching him and watching Ben's hair that I'm playing with.

"A fucking bundle of joy," I deadpan.

About to respond, a familiar popping noise cuts him off.

"Noooo," I moan.

"What the fuck?" someone shouts.

Ben scrambles up in front of me while Ezra and Alex tenses underneath me. Jason and Mikael warily watch the newcomer.

I look to the center of the room where the bane of my life stands with a smile on his face.

"Silly witch," he greets.

I sit up, push Ben aside, and glare at the gremlin. "Gremlin, I thought I left you behind with Perses." I flash my teeth at him in warning.

I feel the guys' confusion.

Want me to kill this thing, angel?

I shake my head and slump back, my arms over my chest. I won't admit I'm secretly glad to see him.

"Er, sunshine?" Ben hesitantly asks.

I sigh. "Everyone, this is Bob. I met him in Perses's world. He's a friend... sort of."

"Bob?" someone asks.

Bob puffs up in anger at the laugh in the voice.

"Bob," I warn.

He sticks his long, forked tongue out at me. "Nice to meet you, silly witch's harem."

I burst out in laughter. Harem?

Bob steps forward and kicks Ben's shin.

He hops on one leg, grabbing it, and shouts, "What the fuck!"

I stand and prop my hands on my hips. "Dude, what the hell?"

"You said no more licking to greet," Bob says, confused.

"So you kick him?" I ask in disbelief.

"That's how you greeted me," he reminds smugly.

I point at him. "You were being annoying."

He sticks his tongue out again. "Silly witch."

I narrow my eyes. "That's it, gremlin," I warn and build a fireball in my hand.

His beady eyes narrow in warning. "You wouldn't."

I smile at him evilly. "Watch me."

"Aurora?" Hesitation fills Alex's voice.

I let the fireball go, but I point from my eyes to Bob's, then turn back to my men. Ben is trying not to laugh, as is Jason. Ezra looks confused, and Alex is caught somewhere between amusement and confusion. Mikael looks like he's about to bust a gut. Darius is still prowling around behind them.

"Yes?" I say sweetly.

Alex raises his eyebrow at me. "Care to explain why there's a hobbit reject in the living room?"

I smile at the reference. "I sort of made friends with him. Perses asked him to look after me while I was there, and the bugger won't leave me alone."

"Silly witch."

I turn back to Bob with a growl and point at him. "I will burn your little ass if you carry on, goblin."

He perches on the now vacated couch and scooches back until his back rests against the sofa. His little legs swing over the cushion.

"Okay, I can't deal." Ben laughs so hard tears track down his face.

I look back at the gremlin.

"Cookies?" he asks.

I groan.

"Yep, he definitely knows Aurora," Ezra says with a chuckle.

We all sit down again, plus the gremlin. No one wants to sit next to him, so I perch on Alex's lap in the middle cushion with Ben and Jason next to us. Ezra and Darius block the doorway.

"Where are we, anyway?" I ask for the second time today as I run my eyes over the room. Ezra said it was a long story, but I've told them mine, so now it's their turn.

Alex laughs beneath me, his hands tightening where they rest of my thighs. "Healer's house, about two hours from ours."

I nod. "Healer?" I tilt my head in question.

I watch Bob devour the cookies, happily swinging his legs back and forth.

"A special type of witch. Usually high up in the pecking order." Alex's voice rumbles from behind me.

I stiffen instantly.

"Yeah, except this one is crazy and doesn't have a house lineage or coven. He has nothing to do with the council," Ben says with a laugh.

I relax instantly. "So, we can trust him?"

Alex squeezes my thigh. "Yes. Otherwise, he knows what will happen. Plus, he sells his services to the highest bidder. He doesn't care about anything but money."

It probably shouldn't make me feel better, but it does.

"What happened to the kid?" Ezra rumbles.

Alex sighs beneath me and strokes my bare thigh. "I sent him home to look for some information. I rang him earlier to let him know it doesn't matter and to finish payment."

"Kid?" I ask.

Jason smiles at me. "Sheldon, the one I was telling you about."

I remember now. They filled me in on what they were doing, and I must admit, it warmed my heart to know they spent so long searching for a way to bring me back.

"Where's Mikael?" I ask, realizing he isn't in the room anymore. It's hard to keep track of this many people.

"He went to rest. He's still not a hundred percent." Ben lays his head on my shoulder.

I try to think of any other questions I have. Honestly, though, I'm exhausted. I shouldn't be after all the resting my body has done, but it seems it doesn't matter.

"Lane!" I shout and bolt to my feet, spinning to face Alex reclines.

"Your human bestie is quite insistent," he says with a small smile.

"You spoke to her? Is she okay?" Panic grips me at how I left her.

His eyes soften. "You're worried about her after all that has happened?"

"Duh. Is she okay? Can I speak to her? Does she—"

"Kitten."

I stop and look at Alex. He crooks his finger, and I step between his parted legs.

He locks them around my thighs and keeps eye contact with me. "She's fine. She was worried about you. We told her we were all going on a vacation when we were in an accident which left you in a coma. I also told her we were paying for medical care and that we needed her there looking after your house and Tom." I follow along, more questions crowding my mind. "We told Tom the truth, and he's been looking after her. I promised to ring her every day."

My walls crumble even more. "You did?"

"Of course. You care about her, and she cares about you." His purrs, and my heart clenches for this man who, after everything, took the time to comfort my bestie.

"I bet she's mad as hell," I say, laughter breaking our moment.

He smiles again. "No doubt. But we're leaving tomorrow to return home, so you can see her then."

Excitement and nerves jumble my emotions. I don't know what he sees in my eyes, but he leans forward. "What's wrong, kitten?"

"I promised her I would tell her everything when I saw her next. What if she doesn't believe me? What if she thinks I'm crazy?" I look down from his probing eyes. "What if she leaves?" I trail off as I voice my fears aloud.

Lane is my family and it would kill something in me to lose her.

He raises my chin with a finger and waits until I look at him to answer. "She will not leave. Lane loves you more than anything. That girl was willing to take on all of us, use anything to track us down, and then would probably have beaten us for letting you get hurt. She's not going anywhere."

I nod, tears in my eyes.

"And neither are we."

I take a deep breath as his words sooth all my fears. I look up and catch Darius's eyes as he turns away and leaves the room, but not before I see the longing in them.

"So, I can see her tomorrow?" I glance around.

"Of course, kitten. In fact, I can't wait because my ass is numb from the constant calls."

I burst out laughing and look at his smiling face. Reluctantly, I step away and turn to the gremlin. "Are you staying?"

"No, silly witch. I came to see if you were okay." I smile before he carries on. "Not for me, stupid witch. For Perses."

I build a fireball, ready to throw, when he pops out with a laugh.

I stand there muttering about gremlins as my men laugh behind me.

When I look at the guys again, I noticed the exhaustion in their faces. I tell them sternly to go and rest, and I'll do the same. There are no complaints. I guess they really are tired.

Ben kisses me on my cheek, as does Alex.

Jason offers me a smile, and Ezra gives me a confused look before leaving.

I find my way back to the room I woke up in and hesitate before opening the door, hoping Mikael waits inside. I step in quietly and see him sitting against the headboard of the single bed pushed up next to the one I woke up in.

I pause in the doorway until his eyes open.

He smiles when he sees me, and it reaches his eyes. "You coming in?"

Voice rough, he coughs with a grimace, and I quickly rush in to pass him a glass of water sitting on a table next to his bed. He accepts it, takes a drink, then passes it back to me.

I place it next to the bed. "Are you okay?"

He smiles at me again. "Shouldn't I be asking that?"

His voice is rougher now than when I heard it in my dreams, probably due to the large scar along his neck. The edges are still red and sore looking, but at least it's closed.

"Hey." He gently grabs my hand.

"It's my fault," I murmur, unable to meet his gaze.

"Like hell it is."

I snap my head up and see the storm in his beautiful eyes. I can't seem to look away. I'm trapped inside the depths.

"I was drawn to you, Aurora. That's why I went to that town. He captured me before I even found you. I was complacent, and I know better than that." His voice evens out a bit when he speaks.

"But if you hadn't been drawn to me, this"—I gesture at his throat— "would never have happened."

"Maybe, maybe not. You saved my life, Aurora, and I don't blame you for anything. You didn't make him torture me. You didn't make him try to kill me."

My guilt weighs heavily on my shoulders. "But—"

"No." he cuts off, voice stern and face serious. "I don't blame you and neither do any of the others. I'm glad I came after you, because then my brothers did, too. Without that, we wouldn't be here with you now when you need us most. Everything happens for a reason, sweetheart, but it's not always good."

He strokes my thumb as he watches me think through his logic.

"You really don't blame me?" I ask, needing to be sure.

His smile lights up his eyes and it's like the rainbow on a raining day. "Never."

I smile back at him, the weight lifting from my shoulders.

"I missed our nightly chats," he admits shyly.

I laugh. "Me, too."

While we only met in a dream, he knows things about me no one else does. There's no hiding from the honesty in his depths.

He pats the bed next to him and slides over to make room. I hesitate before deciding what the hell. I sit beside him, his shoulder behind mine. My legs pushed up against him.

"It feels strange to see you for real. I thought your beauty was because of the dark place I was in, but if it's possible, you're more beautiful than I remember."

My face heats at his words. "You're not so bad yourself."

"Not anymore," he mutters.

I turn to see him gently touching his neck and frown. "Your scar is part of you. I've never felt fear like I did in that moment. Knowing I was going to lose you before I even got a chance to have you." I gesture at his neck. "This is part of you. It shows your strength and loyalty. It doesn't take away from how handsome you are. If anything, it adds to it." I stare in his eyes, showing him the truth of my words.

His smile is blinding, and the darkness in his eyes disappears. "What's your favorite flower?"

I laugh as I sit back, done with all the deep, emotional talk of the day. "Corny, I know, but roses."

He grabs my hand again. "Classic. Would you rather be an animal for the day or a man?"

I laugh again. I needed this. We sit side by side for hours, laughing and joking, sharing our lives and our dreams.

He holds my hand the whole time.

30

AURORA

*L*ater, I lay in bed, my thoughts running wild.

I ordered the others to bed hours ago. I should be doing the same, but my mind won't let me. Mikael eventually fell asleep, and I slipped out so he could rest.

I ran into Alex in the hallway. He didn't say anything. With a knowing look in his eyes, he walked me to a door and kissed my forehead before bidding me goodnight. The new room isn't like the one I stayed in when I was in a coma. I think no one wants me to sleep in there. Instead, it offers a double-bed and an en-suite.

This house is huge. I'll have to remember to thank the healer for letting us take over his home. Wherever he is. Alex mentioned he tends to keep to himself. They only see him once a day when he comes to check on me and Mikael.

The door creaks open, and I bolt upright, squinting to make out the figure who hesitates in the doorway.

I allow my power to trickle through the room until I can identify the intruder. "Ezra?"

He steps in, shuts the door behind him, then stops again.

"Giant, is everything okay?" I ask softly.

As he walks over to me, the moonlight streaming through the curtain reveals him to me. He stands over the bed with the most vulnerable look I've ever never seen in his eyes.

"Baby, can I—" He glances away and swallows before looking back at me. "Can I hold you?"

Nerves fill his soft voice.

A giant chunk of the wall left around my heart shatters at his hesitant words. I scooch over and lift the covers. He sighs and crawls in beside me. Covering him up, I lay down on my side facing him, and he turns on his side so we're inches apart.

"You okay?" I ask softly.

He nods.

I frown. I can feel that he's not. I reach forward, the moonlight allowing me to see him, and cup his jaw.

He closes his eyes.

I gently stroke his cheekbone. "You know you can talk to me, right?"

"I know. I'm not used to sharing." He opens his eyes and looks at me. "I meant what I said earlier. I missed you so much. I need to hold you tonight. I need to know you're really here."

A smile stretches across my face. He might look scary, but underneath, he's all mush. My gentle giant.

"Okay." I kiss his cheek, then turn on my other side.

He moves closer so his body runs along my back and wraps his arm around my waist, pulling me until I'm flush back against him. He gently pushes his other arm under my head like a pillow. His heat seeps in, and I lay there blissfully happy. Safe in his arms. He really is like a teddy bear with a smile.

"Night baby," he whispers against my head and kisses the back of it.

"Night, teddy," I whisper back and cuddle down into him.

Something hard pushes against my ass. Without thinking, I move, pressing back into it. I stop, still half asleep. My nightgown is pushed up, a warm hand cupping my unbound breast. My legs twist with theirs, and it's clear they're happy to be there.

I think back and remember Ezra sneaking into my room last night.

I try to nod off again, but his hand tightens on my breast, causing me to bite my lip to hold in a moan. We've been flirting the edge for a while, and my body is warm and needy, throbbing. I push back again. I swear it's on accident.

He groans behind me and grinds into my ass. It causes my nipples to pebble and my breathing speeds up. My panties are already damp with my need for him, and I try and twist my legs around to relieve the pressure. He grabs me tighter and grinds again.

This time, a moan slips out. He stops, and his deep breathing picks up as he wakes up.

"Baby?" he whispers, gruffly.

I swallow. "Yeah," My voice comes out soft and velvety with lust.

"What—" he stops and inhales when he realizes where his hand is.

He pulls it back, slowly grazing my nipple as he does.

I can't help the little sound that escapes me. He stops with his hand halfway up my shirt.

"Ezra—" I don't even get time to say anything before his large, warm hand strokes down my belly.

He buries his head in the back of my neck. "Tell me no, baby, and I'll stop."

Is he crazy? Lust fogs my thoughts, and all I want is my gentle giant. I want to break that shell he surrounds himself with and lose control. Maybe I'm a little crazy.

His hand slips lower, playing with the edge of my panties. "I mean it, baby."

I don't say anything but push my ass back on him

again. He growls and nips along my neck. I move against him, needing friction. He pushes my legs apart and presses his thigh tight up against me. I moan and rub against him.

"Jesus, baby, if you don't stop—" It ends on a groan as I rub myself against his thigh again, my ass rubbing his hard-on. He bites my neck harder, and I close my eyes in bliss.

He flips me to lay on my back, panting with need beneath him. He hovers over me without touching. I look into his eyes, now darkened with need, his pupils blown. I lick my lips and he growls.

He slams his lips against mine, the kiss rough and hard and everything I need to remind me I'm alive. I wrap my arms around his neck and pull him to me. He falls on me, and I part my legs so he lands between them.

He breaks the kiss, his breathing labored. "Tell me to leave, baby, and I will."

I stop and look at him. "You don't want me?"

With a smug smile, he growls, "Of course, I want you. You're all I think about. Every time you give that smile to me, I get hard. The first time I kissed you, I knew I was gone. I've been imagining this since I met you, but I don't want to rush you."

I smile at his sweet, gruff words, the evidence of his desire between my legs. I lean up and whisper at his lips. "I'm not a child, Ezra. I know what I want. I'm not afraid to tell you. I wanted you, too, and right now I need you inside me, fucking me until I scream. I want to watch you break apart between my legs—"

I don't get to finish before he slams his lips back down on mine.

He nips my lower lip, then sucks it better. I let my hands roam, happy to discover he's not wearing a shirt. I must have been half asleep last night not to realize. Soft skin stretched over muscle meets me, and I run my nails lightly down his sculpted back. As I do, he thrusts against me. I smile smugly against his lips.

He breaks the kiss again, and I'm about to moan in protest when he leans up and grabs the bottom of the nightgown I wear.

With a wink, he rips it over my head.

I'm laid beneath him in nothing but my black lace panties. His eyes run across my skin, heating as they go. Where he looks, a trail of fire follows. He gently strokes my tucked in waist, and his hands move up to cup my heavy breasts. I pant when he tweaks my nipples, and it's his turn to smile smugly at me.

He leans down and wraps his lips around my left nipple, and I arch in pleasure, pushing deeper into his mouth. I grip his hair and hold him to me as he sucks on one and plays with the other. I wrap my legs around him, my panties soaking now. He grins against my breast.

"Ezra, please." My voice is needy as hell.

"Please, what?" he growls against me, the vibration sending another pang of pleasure through me.

"I need you," I gasp.

He leans back, looking down at me. "You're so fucking beautiful. I want you so much. The first time is going to be hard and fast."

I groan when he says that. If possible, him talking dirty makes me wetter. He leans back down and kisses me to death. His hands toy with my panties again, and I growl. I nip his bottom lip, and he rips them off my body. I gasp with an arch.

He stops kissing me and watches my face as he cups my now bare pussy. "You're so wet, baby."

He groans, making me nod desperately.

"This for me?" he asks as I grind into his palm. He stops me by holding me still. "Answer me."

"Yes," I moan.

He leans down and kisses me lightly. "Good girl."

He strokes my nub in circular motions and watches as I writhe in need. I'm about to do—I don't know what if he doesn't hurry up—when he slides a finger into me. I arch again, needing him deep in me, filling me. He slides another in and slowly starts moving.

"Faster," I pant.

He ignores me, prolonging my torture as he slowly works me.

He pulls his fingers out and watches me as he sucks them.

"Fuck." I pant.

His eyes close and when he opens them again, they're predatory. "You taste fucking delicious."

He kisses his way down my stomach, stopping above my aching pussy. He smirks up at me, and I glare down at him. He watches my face as he licks me softly.

I can't seem to look away as he slides two fingers back into me. He keeps his gentle rhythm up and devours me like I'm his favorite dessert. I grab his hair and grind against his face. I look away, and finally, my head smashes back against the pillow.

The pleasure is almost too much. I need him in me so bad. I writhe beneath him as he slowly increases the pace. My moans pick up speed, my release building.

"Ezra," I moan.

He pushes a third, big finger in, and I explode against him with a scream. I lay there panting as he continues to fuck me with his fingers and lick my sensitive nub.

"Again," he growls.

He fucks me faster and curls his fingers inside me, hitting that spot. Before I know it, I'm coming again, screaming his name. I lay there in my post orgasm bliss as he moves away. I don't remember closing my eyes. I open them as he slowly slips out of his sleep pants, watching me hungrily the whole time.

When he stands before me naked, I nearly sob with need for him.

He's stunning. All solid muscle and lines. His cock stands hard, and I lick my lips when I look at it. He's longer than I've ever had, and thick, too. Not crazily so, but I can't wait to feel him in me.

I slowly raise my eyes to his hooded ones. "You going to fuck me or what?"

He prowls to me and climbs over my body. I moan when I feel him at my entrance. He breaths down on my face, and I've had enough of his hesitation. I reach between us and grab his hard cock. I line him up, and he growls. He slams into me, and I arch my back. Fuck, he's big. He stretches me, and I love it. When I move beneath him, he grabs my hips and stills me.

Confused, I look back up at him, my lust-filled brain completely fried. "What?"

"I want you on top next time. Now though, I'm going to fuck you senseless, so hold on to the headboard, baby."

I lift my arms slowly, rubbing my breasts against his chest as I go. I do as I'm told and grab the wooden slats of the headboard. As soon as I do, he moves in me. He starts out slowly, but within seconds, he's slamming into me hard and fast like he can't get enough of me.

He drops his forehead to mine. "Fuck, you feel amazing, baby."

At his words, I clench around him, and he grits his teeth. He slams back into me, and I can't help the noises coming out of me.

He reaches between us and gently rubs my nub. With every slam back into me, he reaches deeper. My next orgasm builds, and by his wild movements, he's close. I toss my head from side to side, gripping the headboard for all I can.

He thrusts so deep and hard in me and I explode around him, my pussy clenching him. He growls as he comes.

We're both panting, slick with sweat. He drops his weight on me, his head buried in my neck.

When he stops breathing so hard, he takes some of his weight off me and looks at me. He gently kisses my lips, and I decide then and there he's mine. He claimed me, body, mind, and soul, and he doesn't even know it.

Ezra keeps his promise. He wakes me during the night again, and I ride him slow and steady. He watches me the whole time, lust and caring in his eyes.

We fall back to sleep sometime around sunrise.

When I wake again, I slowly stretch my used muscles. I feel well and truly fucked, but in the best way. I turn over and find the bed cold. Sitting up, I shiver at the coolness in the room as I frown and look for him.

I tilt my head when I hear the shower running.

Uncaring about my nudity because, let's face it, he's seen all of me, I strut through the open en-suite door.

He's rubbing his hair when I walk in, the glass shower divider fogged from the steam. I slowly open it and lick my lips at his delicious, wet body. He turns to me, eyes lowering, and when he sees I'm still naked, they heat again.

I step over the lip of the shower and face him. The water hits his back, but his eyes are on me, waiting to see what I'll do. It feels different in sunlight. Last night was all about need and pent up emotions. Now, it's about want. I see a sliver of vulnerability in his eyes.

Did he think I'd regret last night this morning? Determination to ease his fears spears through me, and I grin as I drop to my knees.

"Wh—" he begins.

I silence him by grabbing his wet buttocks. I look at him and gently lick the top of his hard dick.

He swallows. "Baby, you don't—"

I lick him again, and he groans, his eyes screwing shut. He braces against the wall behind me, and his head hangs down.

"Look at me," I whisper.

His eyes open, and his mouth parts as his breathing picks up. I slowly lick around the tip of his dick, then slip him into my mouth. I keep my eyes on him the whole time, showing him how much he means to me. I might be too messed up to say it in words, but I can in actions.

He watches me the whole time. He pants, and I rub against the floor for relief, my need for this gentle giant so big.

He reaches down with a growl and drags me up. I start to protest. I loved the feeling of his silky hardness in my mouth. He lifts me up by the thighs and slams me back against the shower wall. I brace against it and wrap my legs around his thick waist.

"Your mouth felt amazing, baby, but I need to be in you," he whispers against my lips.

I groan, then kiss him, the taste of him still in my mouth.

He thrusts into me and stills as I stretch around him. Tangling his tongue with mine, he thrusts slowly, pulling out before slamming back in. He puts his hand behind my head to cushion it as I hang onto his shoulders. His other hand drops to my hip and holds me as he fucks me. Hard and fast, not as desperate as the first time, but every time he drags his cock over the bundle of nerves in me, I moan, which only seems to spur him on.

My nails cut into his shoulders as I throw my head back, trying to push down on him, my feet digging into his ass. He growls and shoves me back into the wall, pinning me there as he slams into me, again and again until I scream as my pussy clenches around him. The orgasm comes out of nowhere. His thrusts stutter, and he slams into me once more, coming with a yell.

Trying to relearn how to breathe, I drop my head to his wet shoulder as he holds me there.

"Fuck, baby," he mutters, and I grin against his skin before dropping a kiss there and lifting my head.

He smiles at me and drops a soft kiss on my lips before lowering me back to my wobbly legs. He steadies me, then turns me to the spray as he washes my body and hair.

The caring way he does it, and the worship in his expression, breaks down that last barrier between us. My magic reaches for him.

"Ezra," I try to warn.

He must feel it. "I'm ready, baby. Bind me."

I don't know how he knows, but he lets his magic tangle with mine and it's like a bomb going off. My mind rushes into his, no barriers in the way. I couldn't stop this even if I wanted to, so I imagine the cut on both of us like I did with Darius. Ezra slams his mouth to mine as I bind us together.

When I come around, we both kneel on the shower floor, panting like we ran a race. I look into his eyes, his mind open to me. His feelings for me rush to me, and I nearly panic at their intensity. His love for me is huge. He would do anything for me, and he was lost when I was gone.

We might not say the words, but there, kneeling on

the shower floor with the water bearing down on us and our magic tangled together, I know he loves me.

And I love him.

Something brushes against my mind, a mocking laugh, and I push it away, unwilling to let that asshole ruin this moment.

31

DARIUS

I feel every inch of pleasure, and when I close my eyes, I see her on her knees before my brother as he fucks her mouth, and it drives me crazy.

Five years is a long time to be celibate, but it's not like there were a lot of options in Purgatory. Plus, my need seemed to have disappeared, only to return when that dark-haired angel appeared in front of me. It came back like a roaring fire, one I can't seem to quench.

Her binding us together doesn't help. All I think about is that fucking mouth, that sexy as hell body, and her on her back underneath me like she was with Ezra last night.

I'm not ashamed to say I peeked at it. Hell, I fucking touched myself to it and came embarrassingly fast.

But underneath it all, my anger stirs. She fucking

bound me then ignored me like I'm nothing but a stranger to her. If only she knew I spent the last six months learning her life. Watching her, seeing her every time I closed my eyes. I don't know how she did it, but she called me from the other side long before she met my brothers. I had to watch months and months of her with that other fucking guy, wishing all along it was me. Watching her struggle, watching her wake up screaming.

I know her better than myself at this point; all her fears, all her secrets, all those embarrassing moments she'd rather not share.

Fuck. I slam my fist into the wall. She didn't even look. I can admit that's what bugs me.

When we bonded, I offered her my mind. It seemed only fair since I saw all of her. But she didn't even look, didn't even peek, before blocking me off from the light and salvation of her head.

The anger and darkness that consumed me in Purgatory is hard to fight; even harder now that she cut me off from her—only allowing me scraps of her emotions and feelings, and only when she doesn't realize she's doing it.

Yet I still drink them up like a drowning man, rushing for each one and the light it throws into me that blocks the darkness. But it's never enough, never for long enough.

The only time I felt like my old self was when we

bonded and were open to each other. For that split second, I was whole again. The monster in me retreated back to the darkness.

God, I don't blame her, though. If she'd seen what I had done, what I became while I was there, before I met her, she wouldn't want me. I'll have to accept that. Maybe find a way to break the binding. It's my only choice, because I sure as shit won't sit here and watch as she falls in love with everyone else but me.

She will never love you, a whisper inside of me speaks, and I know it's true.

How could she? I'm nothing more than a monster.

32

AURORA

*O*nce Ezra and I dry off and dress, we head to the kitchen. He holds my hand along the way, and I expect him to drop it when we reach the kitchen. He doesn't. He keeps hold of it and sits down next to me.

Alex looks back and forth between us, his blank mask clearly in place. "Lucky bastard."

I pretend not to hear, but Ezra smirks at him.

"Yes, angel. Although next time you decide to fuck one of my brothers, could you block me from your mind, please?" Darius says sarcastically as he leans against the counters.

He wants to embarrass me, but I won't let him.

Instead, I make eye contact and smile slowly at him. "You're jealous."

Alex laughs and I feel Ezra's amusement from next

to me, but I don't look away from those brown eyes. Something flashes in them, and a stab of anger mixed with jealousy hits me.

My smile grows.

"Whatever you say, angel." His voice is snarky, and if I couldn't feel his emotions, I would probably hate him. As it is, I'm weirdly glad for the ass wipe's jealousy.

Ben walks into the kitchen and kisses my cheek before sitting down next to me. Jason wanders in behind him and heads to the kettle.

"So, what time are we leaving?" I ask everyone in general, trying to keep my wandering eyes from Jason's ass.

"After breakfast."

I glance at Alex, who smiles about something. Weirdo.

Mikael comes in next, shuffling until he sits down hard across the table from me. He smiles at me tiredly and yawns.

"Someone have a late night?" Alex asks smugly.

I stick my tongue out at him.

As Jason puts a mug down in front of me, I lean back. "Thanks, sweetie."

He smiles before giving Mikael a mug.

He grips it, his eyes half closed. Guess he's not a morning person. I blow on my coffee and watch them. Jason goes about making breakfast and Mikael continues to zombie sip his coffee. Alex reads a newspaper. Darius comments on Jason's cooking. Ben tells awful jokes to me and anyone who will listen. Ezra leans back, watching it all.

My smile grows. It's good to be back.

"Cookies!" comes a scream right in my ear and I jump, throwing my coffee all over myself.

I turn to where the gremlin stands giggling to himself. When I glare and raise my hand, he pops out of existence again.

Fucking magical beings.

I end up wearing one of the guys' shirts and some jeans that are a little too tight. I don't ask where they got them. I help everyone pack up as Alex leaves to speak to the healer. Ezra goes with him.

Ben and I then sit on the front steps to the house waiting to go. I can't wait to see Lane. I lean my head on Ben's shoulder and watch the nature surrounding us. He kisses the top of my head and I smile.

"Missed you, sunshine," he admits, a note of sorrow in his voice.

"Missed you too, Benny," I say softly.

He wraps his arms around my waist, and we sit like that, waiting for the others.

"Why do you never see elephants hiding in the

trees?" He doesn't wait for me to respond. "They're really good at it."

I laugh softly at his bad joke. "What's orange and sounds like a parrot? A carrot."

He groans at my bad joke. "Why didn't the astronaut come home to his wife? He needed space."

I try and hold in my laughter, but when I glance at his face, we both burst out laughing. We nearly stop again, but then one look at each other has us hysterically giggling again. Tears run down my face and I can barely breathe.

"What are you two doing?"

We peer up at Jason who watches us with his eyebrow raised as he watches us leaning on each other laughing.

We glance at each other, then him, and laugh again.

He stands there watching a smile on his lips.

Ezra, Alex, and Mikael come up behind him. At their side, Nev wags his tail. There he bloody went.

"What's going on?" Mikael asks.

"I think they're broken," Jason says, still watching us.

I manage to control my laughter and Ben seems to as well.

"What did the blanket say as it fell off the bed? Oh, sheet!" I shout.

Ezra's lips twitch and Alex smiles, shaking his head. Jason and Mikael both laugh with me and Ben.

"Are we leaving or what?" Darius's grumpy voice comes from behind them.

Groaning at the party pooper, I stand and brush off my ass.

Need a hand with that, angel?

I ignore Darius's voice floating in my head. I really need to learn to block him.

Anger explodes down the bond, making me stumble. As soon as it started, it cuts off, leaving me reeling as an empty feeling replaces it in my chest as Darius stomps away.

I sit squished in the back of a black Range Rover between Jason and Ben. Ezra drives. Alex follows in his car with Darius and Mikael, and Nev rides with them.

"Why couldn't I sit in the front again?" I ask, confused.

"Because then we wouldn't get you pressed up next to us," Ben says happily.

"Perv." I laugh.

When I meet Ezra's smiling eyes in the rear-view mirror, he sends a pulse of happiness to me through the bond.

I lean my head on Jason's shoulder and watch out his window as we drive through the countryside.

A song comes on the radio and I sing along softly to it. Ben joins in and soon all three of us sing along.

When we pull up outside my house, I feel strange. So much has changed since I was last here.

Ben hops out and reaches back in, his hand outstretched for me. I grab it and stand next to him in my driveway.

My front door opens, then a blonde blur flies at me, almost tackling me to the ground But with a grunt, I manage to right myself.

Lane wraps herself around me, muttering about how she's going to kill the guys and how much trouble I'm in.

The feeling of being loved hits me and I squeeze her back. "Sorry, Lane."

"Yeah, you will be," she replies, but sobs disrupt her voice.

We stand there holding each other as Alex's car pulls up. A door opens, and Nev bounds to Lane.

I laugh and pull away as she tries to stop him from licking her.

She looks up from the dog and stiffens. "Who are they?"

I follow her gaze to Mikael and Darius. "Long story."

She glares at me.

I hold up my hands. "I promise to tell you. Can we go inside first?"

She nods, turns with a hair flip, and marches back inside my house like she owns it. I smile, happy to have her here. I promised to tell her, and I will. I'll tell her everything and hope like crazy she sticks around.

Who's the human, angel?

Curiosity laces Darius words, and a pang of jealousy hits me. Lane's beautiful. She's taller than I am. She has the crazy curved body. She looks elegant. She's basically the total opposite of me.

I try and shut my thoughts down. I'm not used to being insecure or jealous.

I prefer my woman, small, dark-haired, curvy, and with a smart mouth.

I try and ignore the flipping sensation in my stomach his words cause, even as my jealousy retreats at his words. Not looking at him, I follow my best friend into the house.

33

AURORA

"So, let me get this straight. You're a witch and you went to visit a god realm and then to Purgatory?" Lane's voice is flat, and I can't get a read on her emotions.

We sit in the living room while the guys hang out in the kitchen, giving us some space.

I watch her like a wild animal. "Err, yeah, pretty much."

"All this time! Every time we watched Harry Potter and I said how cool it would be to have magic! And you're telling me now that you have it?" She ends on a screech, and I wince.

She paces in front of me, muttering, "Wait, is Hogwarts real? Did I miss my letter?"

She turns to me, and we both burst out laughing.

There's a hysterical edge to it, but I'm relieved she hasn't run out of the door yet.

She sits opposite me on the sofa. "Why didn't you tell me?" she asks softly, staring down at a cushion.

I fight the urge to make a joke. "I was scared you would think I'm crazy. Or you would leave." Now I'm the one looking at the cushion.

She sighs. "I'm not going anywhere. I might not have known you were a witch, but I always knew there was something different about you." She grabs my hand and stills it as I pulled at the threads of my jeans.

I look at her. "You mean it?"

She nods. "Yeah, you always had—"

I interrupt her with a smile. "You're not going anywhere?"

She snorts. "Like you could get rid of me. Especially now." We smile at each other. "So, tell me everything again and don't skip any details."

She settles down, and I start from the beginning.

As we wait for pizzas to arrive, Lane grills the guys and gives Alex the stink eye. Apparently, he put the phone down on her. It's hilarious watching my skinny, bubblegum pink human best friend glare at the huge witch.

She tilts her head in curiosity. "So, can you do anything you want with your magic?"

"We use spells and words of power, but essentially, yes. It also depends on power levels. The stronger the witch, the stronger the spells," Alex answers.

"What about you?" Lane asks me.

"I never really need spells or words. I sorta wing it."

She snorts. "Of course, you do."

I carry on. "My power is different, though. It's not completely witch power, so maybe that's why?"

Ezra grunts next to me. "I don't know."

We all look at him.

"What do you mean?" I ask.

"Since we bonded, my magic is stronger, and I don't need any of that, either."

I stare at him in surprise.

"Me, either," Darius mutters.

"So, it might be because of this blessing that she has? Maybe it unlocked her power?" Jason offers. "I've been doing some reading, and apparently we didn't always need to use words and spells. The strongest of us had control over their magic. It would stand to reason that Aurora would have control over hers, too, and I'm guessing with her magic touching you two, now you do as well."

"Why doesn't everyone know we didn't used to?" Ben asks, confused.

"It's hidden in ancient books. My guess is the

council doesn't want anyone to know how far we've fallen. If what Perses said to Aurora is true, they've corrupted their power," he muses.

"So, basically, we bind with Aurora and become like some mega transformer?" Ben ask.

I laugh at his description.

Jason shrugs. "Maybe, but it's a theory."

"A good one. We need to know how it works. I don't think Aurora should bind anyone else until we know all the side effects." Alex looks at all of us.

I glance down guilty. In all honesty, I hadn't planned on binding Ezra. But it felt right, like my magic was in control.

"Awwww, I wanna bind to my sunshine," Ben whines, and I shake my head.

"So, what is this binding, then? And who are you bound to?" Lane asks, curious.

"I'm bound to Ezra and Mister Bag-of-Fun over there." I jerk a thumb in Darius's direction.

He sneers at me. "Cute, angel."

"Jackass," I mutter. "I had to bind Darius to bring him back. The dead can't cross without the living. I bound to Ezra the other night." I smile at him, and he smiles back.

"Uh huh, and why is that?" Lane laughs with a knowing look on her face.

I lean back casually. "I don't know what you're talking about."

"No?" she says innocently.

When she wiggles her eyebrows at me, I laugh.

"So, you didn't sleep with him?" Amusement fills her voice but her face turns red from talking about this.

All the guys glance between us.

I don't look at them, scared of the expressions on their faces. I'm not ashamed of sleeping with Ezra. Hell, it's the total opposite. But I don't know how they'll all react. Perses mentioned the bonds don't need to be sexual, but if I'm honest with myself, I'm attracted to all of them, even Jackass.

I decide to go with humor, hoping it will cut the tension. Plus I've never been shy, and I don't want Ezra to think I regret it. "Want all the details? Because he did this thing with his tongue—"

When she flames bright-red and covers her ears, glaring at me, I cut off in laughter.

But I still don't look at the guys.

"So, is that part of the binding? 'cause if it is, I'm so down to test it." Ben winks at me.

I smile at his attempt to cut the tension. Jason stares at the floor. Mikael watches me carefully, and Alex's eyes run over everyone.

The silence stretches until the doorbell rings.

I jump up and jog to the front door, calling over my shoulder, "I'll get it!"

Well, that was awkward.

34

AURORA

*A*s we all eat together, the tension lessens, but it's full of unspoken things.

Lane leaves after grumbling and making me promise to call her tomorrow.

I make an excuse about showering and flee to get some space.

The spray from the shower flows over my tired muscles. My hands brace the wall in front of me, and the water hits my head and flows down my back. I spend the time trying to block Ezra and Darius from my mind without cutting them off completely, especially when I remember how painful for Darius this has been.

I imagine a steel wall surrounding them. I never noticed before, but I can feel them there, like a warm presence. As soon as I shut them out, it seems almost empty, but I need to be able to think without them pushing in and without Darius's attitude.

I know I should be an adult, sit them down, and ask how they feel about the binding of me and Ezra. Instead, I hide out in the shower, allowing myself one last minute of peace. Lost in my thoughts, I don't hear the bathroom door open and close.

"You know, you ran away pretty fast."

I spin in shock and stare at Alex where he perches on the counter next to the sink. "Seriously? Can I have no privacy?"

I don't bother trying to cover myself. Maybe I should be embarrassed and grab a towel, but I don't really care.

He looks at me, his amber eyes glowing. "If you really wanted some, yes, but I know you're trying to shut us out and feeling unsure."

He lets his blank mask fall to reveal the Alex I've come to love so much.

Wait, what? Nope, not going there.

"You know, I never apologized while you were conscious for the things I said to you," he continues.

I sigh and grab my shampoo, knowing he won't leave. "You don't need to."

I lather up my hair and the scent of strawberries hit me.

"I do. I didn't mean it. I let my fear and desperation

cloud my judgment. It was wrong of me. So, I'm sorry, kitten."

I stop lathering to look at his serious face. I can tell it's bothering him.

"Apology accepted," I say and turn so the water washes away the shampoo.

His eyes burn a hole in my skin as he watches me, but it's oddly comforting to have him here, to know I can't block him out. Alex would never allow that. He doesn't speak as he watches me condition my hair and rinse it out.

When I turn off the water and turn to him, he waits on the other side of the glass shower screen with my black towel in front of him, open.

I smile and step out into it.

He wraps it around me, then steers me to stand in front of the mirror.

I wipe the fog away to see him. "What are you doing?"

He smiles at me in the mirror and goes back to rummaging through my drawers. When he finds what he wants, he turns around.

I raise my eyebrow at the hairdryer and brush, then laugh. "You're going to dry my hair?"

"If you'll let me." He walks closer and perches his head on my shoulder, gazing at me in the mirror. He looks so open and eager, I can't say no.

"Let me look after you, kitten," he whispers softly, and I nod.

He smiles and plugs in the hairdryer. He runs it over my hair, and I feel loved. It's a strange intimacy. I feel more vulnerable now than even during sex. It isn't driven by need or lust, but by kindness and caring. He concentrates so hard, his tongue caught between his teeth as he dries my hair.

In this moment, I'm open, too. No walls between us, just the sound of the hairdryer as he blows away my worries. I watch him in the mirror. He catches my eyes and smiles, soft and slow. His eyes burn with tenderness, and I let myself fall in.

When he finishes, my hair hangs in soft, sleek curls down my back, and with a frown, I realize it's almost at my bum now.

Without a word, he leaves me to dress. I choose comfort over sexy and put on pants and a tank top. As I pull on my fuzzy socks, he returns and sits by my side on the bed.

"I saw your face earlier, Aurora. I know you're worried about how we'll react to this binding and your relationship with Ezra."

How does he see so much?

"You need to ask them, but I can offer you some advice and truth."

I nod, not looking at him.

"Those men, all of them, were devastated when you

were gone. And not in a friendly way. Ben might hide it well, but he went to a dark place, and he's still not back completely. He needs you now more than ever. Jason barely held it together. He might be the quiet one, but he needs to hear from you that you want him as much as he wants you. I don't know how you did it, kitten, but you thawed Mikael's heart. It's his story to tell why it was frozen in the first place, but know he's fallen for you as well."

I digest his words.

"You?" I ask softly. I need to know.

"I promised myself, if you ever came back, I would kiss you like I should have done that night. I might act closed off, kitten, but that's only because they need someone to lean on. I have to be that person, but anytime you need to know how I'm feeling or whether I care, all you need to do is ask. I won't hesitate to show you, even if it's not what you want. I once told you I would never lie to you, and I meant it."

He takes in a breath. "I'm not light, I'm not funny, and I'm not smart. I have darkness in me, Aurora. I would do anything in this world to keep my family together. I would kill. I would destroy. I won't always do things the way you want, but I'm always doing it with your best interests at heart, even when it seems like I'm not."

With that bombshell, he stands and goes to leave.

Bravery hits me and I stand. "What about your promise?"

He stops still like a statue. "I won't kiss you until you know how you feel about me, kitten. Because when I do, I'll be lost, and you will never get away from me."

I watch as he leaves, and my heart thumps hard. I sit down on the bed and think over everything he said.

He's right. I need to talk to the others. I had already noticed the shadows in Ben's eyes and that Jason has been quiet. I need to spend some time with them. The idea that they're hurting because of me fills my eyes with tears.

Everything over the last couple of days hits me.

A wet nose nudges my hands, and I glance down at Nev. He places his head in my lap and looks at me.

I lean down and kiss his furry head. "I missed you so much."

As I rain kisses down on my fur baby, he barks, and I know he's saying he missed me, too.

When I reach the living room, the conversation stops. I roll my eyes and slump on the corner seat of the closest sofa and watch them.

"How about a movie night like old times?" Ben grins at me, shadows in his eyes.

"Sure."

As he goes over to the movies to pick out a few out, his shoulders are tense.

Jason sits down next to me and passes over a bag of cookies. My smile is genuine, and I'm happy as I grab them.

Darius makes a disgusted sound. "Are there any bars around here?"

I don't bother looking at him, but my shoulders tense up. Ezra stops behind me to massage them.

"Sit down and enjoy the movie," Alex orders.

Darius sprawls on the floor in front of the telly, ignoring us all.

Mikael hesitates in the doorway, and I scooch over, moving Jason across the seat, and pat the free space. Mikael glances at Ezra before coming to sit next to me. I offer him a smile and turn back to the others. Ezra moves to sit next to Alex.

Ben puts in the film, then turns around and looks so disappointed that I stand up.

"C'mon, Benny, before I miss the movie because your fat ass blocks the way." I grin at him.

He smiles shyly before sitting in my open spot. I plop myself onto his lap. He hesitantly wraps his arms around my waist, and I cuddle into him. I don't like this shy Ben. I miss my mischievous one.

Shut up, will you, angel? You think so bloody loud.

I narrow my eyes on Darius.

He watches the television, ignoring me.

Shut up, asswipe. If you don't like it, get the fuck out of my head.

With a start, I glance at Ezra who watches the movie. He's not spoken in my head yet. Can he hear our conversation?

I don't think so. Now, be quiet, will ya?

Jackass.

Princess.

Bucket of cum.

I feel his amusement. *Tinkerbell.*

I try to stop my lips from twitching. *Bum bandit.*

His silent laugher roars through my head. *What the hell is a bum bandit?*

You, I think smugly.

I make sure to project my thoughts loudly to him about how hot certain characters are as we watch the movie. He ignores me, but I find myself funny.

Eventually, I fall asleep on Ben's lap and wake up halfway through the movie when Ezra says he'll take me to bed.

I remember my plan to cheer Ben up and make a decision.

"Benny, will you sleep with me tonight?" I ask around a yawn.

I feel the room hesitate.

After a while, he replies, "Sure thing, sunshine."

He lifts me and carries me out of the room.

Raised voices sound behind us and anger smashes into me from one of the bonds.

Before I know it, the front door slams and my heart and bond tug like they want me to go after Darius. I feel him slipping farther away as he heads into the night. I hope he's okay.

I project the thought, but a barrier slams down on me hard, cutting me off and making me gasp in pain.

Ben stops and looks down at me with a worried expression. I don't know what he sees, but his face contorts in anger.

I wave my hand in the air. "I'm okay." Unwilling to let that jackass ruin my night, I raise my voice to the others and shout, "Night!"

I hear their replies, but I'm already burrowing down against Ben's chest again, even as part of my heart aches like it's being torn apart. Is this what it felt like to him when I blocked him out?

Fuck, Darius. I'm sorry.

Of course, I get no response.

"Sunshine?" a soft voice whispers.

I ignore it.

"Sunshine?" It comes stronger this time.

"Hmm?" I ask sleepily.

"You sure you want me to sleep in here tonight? I

can go get Ezra." Hesitation fills the voice and it wakes me up quicker than anything.

I open my eyes to meet Ben's ocean blue eyes, shadowed and full of something I can't name. His head is on the bed where he must have laid me down. He sits on the floor. I frown at him. Ben wouldn't usually hesitate to climb into bed with me.

I move farther back and pat the space I was in, my voice thick with sleep. "I want my Benny."

He smiles, but it looks forced. He gently climbs in, keeping distance between us, and I hate it. I shuffle closer until I lay at his side and rest my head on his chest.

Under my ear, his heartbeat speeds up.

"Aurora?" His voice sounds almost strangled.

"Yes?" I whisper softly, feeling him hesitate, and I fully wake up. "What's wrong Benny?"

"I—you don't—I mean…"

I sit up and study his downcast eyes. I cup his face in both hands and wait for him to look at me. He continues not to, so I straddle his waist and tilt his head up. "Talk to me."

He sighs and looks at me. "You don't have to play with me, anymore. I know you've chosen Ezra."

I sit back and drop my hands. Is that what— Sighing, I watch him closely. "Benjamin, look at me."

He swallows, but when his eyes finally meet mine, I realize what I've been seeing. Fear. He's afraid he's going to lose me. "I haven't chosen Ezra. I haven't chosen anyone."

He looks at me, seeing the truth in my words. "But you slept with him and bound him?"

I nod. "I did. I care about him." He looks like a kicked puppy, so I quickly carry on. "But I care about you, too, and Alex and Jason and Mikael, and yes, even a little bit for Darius."

"But—"

I put my hand over his mouth and tell myself to talk to him, to trust him. He needs me right now. He's hurting and it's the only reason I open myself up. I usually shy away from emotions and feelings but I'll do it for him.

"Perses says I'm bound to all of you, but it's only been completed with Ezra and Darius. I want you, Benny. You make me smile and laugh until tears fall. I missed you so much when you were gone. I love that you don't take me seriously. You lighten me up. Yes, I slept with Ezra." I force my eyes to his. "But I want you, too, so much. It might not be today or tomorrow, but I will bind you to me if you'll have me." My words trail off in hesitation, my bravery cracking under my own fears.

He leans up and puts his head to mine. "Always." He gently kisses my lips and then his usual brilliant smile breaks out. He wiggles his eyebrows at me. "So, you want me, huh?"

I laugh with him and see his eyes have cleared a little, their usual twinkle back. I slap his chest lightly. "C'mon, Benny, I'm tired."

He smiles and lays back down, taking me with him. I lay my head on his chest, our legs tangled together. He kisses my head gently.

"I will wait for that day. I'm yours," he whispers against my head.

I smile into his chest.

"I have an addiction to cheddar cheese... But it's only mild," he deadpans.

I giggle at his corny joke. "Why shouldn't you write with a broken pencil? Because it's pointless!"

His chest moves under me as he laughs.

I smile as I fall asleep in his arms.

Something wakes me in the middle of the night, and at first, I don't know what it is.

When I figure it out, a tear drops down my face.

I can feel him, all his pain and rage. It batters me, and I can only imagine what it's doing to him. He might not even know it, but he's calling to me, and I would never not answer.

No matter how much he hurts me.

I slip out of Ben's arms, who turns over and cuddles

into Nev who must have snuck in sometime during the night.

Silently, I make my way downstairs and pass my other sleeping men before stopping at the front door and slipping on some shoes. I hesitate only for a second, reminding myself the reaper is dead and he can't hurt me anymore.

Opening the door, I wince when it creaks. I hold my breath, and when no one stirs, I slip out into the night.

Frowning when I can't see him, I allow our bond to guide me up the drive, through the trees, to the left.

I narrow my eyes to see better.

Ten minutes later, I find myself at the edge of a clearing where Darius is beating the shit out of a tree. I stumble back at the pain radiating from him with each punch, like a blow to my heart. He's so lost, I can feel it. So fucking hurt and scared. I can't help myself.

He probably doesn't want me here, but I step out anyway, and when he senses me, he freezes with his back to me.

"Darius?" I ask softly, and he shudders, still not turning around.

Blowing out a breath, I summon courage and walk closer until I stand at his side.

I can only see half of his face, but when I do, I gasp. He looks like he's been in a fight, with one black eye and a split lip. Looking down, I see his knuckles are split and covered in blood.

Unable to help myself, I reach out to touch his face, and he throws himself back like I'm poisonous, making me flinch.

"What happened to you?" I demand.

He stares at the ground with his fists clenched by his side, breathing heavy and not speaking.

"Darius?" I demand, getting angry but also worried.

He slowly lifts his head, and I gasp. His eyes are pale, like the skeletons from Purgatory, and an animalistic snarl twists his face. He doesn't even look human.

"Run," he snarls at me, spittle flying from his lips.

I stumble back, a mistake really. Everyone knows you don't run from an animal.

He pounces, no hint of Darius even left in his eyes. I try to move, try to scramble away, but I don't want to hurt him, so I don't attack. I end up on the ground with him pinning me, grinning down at me evilly. I know it's still him. I know it is, but fear winds through me.

"Darius, what happened? Please, it's me," I beg.

He growls, darting forward in warning, and I shut my mouth.

Okay, so talking is out of the question. I could pull on my bound with Ezra, but it would probably be too late. I already decided I can't attack Darius, so what am I left with? The bond.

Fuck. I'm so stupid.

But when I try to open it, I meet a steel wall and remember he blocked me earlier.

Okay, so maybe Perses's lessons will come in handy. Closing my eyes—a stupid move, but what else can I do—I concentrate on Darius's mind. Darkness swirls there, filled with hate, pain, and hunger. It's so strong it takes my breath away. As I push past, it feels like it clings to me with every step until I reach the steel barrier of his mind. Praying to the gods this works, I lay my hand on it gently like I did with Perses.

The wall starts to slowly drop, and inside, I find Darius, scared and alone.

Angel face? he asks weakly, and I feel the darkness feeding off him.

There's only one way I can stop him from progressing further. I knock him out using the bond. He lands on me with a thump, and my eyes fly open as I try to breathe.

Fuck, he's heavy, but I close my eyes again and check. The darkness seems to have stopped, frozen like it can't move while Darius isn't awake.

I poke around it, but when it snaps at me, I retreat back into the real world.

"Holy shit," I gasp, pushing Darius with all my strength.

He doesn't even budge.

A pop sounds, and I've never been so thankful when a certain gremlin face looks at me upside down.

"Bob, help," I wheeze, and he grins.

"Silly witch." He touches my head, and everything explodes into white.

I land on a hard, marble floor with a thud and groan as my head spins and my stomach rebels. Hanging my head low, I breathe through it until I feel normal again.

Sitting back, I grin when I realize where we are.

"Bob, is that you? Did you check on—" Perses stops in the doorway, his eyebrow arching and mouth snapping shut. "Okay."

"Hey there," I greet lamely, waving my hand.

Perses blinks before looking at Darius's still form next to me. Then, his eyes turn all business as he walks closer. "What happened?"

"I don't know. One minute he was fine. Then he went rabid." I crawl closer and hesitate to touch Darius.

Perses has no such issues. He closes his eyes and holds his hand to Darius's forehead before crying out and stumbling back. A look of horror dawns in his eyes as he stares at me.

"What?" I ask, panicked.

"What did you do?" he asks.

"Me? I did what you said! I brought him back, and he was fine, then this happened!" I wave my hand at Darius, my voice rising.

Perses shakes his head and crosses his legs on the floor, looking at Darius in sympathy. "Did you block your mind to him?"

"Well, erm, slightly? Only so I could have some…" I trail off as Perses shakes his head.

"Aurora, you can't do that. The only reason you could bring him back and stop the change was for him to be connected to you. I made that clear. When you blocked him from your mind, you basically cut off the only thing keeping him human."

My face pales as my hands shake. "I did this?"

Perses nods.

Feeling sick, I blow out a breath. "What is he becoming?"

Perses looks at Darius sadly. "A soul eater, like the ones that wander Purgatory."

"I met them," I say with a numb nod. "What can I do?"

Perses contemplates my question, making me want to kill him. "Are you still blocking him?"

"No. He blocked me," I whisper.

"Probably because you blocked him first. I'm betting the hate and darkness started taking over, whispering bad things to him. It would make him different, angry and hateful. He would do it to spite you."

"So, I can't close our connection, or he dies?" I ask slowly.

"Not dies. Becomes a soul eater." Perses blows out another breath. "I don't think the connection needs to be open all the time, but I bet there's a way you could sort of mute it, so essentially, yes."

I nod. A problem to deal with later.

"Okay, so what do we do?" When Perses raises his eyebrow at me again, I get angry. "We have to save him! I'll leave my mind open. I'll do whatever. Just, please, help me."

He jumps to his feet with a clap. "Okay, I have an idea."

35

AURORA

*D*arius lies still on the cloud bed. Hovering over him, I think back over the last few days. I should have noticed. I could feel the anger. It was leaking into me, but I never thought anything of it. Nor could I see the pain closing the bond caused.

Leaning forward, I dab at the sweat coating Darius's forehead. He's burning up. Fuck. I hope Perses hurries the hell up.

The door slams open, and Perses strides in with an open book in his hands, muttering to himself. He stops at Darius's bedside and snaps the book shut with an anxious look.

My hands tighten around Darius. "Can you do it?"

"Yes and no," he says, distracted.

"Now is not the time for your fucking riddles!" I scream, and he throws me a disapproving look.

"Yes, I can do it, but I need your help." He crosses his arms. "And it's not a hundred percent that it will work."

"Do it, I don't care," I beg and I let him see all the emotions fighting for control in me right now.

His eyes soften, and he takes a step closer. "We will help him." With that, he turns to Darius. "Okay, it seems simple enough. I need to suck the darkness from his soul and mind, and you need to be there with your mind open, ready to protect him and call him back."

I frown and stare at Perses. "Won't the darkness stick to you?"

Perses throws me a cocky look as his eyes shift color, making me dizzy. "God, remember?"

Shaking my head, I turn back to Darius. "Okay, let's do it."

I close my eyes and concentrate on my connection with Darius, holding it hard and fast. I feel the moment Perses enters his mind, but I keep my eye on the worn thread between me and Darius.

As Perses sucks out the darkness, Darius's soul tears, and I surround him with my energy and connection as much as I can to help. It works a little and Darius settles down.

I don't know how long we work, but when Perses leaves Darius's mind, I quickly call to him. I feel the moment Darius returns. He's weak, but there.

Thank you, angel face, he whispers in my mind before he passes out.

I open my eyes and look around. A weak, sweaty Perses perches on the end of the bed, looking exhausted. My head is heavy as well.

"Magic like that takes its toll. We all need to rest. You're safe here. I'll get Bob to return you in the morning. Aurora, beware. Not all of the darkness may be gone," Perses says slowly, like each word hurts.

Then he stands and stumbles to the door before shutting it behind him.

I focus back on Darius. He looks better now, his color better and no longer sweating. Some of the weight even returned to his body and face.

"I'm so sorry," I say before laying my head down and keeping my eyes locked on his face, watching him as he rests. My eyes slide shut even as I fight them.

Something strokes my hair.

I mumble and bury my face into the softness beneath me.

The bed shakes as someone laughs, and I raise my head with a glare to find Darius sitting up and staring at me.

I jump up, running my hands over him as I panic.

"Are you okay? How do you feel? Do you need anything—"

When he laughs, I cut off and narrow my eyes.

He winks before leaning back again. "Never knew you cared so much, princess."

Well, I guess it didn't hurt his fucking attitude, asswad. Laughter brushes my mind.

I heard that, angel.

Fuck, I need to shield my thoughts better. I find my eyes running over him. He looks good. He looks like I saw him in the memories. His face is filled out, his lips plump, and his eyes sparking.

You checking me out, your highness?

"Stop fucking listening to my thoughts," I grumble, and he grins in real life.

"Sure thing, princess."

I huff as I sit back. "Fucking asshole." Blowing out a breath, I look at him seriously. "Darius, I'm sorry. I didn't know blocking you would do that. I really didn't. I'm sorry. I won't block you from now on."

His face closes down as he stares at me, that cocky expression firmly in place. "Don't worry about it, angel. We both know we don't want to be bound to each other. We'll stay this way until we can break it, and then we can be rid of each other." I gape at him as he slips from the bed and stretches casually. "Now, can we get back? I'm craving bacon."

I stand slowly and swallow down all the arguments

bubbling on my tongue, but hurt sears through me, and he flinches before looking at me. Gritting my teeth, I storm away. No way will I let that asshole know how much he hurt me. If he wants to find a way to unbind us, then so be it. I don't need someone who doesn't want me, anyway.

Angel.

I ignore his pained whisper in my mind and set off to find Perses so he can send us back home.

Please don't tell the guys. They'll panic. Promise me. The whisper brushes my mind like a truce, but I'm still so angry and hurt.

Against my better judgment, I answer him. *I promise.*

36

JASON

*W*hen I hear footsteps near the front door, I shut the fridge and edge down the hallway, hiding behind the living room door in case the person is here to hurt Aurora and my brothers. I hold my breath when they turn the door handle and push the door open, their shoes light on the wooden hallway floor.

When Darius storms past, I let go of my magic and breathe out.

He heads straight down the corridor and slams the kitchen door. Looking around, I spot Aurora in the hallway. She looks so lost and alone, and before I know it, I take a step toward her.

Those eyes, those deep eyes, swing my way, and when I see the pain and vulnerability in them, my heart stutters. She might not know it, but I'm crazy about her. She's so amazing, so strong all the time, and yet so kind, and right now, she's hurting.

I open my arms, and she runs into them. I hold her there as she presses her face into my chest. Kissing her head, I tighten my arms.

"Shh, you're okay," I whisper, and when she shakes, I keep on whispering to her.

When she calms down a bit and pulls away, her eyes are red-rimmed, and I cup her face. God, she's beautiful. With twigs in her hair and tears staining her face, she makes me feel like a giddy teenager again. I can't help myself.

I lean forward and run my lips gently across hers. Fuck, she tastes amazing. All sweet with the slightest hint of salt. I pull away as my cheeks heat, realizing what I just did.

Good going. She's upset and you're—

Her lips meet mine, and I lose all rational thought. I can't help myself. I grab her cheeks and deepen the kiss, and when she moans into my mouth, I walk us back until she meets the hallway wall. Her hands wind in my hair as I pull back and search her eyes.

I don't want her kissing me unless she wants to, but when I see her blown pupils and face coated in passion, I dive back in, having to reach down and rearrange my cock as it presses against the front of my jeans tightly.

"Jason," she groans, and using the wall, I hoist her up and jam my leg between hers.

I devour her mouth, my mind caught on those moans I heard from her through the walls when she was with Ezra. She probably wouldn't care that I listened in. I couldn't help it, but I'll never tell her I jerked off to it. She was so hot and those noises drove me crazy.

She pulls back, and I open my eyes to see her staring at me in wonder.

My cheeks heat even as I grin at her.

Blinking, she watches me before biting that plump lower lip. "I thought you were shy."

Leaning in, I sweep her hair to the side and kiss up her neck before whispering in her ear, "I am, but I know exactly what I want. You beneath me, screaming your orgasm as you ride my cock."

She pants at my words, and with a groan, she yanks me back to her, her soft lips exploring mine.

"Jason," she moans, and the sound of my name on her lips drives me wild.

Bolstered by her moans, I drop my hand to the bottom of her top and slowly lift it, running my hand up her toned stomach and curves until I reach her lacy bra.

Her back arches, and I take it as permission, hooking my fingers under the cups and dragging them up until I can reach her breasts. She groans into my mouth as I curl my finger around her nipple, moving against my thigh in a way that makes my cock jerk. I can't help but imagine her riding me like that.

Tweaking her nipple, I sweep my tongue inside her mouth.

She pulls away, breathing deeply, and watches me with wide, lust-filled eyes. Her eyes sweep across my face as she puts some distance between us.

"Everything oka—" I cut off mid-sentence as she darts forward, her hands running under my shirt and across my stomach, causing me to freeze. My eyes stay locked with her as she explores me, her hands running up my back before circling around and cupping my face.

"I missed you so much," she says softly, causing my heart to stutter, and I see the truth in her eyes. She really means it.

Swallowing hard, I stare at her as her lips rise to mine, and with that touch, I'm lost again. I've been trying to fight it, to push it away. Knowing how crazy the others are about her, I tried to stay the smart one, but she knocks down my walls every single time. That evil little smile, those sparkling eyes, her wit and loyalty. I might not have realized it completely, but this little witch is buried so deep in my heart I couldn't separate us if I tried.

I'm hers, if she'll have me.

I draw back to tell her that when a crash sounds

from the kitchen. We pull away and whirl at the same time, me stepping slightly in front of her.

She snorts and pats my arm.

"You don't have to protect me, sweetie. I'm a total badass, remember?" With that, she leans on her tiptoes, drops a kiss on my cheek, and pushes past me to investigate.

37

AURORA

I quickly right my bra, ignoring the throbbing between my legs created by Jason's masterful fingers, along with his dominant mouth. Who knew it? My shy witch, the guy who blushes when I wink at him, has a dominant side. I can't wait to explore that.

Shuffling down the hallway, I push into the kitchen and stop with my mouth hanging open. What the…?

I stare around incredulously. "Bob?"

Jason stops at my back. His body pushes up against me; his heat makes me shiver. Pushing my horniness aside, I stare around again. The gremlin, doubled his normal size, is throwing every utensil he can get his hands on at Nev, who growls at him with his fur standing up and his eyes glowing.

I grab Jason's shirt and drag him down in time to duck a fork flying through the air.

"Bob, stop it right now!" I yell when he chucks a cheese grater at Nev.

The gremlin turns toward me and seems to lose some of his air, shrinking back down a bit.

"Silly witch." He nods before glaring back at Nev.

"What's going on?" I ask, confused.

"Silly witch was busy sucking face with other silly witch." He picks up a rolling pin when Nev growls again.

I roll my eyes as Jason coughs behind me, obviously covering a laugh.

"Okay, so why are you attacking my dog?" I frown at Nev as he growls again. "Nev, heel," I command, and he growls once before sitting down and tilting his head at me with his tongue hanging out.

"Silly witch, this isn't a dog." Bob rolls his eyes and stares down at Nev.

"Erm, gremlin, say what?" I choke out, staring between him and Nev like my dog can give me all the answers.

Jason freezes, and I almost hear his mind whirring.

Bob huffs and shrinks back down to his normal size but still holds the rolling pin like a weapon. He sticks his tongue out at Nev, then turns to me. "Silly witch, silly witch."

At his laugh, my eyes narrow, and I hold my hand up, conjuring a fireball.

He points the rolling pin at me, his skin shifting as if to expand again. "Don't do it, silly witch."

"Try me, gremlin," I growl, and he starts to mutter.

I don't even see Nev move. One second, he's sitting with his tongue lolling out, and the next, he appears mid-air, snatching the rolling pin from Bob and throwing it to the other side of the kitchen.

When Nev turns to me, I choke out a breath. The puppy I saved and the dog I love looks nothing like the beast that stares at me right now.

His eyes glow, I mean actually glow, bright-blue with a ring of purple in his left eye and a ring of black in his right. He's huge, double his normal size, and seems to dwarf my kitchen as he looks at me.

Bob moves, and Nev growls, opening his mouth to reveal sharp fangs I've never seen before. They hang down over his bottom lip and his tail swishes forward, drawing my gaze. It's as bushy as normal, but where it was hair before, it now has spikes coming from it. At the end, a giant one hangs off, sweeping along the floor as he growls. Even his fur is darker, almost midnight black; the same kind of darkness my magic has when I let it out.

Nev turns back to me, watching me with way too intelligent eyes.

"What is he?" I step back into Jason, who wraps his arms around me and plops his head on my shoulder.

Nev whines sadly and sits as he watches me. The sound goes straight through to my heart, and I have to remind myself not to run to him.

"I did wonder if there was something different about him," Jason murmurs, almost talking to himself.

Bob huffs and disappears, only to reappear on top of my counter with my bag of cookies in his hand.

"Silly witch, he's a bonded hound." He munches on my cookies, and it's a testament to how freaked out I am that I don't flame ball his ass.

"What does that mean?" I shout, freaking out.

Still watching me sadly, Nev lays down and puts his head on his enormous paws, which have also grown curved, lethal-looking claws.

"I toldss Perses you were stupid," Bob starts, and I glare at him. "Finness, silly witch. A bonded hound is a magical creature. They only appear to people they think are deserving; it's like a soul matess. They feel that person when they are born, and they appear when they need them the mosts."

With that, he shoves a cookie into his mouth and watches me like he explained everything.

Jason hums, and I slip out of his arms and turn to keep everyone in my line of sight. Jason looks like he's thinking hard, his focus on Nev before his eyes clear and a smile forms. "Yes! I remember reading about them now."

"Care to enlighten me?" I ask shrilly, but what else is a girl to do when she finds out the dog she rescued is some sort of magical being who selected her at birth?

Jason smiles at me and it calms me down a bit. "They're said to be extinct many years ago. Right before the coven lines started dying and losing power."

"Silly man witch. Not extinct. They tooks themselves from thiss world because of the taint to your magic. It tainted them as wells, so they hides away," Bob interrupts before going back to his cookies.

Jason inclines his head, but I see he wants to ask questions. Luckily, he keeps his train of thought. "Of course. They were said to only appear to the strongest of our kind, men and women destined to be leaders and saviors. Only three were ever recorded. It's like Bob—" he stumbles over the name, and I snort, "pointed out. They pick someone at a young age, and one day they appear." He stares at Nev. "Though I've never heard of them camouflaging like a dog before."

"Silly man witch. It's called glamour. He knowss his witch was hiding, so he hid, too. But once the glamour is on, it iss hard to get off. Especially for a young one."

I rub my head, a migraine starting. "Okay, so Nev is some mythical being who picked me at birth because I'm destined to be powerful and all that shit. We're bound for life, and he protects me and boosts my magic, blah blah blah. Am I right?"

Bob nods. "Pretty much, silly witch."

Groaning, I lean back against the wall. "That doesn't explain why you two were attacking each other."

Bob shoves the bag in his mouth and chews, and I wince. "I wass trying to help the silly doggie's glamour come off. He didn'ts like it. Thoughts Bob was trying to hurts him. Misunderstanding."

With that, he hops down again.

"Right, of course. So, is there anything I should know about bonded hounds?" I trip over the words.

Bob sighs again. That popping noise comes, and he's gone.

When he doesn't reappear straight away, I swear. "That mother fucking gremlin."

He appears right before me, kicking my shin, and I scream.

Hopping on one leg, clutching my throbbing one, I glare at him.

"Silly witch should be nicer. Here!" He thrusts a book at me and throws me a wounded glare.

Looking down at the book, I groan. Great, more reading.

Jason comes to my side and holds his hand out with a soft expression. "Here. I'll find the right parts and give you two some time." He gives me a meaningful look, and I follow his gaze to a sad looking Nev. I nod, and

Jason takes the book and shuts the kitchen door after him.

I stare at Nev and he stares back. I don't really know what to say.

He whines again, like his heart is breaking, and it sends a sharp pain through mine.

Shaking my head, I walk toward him and plop my ass down into a crossed legged position. I take in his changes and decide what the hell. "Look, buddy, I was surprised, okay? I mean, I knew you were smarter than a normal dog, but I never expected this. I guess we're both full of surprises, huh?"

He tilts his head, and I take that as a good sign.

"I'm sorry for freaking out, I really am. You know I love you. You're the only reason I survived this long without going crazy. So what? You have a barbed tail and cool glowing eyes."

He crawls closer and stops when his head rests on my legs.

I automatically reach down and stroke his coarse fur. "Baby, it only means I love you more. I can't believe you picked me out of all the witches and magics in this world. You came for me." I start to choke up, so I clear my throat nervously. "I guess your name makes more sense now, anyway. Neville was always looking after everyone, and he was a magical being so..."

Nev's tongue rolls out and licks my other hand, making me grin.

"I'll take that as you accept my apology."

He huffs, and I laugh again. "Love you too, buddy. Come on. Let's go find out all about you. I sure as shit hope you're allowed to eat cookies, 'cause you've eaten enough to feed an army."

When I make my way from the kitchen, Nev happily trots at my heels. I find Jason pouring over the book in the living room, so I sprawl next to him, my head on his lap. He doesn't look, but his free hand plays with my hair.

Footsteps sound on the stairs, then Ezra and Alex appear around the corner of the sofa. They look from Nev to me.

"Interesting," is all Alex says, almost like he can't help himself. He pushes past Ezra and lifts my legs before sitting down and putting them back down on his thighs.

Ezra rolls his eyes, and I blow him a kiss.

I hear more footsteps and smile to myself. It's like they always know.

Mikael and Ben come down, arguing between themselves. I tense before I realize what they're arguing about. Then I laugh.

"No, the older Sabrina is better," Ben defends, walking in and slumping on the floor in front of me. "Baby, tell this heathen."

I shake my head and reach down. He sighs as I pull out his hair tie to play with his hair.

Mikael grins at me and finds a spot near Ezra. Only Darius is missing...

Missing me, angel face?

I snort and ignore the guys' confused looks. *Like the plague.*

His laughter floats through my head even as he appears, his face blank, and leans against the wall. "What's with the family meeting?"

"It turns out Nev here"—I ignore Darius incredulous look at the name and carry on — "is a mythical creature who loves me so much he bound himself to me."

Nev huffs before laying his head down on Ben's knee. It warms my heart when Ben doesn't even hesitate to stroke him, completely ignoring his new... bits.

"Jason?" Alex leans forward with his eyes locked on the other witch.

"She's partly right. He's a creature we thought long since extinct. It seems they're not gone, just waiting for a 'pure' witch; one who hasn't, as Bob said, tainted their power. He's a bonded hound," he says, and the others react to the name.

Wow, so I was the only one who didn't know. Guess Bob was right.

You named a great, mythical being, one who's spoken in reverence throughout our community, Nev?

Fuck off.

Not my best come back, but he's right.

Darius laughs again in my head, fucking cumbucket.

You seem to have an obsession with my cum, angel face.

I ignore him this time and feel him grinning at me. I'm still hurt over how we ended things when we last spoke, but I'm beginning to understand that's who he is. One minute he's hot, and one minute he's cold.

Princess, I'm always hot. Why don't you come and find out?

Ignoring him, I concentrate on Jason, who continued talking while Darius distracted me. "It seems he had some kind of glamour to help blend into the human world while our girl was hiding out here."

Jason flushes when he realizes what he said.

Our girl?

Nope, ignoring him.

"Okay, Nev. Can you conjure this glamour again? You might need it. Plus, we don't want to go around tipping the humans off," Alex says, holding a full conversation with my dog… or my bonded hound.

Nev huffs and gets to his feet, stretching out and showing off his true form. He stands there and I watch, entranced, as purple and black dance along his fur. My magic seems to feel its call and rises as well, causing me to gasp.

It's over in seconds, and sitting at my feet is a normal looking Nev.

"Good. Keep practicing turning it on and off so you don't get stuck again," Alex says and Nev nods.

"It says here that your two magics will be connected and you can draw power from him and vice versa. It also says—" Jason stops mid-sentence.

"Says what?" I sit up, looking over his shoulder.

"That if you die, so does he. But if he dies, you don't, but you'll be weakened."

Alex wraps his arm around my waist as I shiver. So, I could have killed Nev when I almost died saving Mikael.

"We won't let anything happen to either of you," Alex whispers in my ear, and I nod before snuggling into his side.

Jason reaches out and squeezes my hand. "I'll do more research and let you know what I find."

"Thank you," I say, and we share a soft smile as someone's phone starts to ring.

*L*ooking around, I grunt when Alex pulls his phone out and sighs. I expect him to stand and move away from Aurora. It's what he'd usually do.

Instead, he shakes his head and leans back, pulling her closer to his side before answering the phone with a curt, "Alexander."

Ezra and I share a grin. He's starting to let her in, starting to trust her. Something I thought he would never do, not because she's a woman, but because he doesn't let anyone in.

When her hand weaves through my hair again, I sigh and lean my head back to allow her easier access. I'm not the least bit bothered by how whipped it makes me look.

I catch Darius's angry eyes as he grinds his jaw,

looking at her hands on me. What's his problem? It makes me sad. We were always so close. I'm close with all of them, but he and I were inseparable.

Alex always used to say if you saw one of us it wouldn't be long until you saw the other. When Darius died, it took something inside of me. It made me angry, but underneath that was heartbreak. I lost my brother, my other half.

When Aurora brought him back, my heart soared and my soul jumped, but he's not the same. I guess I can't expect him to be, but I feel like I don't even know him anymore, and that hurts. He's a stranger with the face of someone I loved.

He catches me staring, and his face wipes clear. I quickly look away, not wanting him to see the tears gathering in my eyes. I don't know if it was for the best that he came back at all.

"Benny, you okay?" Aurora whispers, leaning into me.

I nod and look down as Nev plops his head back on my lap like he feels my pain. Hell, maybe he does if he's some mythical, magical being. I stroke Nev's head. "I'm fine, baby."

Aurora sighs, and when I glance back, I see her fighting her way free from Alex's arm. He frowns down at her, trying to keep her by his side before she grins and wiggles free. She scoots to the edge of the sofa before sliding down.

I have to shuffle forward as she wraps both arms and legs around me, holding me tight.

Her head lands on my shoulder, and I shiver when she whispers in my ear, her perfect lips meeting my lobe. "He'll be okay. He needs you guys right now. I saw him there. It was horrible. Give him time."

I nod, trying to breathe back the tears as she holds me.

"No. Yes. Well, we don't need him anymore," Alex says, low and quiet, the way he only does when he's really angry. "Don't you dare." He huffs out a breath. "Fine."

He throws his phone down and pinches the bridge of his nose.

"What's wrong?" Ezra asks, his voice rumbly and tired.

"It seems our friend found the dream walker we were seeking. He doesn't care that we no longer require him, he's calling it even. He wants to meet tonight." Alex sighs as he tips his head back and stares at the ceiling.

Ezra swears and I shake my head. That good for nothing. I knew he would find a way to play us.

"What's the plan?" Jason asks from behind me, but I don't want to move. I'm so warm and comfy in Aurora's arms.

"We'll go to see what he suggests," Alex says slowly, his mind obviously thinking through the plan.

"Right, 'cause that's a good fucking idea," Darius grumbles from the corner.

I turn to glare at him, getting angry. "We all know Alex's ideas are the best, and we will follow him. You don't have to come."

His gaze snaps to me, and we have a stare off. His eyes soften as something akin to regret enters them, but it's too late.

"I never said we would do as he asks, just that we will turn up," Alex interrupts. "Until then, I want to spend some time on Aurora's magic."

We all look at him this time. He has his no-compromise-face on that makes us all smile.

"Welcome to the coven, baby," I say with a laugh.

I'm going to enjoy this. It's something we all had to go through, and Alex is tough as shit. I ignore the gaze burning into the side of my head and lean back into Aurora more.

She giggles, and when I look over my shoulder, she's smiling softly at Darius. When I follow her gaze, he's watching her with stars in his eyes, his face happy and open like it used to be.

Huh. Maybe there's a chance after all.

39

AURORA

*M*uch to Alex's chagrin, Lane turns up super early, a panicked expression on her face like I might disappear overnight again. She hugs me for the longest time and even brings me cookies.

I sit on the sofa munching them and eye her. She looks sad and lost, and the others don't know what to do with a human around.

I polish off the last cookie and stand. "Right, so let's practice some magic. Then, I need to go see Tom before he goes all bear and kills everyone."

Lane jumps up, almost bouncing on her toes. "I get to see magic!"

At her screech, Darius covers his ears. I glare him at before turning back to her.

"Sure do. Let's magic this shit up!" I shout and laugh when she giggles.

I hook my arm through hers and drag her outside, the boys and Nev close on our heels.

We make sure to stay away from the forest, keeping to the back garden instead. The boys sit on the grass while Alexander and Jason stay with me.

Jason surprised me. Apparently, he's the best teacher. Makes sense.

Lane sits off the side, way back just in case, with Nev sprawled on her lap. Grinning, I turn to the makeshift targets they created. I'm excited to see them use magic as well. Even though they know what I am, they're tight-lipped about their powers, probably because they don't want to scare me off. But it will be nice to see what they can really do. It also reminds me of my training with Perses, which sends a pang through me. I miss the old god.

"Okay, we're going to cover the basics," Alexander begins. "Magic can come in many forms; no witch is the same. Yes, we use words and nearly every witch can master whatever they put their mind to, but we tend to have one stronger aspect than others. The main types of magic are defensive, protection, conjuring, healing, and transfiguration. There's more that tends to mimic the old gods, but don't mention that to anyone else. You can master more than one, but each witch feels a stronger pull to a certain… power, shall we say. We're a coven because we each have that. It's what makes us stronger than most, with one element standing out rather than just being good at most."

I turn and look at Alexander in surprise.

He gestures to everyone. "See if you can match up who we are. Use your magic if you have to, to feel us."

I look at them, closing my eyes and feeling with my magic like he suggested. Not bothering to open my eyes again, I call out. "Ezra feels strong and sure. Defense. Alex, you feel like home and safety. Protection. Benny, you feel like happiness and growth. Healing." I browse over the others. They're a little more difficult. "Jason, you feel like when you master a new topic and wisdom. Knowledge. Mikael, you feel like the ground is rushing to you, the water is calling you, and the air is worshiping you. Elemental?"

"Good, and Darius?" Alex asks, his voice soft as if trying not to disturb me.

Scrunching my eyes, I concentrate on the stubborn witch.

What am I, princess?

"Transfiguration," I call and open my eyes when I hear a whoop.

Ben grins at me, as do most of the others, all apart from Darius who winks.

I turn back to my teachers for the day. "So, what am I?"

"That's what we need to find out." Alex grins as he

steps back. "Each of us will show you an aspect of our magic, and you'll match it. Whether you can do it at all or how easy it is for you will show us what magic is yours."

I nod. Makes sense. "Okay, who's up first?"

"Me." Ezra strides over. He offers me his smile as we face off, and the others step back. "Watch and try to replicate."

I nod, watching him closely.

"Alex," he says and a gold ball comes flying at him almost too fast to see.

He doesn't even break a sweat as he waves his hand in a circle. The power stops and covers his hands before shooting back toward Alex.

"That's defense. I can turn magic back to the user whilst more powerful fighting, what we call disarming spells, come easier to me. There will always be a crossover with magic. For example, I'm good at creating fireballs, which Mikael is also good at because of elements, but I can also stun another magic user faster. Most other witches struggle to master such spells. I can also cut off their magic all together and stop them from attacking. It's painful for a witch but necessary sometimes," he says with a matter of fact tone. He's not trying to show off; he's telling me what it means to be him.

"Alex is going hit you, but he'll go slow," he explains as he walks toward me. "Envision the power in your mind. Imagine it stopping, then turning back. It's that simple."

He stands at my side, offering me more confidence in case anything goes wrong.

I face Alex, who waits with his hand up.

At my nod, he gives me a second to notice the ball that forms in his hand. He throws it at me, and I let Ezra's words guide me. Before it hits me, I raise my hand. It stops, hovers in midair, and reaches toward me with gold tendrils. Gasping, they wind around my hand.

My magic reaches out automatically, and the guys swear when my magic overtakes Alex's. The color turns purple, swirling with his gold underneath.

"What the fuck?" Ezra asks as I look up into Alex's eyes, giving him a warning.

He nods, and I fling it back to him. He stops it just before it strikes, but when it touches his skin, it crawls up his arms, around his neck, and down his chest before seeming to disappear inside him.

He stumbles back, his eyes wide as he pants.

"You okay?" I ask, and he nods, staring at me strangely.

"Alex," Ezra barks, and our usually stoic leader blows out a breath and nods, straightening himself again.

"I'm okay. It was... playing," he finishes.

I tilt my head at him in confusion.

"No matter. You can obviously master defensive, so let's move on." He starts briskly. "Ben, you're up next."

Over the next two hours, I learn more about the others' magic.

Ben shows me healing magic, and Ezra cuts himself and works his magic. I'm okay at that one, but not the best. I make a mental reminder to practice it.

Mikael's magic is the most fun, and I find it easy to master. The earth rushes to my bidding as does the water and the air.

Darius refuses to take part, which I respect, especially when I feel how hard it is for him to try and control his magic since he got back.

After we practice all the basics, we start playing.

I show them what I learned with Perses. It's so much fun, exploring my magic more.

The proud looks on their faces urge me to keep pushing myself until sweat drips down me, and I'm exhausted.

40

EZRA

*W*hen training ends, Aurora sees the human off. The look the little blonde throws at Alex is hilarious. Clearly, she's not over the whole kidnapping her best friend thing.

After her friend leaves, Aurora slips upstairs.

Jason talks with Alex, working through what we learned about our girl's magic. Darius goes off to sulk somewhere, and Mikael and Ben whisper together in the kitchen.

While no one pays attention to me, I slip upstairs and follow the bond tugging at me.

Aurora closed down her side a little, and I'll admit I miss the feeling of her magic and mind rubbing against me.

Shutting her bedroom door softly behind me, I spot

the half-closed bathroom door with the clothes trail leading up to it.

A grin spreads across my face as my cock stands to attention. I haven't had a chance to have her since the bonding. We've been too busy, but I can't stop thinking about that mouth of hers and the way her pussy clamped down on my cock. Those little noises she made as I fucked her.

Shit. Readjusting my trousers, I open the door to see her bent over, testing the water of the shower in nothing but tiny black panties.

I soak up her body before shutting the door.

She turns, and when she spots me, her eyes flare and a naughty little smile turns up those lips. Everything about her is meant for me, and I plan on reminding her of that.

She meets me halfway, rising on her tiptoes as I lower my head, our lips meeting, and we both groan. Her tiny hands land on my shoulders, digging in as I reach down and hoist her up, her lush ass in my hands.

Her tongue tangles with mine as I stride over to the counter and drop her down, my hands already stroking her soft skin. My cock is so hard at this point that I have to reach down and flick open my jeans.

When her hand skates down my chest and into my underwear to wrap around my length, I shiver. She squeezes, and I gasp into her mouth as I thrust into her soft hand.

Fuck. If I'm not careful, she'll have me coming in no time. My cock already pulses and my balls tighten. I force myself to stop moving and reach down to cover her hand. Pulling it from my pants slowly, I hold it to my chest as she smiles at me, that little fucking innocent one, like she wasn't trying to make me bust a nut in my own jeans.

"Well, this brings back memories," I laugh, and she giggles, leaning against my chest.

"I missed you so much," she says softly, her fingers twining in mine as she holds me to her, like I might disappear if she doesn't.

It makes me swallow hard, and I tilt her chin up with one finger while I stare into her eyes.

"I missed you, too, but I'm never going anywhere again, and neither are you. Together," I promise, and she gazes deep into my eyes, letting me see the fear and desperation there.

"Don't make promises you can't keep." Her soft words send a lightning bolt to my heart. She might not know it, but they felt too much like an omen to be coincidence.

Does she know we're keeping something from her? Unsure of what to say, I lean down and show her how much I care in the only way I can. Kissing her deeply, I tell her how much I care. How much I love her.

Her hands wrap around my neck as she brings me closer, her legs wrapping around my waist. I sense her desperation in her touch. Does she feel it, too? That something big is coming? We've all been on edge. That's why Alex insisted on training today. I wish I knew what was coming.

I try to bring her mind back to us, wanting nothing between us. I drop her to the floor and she starts to protest so I silence her by reaching down, I grab her panties and pull them down her legs. She kicks them off, and I pick her up, my hands on that ass that drives me wild, and walk us into the shower, our mouths still fused together as we taste each other.

The shower spray hits us as I pull away to breathe. Gazing into those eyes, I try to tell her with mine how much she means to me. She smiles and reaches up, her hands running across my face, making me close my eyes in bliss.

Shivering against her, I push her into the shower wall, quickly shuck my clothes, and plaster myself against her. My cock jerks as I push it against her stomach, and I force myself to slow down, needing to taste her as much as I need to be inside her.

She lets out a breathy moan and rubs herself against me, making me groan. I love how wild she gets, the way she lets go when she's in my arms. Her pupils are blown with lust and her mouth bruised from my kiss.

Groaning, I push her head to the side and kiss down her neck, licking a line across it as she clutches my shoulders, breathy moans and words falling from her mouth as I nip.

Grinning against her skin, I nearly laugh when she slaps my shoulder.

"Stop teasing," she demands, and I pull back.

"No teasing?" My eyes darken with need, my voice almost a growl.

She has to be sure of what she's asking. I can be sweet. I can be soft. But right now, all I want to do is sink into her wet heat and fuck her hard and fast as she comes apart beneath me.

"No, I want you inside of me. Stop fucking playing," she growls back, and I smirk.

"Whatever you say, baby." I lean forward and leave a gentle kiss on her lips.

Pulling away, frustration and amusement fill her eyes. It turns to shock when I drop her and push her to the shower floor tiles, following after her and pinning her to the wet porcelain.

Without waiting, I grab her legs, hook them around my waist, line up, and thrust into her ferociously. She screams, writhing beneath me, but I don't give her time to adjust. I pull out and ram back in, holding her shoulders so she doesn't slide across the floor.

"Fuck, yes, yes," she chants, her eyes unfocused and her mouth open in a pant as I pull back and fuck her.

Hard and fast. Again and again.

Her pussy tightens around me as she arches beneath me.

Leaning down, I nip at a nipple and she bucks, trying to push me deeper inside of her. Grunting, I speed up, my balls tightening as I hold back my own orgasm.

She always comes first.

Licking around her nipple and leaving stinging bites, I reach down with my other hand and flick her clit. She groans and pushes harder, her nails scratching down my back as I keep up the punishing pace. Fuck.

Rubbing my thumb in her wetness, I run it down her pussy, past where my cock spears her, and down to her ass. She freezes against me, but I nip at her nipple harder in punishment, and she moans.

"Don't worry, I won't have your ass today. I'll save that for when Alex and I are together with you," I warn and she moans, riding me as I fuck her senseless.

She tightens, close to coming as I circle her hole. Pushing the edge of my thumb in, I bite her nipple at the same time, and she screams. Her whole body lifts from the floor as she fights against me. My pace quickens, and I crush her back into the floor with the force of my thrusts.

Something smashes into my mind; jumbled thoughts, and when I feel her pleasure, I yell out my release, stuttering as I pump into her.

Yes, yes, god, yes. More. I need everything. Please, Ezra. Please. So good.

Our pleasure and minds mix together until I don't know where we are or who we are, tumbling together into nothingness, clinging to each other's minds until I fall back to my body with a gasp. I drop down beside her as I try to catch my breath.

"What—what the hell was that?" she gasps, her chest heaving next to me as we both stare at the ceiling.

She turns her head to look at me, and I start to laugh. She joins in, then moans, wiggling against the tile. My smile softens at the joy on her face. Leaning forward, I brush away a wet tangle of hair and cup her face.

She gazes at me, still giggling.

"Our minds melded. I guess you brought down the wall between us fully."

She looks shocked but nods.

"It was fucking amazing. I could feel everything you did," I admit, and she bites her lip.

"Me, too." She searches my eyes for signs of displeasure for her barging into my mind.

I can still feel her lingering there.

You're always welcome here. There's nothing I wouldn't share with you, let you see. I'm yours. I send the whisper through her mind, meaning it.

I leave mine open, letting her look. She stares at me, fighting herself. I know she has a hard time trusting and letting people in, but I can't help it. I have to tell her how I feel. I can feel the pain and longing in her mind.

"I love you," I force the words out of trembling lips, giving her my heart.

It's terrifying.

The silence only lasts for a few seconds, but it feels like forever.

Staring into my eyes, she leans up to my mouth. "I love you, too."

She seals it like a vow with a kiss as her mind crashes into mine again, filled with such love that I gasp into her mouth.

41

AURORA

*A*fter our confession, I manage to untangle myself from Ezra with one more kiss and dry off before the others coming looking for us. My heart still pounds.

He loves me? Why does that feel like an apology, and why, when I mentioned promises, was there a shadow in his eyes?

Shaking off the bad thoughts, I dress, needing to go see Tom today.

I leave Ezra getting dressed again and head downstairs. Ben is the first one I spot, and I bound over to him, flinging myself on his back like a monkey. "Benny, wanna go on an adventure?"

His hands grab my legs and hold me to him as he laughs. "Sure, what sort of trouble are we getting up to?"

Trouble, princess? Count me in.

I stick my tongue out at Darius as he comes into the room. Mikael follows after him, and when he sees me, his face breaks into a wide grin.

"Want to join the adventure?" I ask him and he laughs.

Alex comes into the room. "And what adventure is that?"

I wince but smile sweetly. Leaning down to Ben, I whisper into his ear, "Uh oh, Daddy's mad."

Ben bursts out laughing.

I hop down and flutter my lashes at Alex. "Nothing dangerous."

Alex arches his brow like he doesn't trust me. "I better come with, to make sure."

When he turns, I stick my tongue out at him.

"I saw that. Next time, I'll spank you," Alex warns as he walks away.

I would be so down for that.

"Shotgun!" Ben calls and runs down the hallway.

Cock it.

I chase after him. "Benny, you little shit!"

He laughs as we chase him outside.

Alex leans back against his car, typing on his phone. Grinning, I form a ball in my hand and throw it.

It hits Ben and he goes down, freezing from the stun I put on him.

Giggling, I race to the passenger side and look up to find the others gawking at me.

"He cheats, too!" I call and slip into Alex's car, their laughter following me.

The pub hasn't changed. I know it's only been a few weeks, but with everything else changing, it feels like this should have as well.

Walking through, I spot Tom towering over two teenagers, looking like he's tearing his hair out. When I spot their uniforms, I giggle.

His head snaps around supernaturally fast, and when he spots me, his face breaks into a wide grin.

Striding across the pub, he grabs me in a bear hug and spins me around as I wrap my arms around him and laugh. Obviously remembering everyone else, he drops me back to my feet, his smile massive.

"Missed you kid, are you—" He looks around before lowering his voice, "better?"

We have an unspoken agreement not to talk about why we're both running from our species, so I nod and smile. "Missed you, too, old man. Now, think you can get us burgers? I'm craving one!"

He shakes his head, smile still in place. "You know where the fucking kitchen is." He grins, then turns around when something crashes. Looking around him, I spot the red-faced young man who dropped a plate of food. "I better get back before they destroy the joint."

I nod as he walks away, his face turning angry as he goes to clean up the kid's mess.

I lead everyone to a table, and once they sit, I make my way to the kitchen, almost skipping with every step. For all the weird, magicy shit going on in my life, it's nice to come back to a bit of normalcy. And when I hear a Britney Spears song being belting out of tune and see a twerking ass getting spanked with a metal spatula, it feels like home.

Leaning against the swinging door, I laugh as Eddie dances around the kitchen. "Nice moves."

He yelps and turns to face me. "What did we talk about, missy?"

I grin, dropping into the chair near the door. "That you're sexy?"

He smirks while flipping a burger. "That, too. Tom told us you were off sick? You better? Otherwise, get your ass out of my kitchen."

Despite his jokes, I hear the concern underneath.

"I'm better," I lie.

He nods, grabs some fries, and dumps them into the fryer before turning and opening the grill.

Grabbing an order pad, I jot our order down and add it to the spiked list behind the counter.

On my way back around, I kiss Eddie's wrinkled cheek. "Thanks, old man."

I dance out of range as he chases me with the spatula, and I fall out of the kitchen laughing, only to bump into a hard chest.

Apology on my lips, I look up into a vaguely familiar face. Blinking hard, I try to place him, but it's like my mind won't cooperate.

Stepping back, I smile. "Sorry."

"That's alright," he rumbles.

Eyes as dark as the night sky meet mine as the memory of John and where I saw this man flashes into my head.

"It was my fault." I grin and step around him, but his hand darts out and grabs my arm.

Gasping, I try to pull away as memories bombard me. Looking into his eyes, I pale and almost stop breathing.

"Reaper," I choke out and he nods.

When he makes no move to out me or scream, I let out a jagged breath.

"I wanted to see if you were okay and to let you know that not all of us are like him." He lets go of my arm, and I rub the place he grabbed, feeling like death itself touched me.

"Him?" I ask dumbly.

"Redmond, the reaper who attacked you. He was a bad egg. Know that if you ever need us, there are some who will support you." He nods at me again and turns, strutting down the corridor to the toilets.

I stare at the spot where he stood, debating whether to chase after him, when a hand drops on my shoulder.

I jump and spin, magic already forming in my hand.

Darius glances down at it and back to my face with an arched eyebrow.

Swallowing hard, I extinguish the ball. "Sorry."

He nods but doesn't step back as he looks over my shoulder. "Everything okay?"

His voice is rough and scratchy, making me realize he usually talks in my head.

"Fine." I look away, feeling horrible for lying.

"Princess, you can talk to us," he says.

I force a smile. "I know, but seriously, it's fine. Let's get back."

I nudge him and we walk side by side, his face closed down. He feels a million miles away. Our bond is strained, and I almost groan with the realization I probably didn't block him from my mind and now he knows I lied to him.

"Darius—" I begin, but he walks ahead of me, ignoring me completely.

Great, our bond is going brilliantly.

Sighing, I follow after him and slip into a seat between Jason and Ben. They give me searching looks, but I avoid their eyes.

Fiddling with the beer mat on the table, I zone out of the conversation.

What's wrong? Don't want to lie to them again?

I grit my teeth at the mocking voice in my head and ignore him as our meals arrive.

Working my way through my burger, I look up and grin when I meet Mikael's eyes. Ever since I woke up, he picks at his meals, like he savors them, whereas Darius shovels it in as fast as he can.

Alex catches my eye and frowns, so I purposely take a big bite of my burger and groan.

He shakes his head and smiles.

We sit and laugh and joke. No talk of magic or anything else.

We enjoy our time together until Tom kicks us out when the pub grows busy.

Kissing him on the cheek on the way out, I promise him I'll be back to work next week.

He tells me not to rush, but I wink and waltz out.

It looks like my life is finally getting back to normal. With a tad more magic involved.

42

MIKAEL

*W*hen we get back to Aurora's, I follow Nev outside where he leaps into the forest and chases a squirrel. Laughing, I lay back on the grass and watch him.

The back door opens, and I know it's her.

We haven't been alone since she came back, not really, and it feels awkward.

I see the way my brothers watch her. They found her first. I can almost taste the love on them. Even Alexander, no matter how much he fights it. I'm the reason she almost died, and although I know no one blames me, I still blame myself. I manage to keep my distance, even as I long for her to look at me, to come and sit with me and play our little games.

To talk, like we did for nights on end. Just me and her.

She sits next to me, close, her hand between us next to mine, almost touching but not.

Swallowing, I keep my eyes on the trees. I have no right to her heart or body. Hell, not even her mind, But I want them. I want them all so bad. I want to know her inside out. I want to know what makes her laugh like with Ben. I want to know what makes her smile with Ezra. What makes her angry like with Darius? I feel like I know everything about her past, tidbits from our many conversations. Everything but how to get her to love me.

"How are you?" she asks, that velvety voice from my dreams wrapping around me, reminding me of the hope and need she brings me every time I see her.

The first time I heard that voice, I thought she was an angel. I thought she wasn't real. Even now, my fingers itch to touch her, to make sure she won't disappear again.

"I'm okay." I feel her hard stare, and my lips twitch, remembering that Alexander told me she has claws and doesn't like to be lied to. "My throat hurts every now and again. And when I close my eyes, I find myself back in that fucking room. Then, I wake up and I know I'm safe."

Her hand covers mine, and I grip it like a lifeline.

"Why didn't you say anything?" she asks sternly, making my lips twitch.

"There's nothing that can be done. Nightmares… Everyone has them."

"Yes, but fuck. I could have ridden them out with you, or one of the guys," she mutters.

Turning my head, I face her as she watches Nev. I'm struck by her beauty again. Every time I look I am. She looks like heaven and hell wrapped in one dangerous little package. All dark hair and pouty lips. My throat dries up like it always does around her.

"Would you?" I force out, and she frowns, glancing over at me.

"Would I what?" She tilts her head adorably in confusion, and I realize I'm stroking her hand, but I don't pull away.

I'll take whatever scraps of attention she throws my way. I know she will bond my brothers, and I'm happy for them. They deserve it, but it doesn't mean I can't wish she was my girl, too.

"Ride it out with me?" I ask, needing to know.

She watches me, nibbling on her lip nervously before she nods. "I would. You know I would. Why do you think I came back every night? It wasn't for your bad attempt at flirting. I needed to know you were okay. I needed to be at your side no matter what was happening."

Her words hold truth, and I smile the first real full smile since she saved me, and it's all for her.

"Bad attempt at flirting?" I tease, and she nods, her face serious.

"It was terrible. Really bad. But you're pretty, so you can make it work," she says seriously, and my face drops.

"Not so pretty anymore," I choke out, my other hand raising to the scar, but I drop it back to the grass and stare at the forest, not wanting to see the pity.

She grunts, and I blink in shock as she gets up and jumps into my lap, her knees on the grass on either side of me.

She grabs my face and forces me to look at her. "Now, you listen the fuck up. I don't give a shit if you have a goddamn penis tattooed on your face. That fucking scar is from surviving something horrible, and every time I see it, all I think is *thank god you're alive.* That I got there in time, that you still get to be here with us—with me. I will tell you it every time you need to hear." She huffs the last word, ending her rant.

I watch her intently, running her words through my head, trying to work through the logic. "Why? Why do you care? Is it because it would hurt them?"

She rolls her eyes, staring at the sky as if for help before she tightens her hands and puts her face in mine. "No, it's not because it would hurt them. Yes, you're terrible at flirting and your jokes make me cringe, but you also know more about me than even Ezra. You know all my fears, my dreams, my nightmares. I shared that part of me with you, no one else. I want everything you promised. So no, it's not for them. It's for me. You promised me a Christmas and a birthday, and a holiday, and you're going to fucking keep that promise because I care about you."

My grin is slow but grows bigger and she huffs, letting go of my face and sitting back, her face heating as if her words only now catch up with her. She's so strong, so sure. She's willing to lay everything on the line to make someone else feel better even when it means hurting or showing herself.

"I did promise you a Christmas," I joke, and she groans, leaning forward and laying her head on my chest.

I can't help it; I wrap my arms around her and hold her to me. From inside, my brothers' laugh as they tease each other. No doubt they'll come on the hunt for her soon. But for now, she's all mine.

"Favorite space film?" I ask, and she laughs in my arms, her fingers stroking my shoulders and chest.

"Star Wars, duh. Worst party?"

I grin, happiness exploding in my chest, and she pokes me. "Sorry, what was the question?" I ask, and she lifts her head and grins at me.

I can't help but swallow hard.

She opens her mouth, but I don't hear a word. I'm too busy staring at her. I'm lost.

"Tell me about your family?" she asks, and I freeze.

She lifts her head with a frown, and I force myself to blow out a breath and relax. "What about them?"

"Well, do you have any siblings? What about your parents?" She tilts her head, squinting at me.

Wrapping my arms around her tighter, I watch Nev as he rolls in the grass. "I don't have anyone but my coven in there. Not anymore."

"Mikael—" she says softly, and I smile sadly at her.

"Sometimes I forget you don't know us all. It's not a good story, Rora, but I know your past. You should know mine," I admit.

"You don't have to—"

I shake my head and look at Nev. "I had an older sister; her name was Jules. When she turned sixteen, she caught the eye of another coven's witch. She was destined to follow in my father's footsteps and lead our house. He was the same. Their union was blessed, but she was so young, and he was... more evil than anyone could have ever imagined. They went on a date. She told him she wanted to get to know him before they joined, but he had other ideas."

My sister's face, when I found her, flashes in my head, and I push it away, telling it like a story so I don't breakdown, even after all these years. "He raped her, then killed her. He tossed her body outside of our house, and I found her."

Aurora gasps, and when I look, tears track down her face for my pain.

It softens me and I cup her face. "She was my best friend, Rora. She really was. I looked up to her. She always made time for me no matter how busy she was. Her loss broke something in my mother. Not two weeks after we honored Jules, my mother killed herself."

"Mikael—"

I smile sadly. "My father was never a big family man. Hell, he was hardly ever there. He was the head of the house and it was an important role, but it made him distant and uncaring. After Jules and my mum, he disappeared. Left me the house and everything and stayed with the coven and council. I was alone. That's when I met my brothers."

"What happened to the man who hurt your sister?" Rage fills her voice.

"He went rogue. He had harmed a chosen one, after all. My father would not allow him to live no matter who he was. Hunters tracked him down, and he was executed in front of everyone; a reminder of how powerful the council is." It's why I become a hunter in the first place, but I don't tell her that.

"I'm so fucking sorry," she cries, wrapping her arms around me.

I hug her back and breathe in the smell of her. "Life has its reasons. Maybe all the bad happened so it could lead me to the good. To you."

Eventually, she scrambles from my lap and I sigh, knowing she'll go back to her men now.

She surprises me by reaching down and offering me her hand. I accept it, and she helps pull me to my feet and keeps her hand in mine as we stroll back to the house where the smell of food wafts out.

Opening the back door, she calls to Nev over her shoulder.

He bounds to us, nearly knocking us over in the process, and butts his way into the kitchen.

We share a smile as Ben yells.

Shaking my head, I laugh. That dog has made it his personal mission to annoy Ben.

I follow Aurora into the kitchen and grin as my brothers joke and laugh. They're more at home in her kitchen than they ever are at home.

Ben cooks with Jason, and Alex and Ezra sit at the table, a seat left between them with a mug in front of it.

Aurora ignores it, dragging me after her as she goes over and steals a taste of food, earning her a smacked hand from Jason.

He looks at her, and her cheeks heat and eyes flare. It seems my quiet brother showed her his dominant streak. She dances away when Ben tries to spank her.

She winks at me and drags me over to the table.

I go willingly, as long as I get to still hold her hand.

Instead of dropping into the seat between Alex and Ezra, she sits next to Alex and I slip into the one on her other side. Ezra smiles at her, a soft little thing that I didn't know the big guy was capable of.

Alex pushes the mug toward her, his eyes sparkling when she refuses to let go of my hand to lift it.

I look back at him blankly, almost nervously, but he sits back, throwing his arm across her seat and nurses his coffee, watching her.

"We need to leave about nine. The club is called Encore. Heard of it, kitten?" Alex asks, his fingers playing with her shirt.

"Sure. It's in the next town over, about forty minutes away." She leans into his touch like she doesn't even notice, but he does.

I might have her hand, but he has her completely, and he hasn't even kissed her yet.

When I try to draw my hand back, she grips it tighter, refusing to let me go.

"Okay, then we leave at nine." Alex rubs her shoulder and winks at me.

Cheeky bastard.

"Sounds good. Who's this person we're meeting?" She sips her coffee as she looks around.

When she catches my eye, she smiles.

"He's someone everyone in our community uses if you need to find a certain... job. He's a rat bastard, but he gets shit done. On Sheldon's orders, we asked him for a dream walker. It seems he's found one and is calling in his debt."

She nods. They must have filled her in on what

happened while she was saving Darius. Speaking of him, I wonder where he got to.

Aurora must think the same thing. She searches the kitchen, a worried frown tugging at her lips before she snorts and shakes her head. Even as her lips lift in a smile, her eyes look far away, like she isn't even in the room, anymore.

I don't understand her relationship with Darius. I don't think any of us do. He's different since he came back. One second he's hot toward her; the next he's cold, but he's always here, like he can't stand not to be in her orbit.

As if she summoned him, Darius slinks into the kitchen and drops into the chair opposite her, his legs stretching under the table.

"Glad you could join us," she remarks casually, leaning back.

"Sorry, angel face. Didn't realize you were missing me so much. With how you were screaming earlier, I figured you were occupied."

At his voice tone, I sit straighter, tightening my grip on her hand.

We all heard her with Ezra. Fuck, we'd have to be deaf not to. Her moans are burned into my head, but she has every right. She's bonded to him after all.

Alex glares at Darius, his mouth opening in no doubt ready to rip him a new one, but Aurora laughs and winks at Darius.

"I was. Jealousy doesn't look good on you, princess," she mocks.

Darius narrows his eyes at her, and they have a staring contest.

The silence stretches around us, and we're unsure of how to process this.

Darius looks away first, and Aurora puts the mug to her mouth, but I see her lips twitching behind it.

Little minx.

43

AURORA

*D*inner runs without a hitch. I have to let go of Mikael's hand eventually, and I find myself missing his comforting warmth. Darius inhales his food, his eyes locked on me the whole time, but I ignore him. Dude is mardy as fuck today, and I don't know why.

Bloody man. I'm going to get whiplash from his emotions.

Once Alex finishes eating, he leans back in his chair, his hand landing on my thigh under the table. Hiding my smile, I shove a fork full of pasta into my mouth as he runs his palm up and down my thigh, landing closer to where I wish he would touch me each time.

Before I'm done, the others finish and watch me eat, weirdos.

Sitting back, I pat my stomach, nearly in a food coma. "I don't think I can move ever again."

Alex laughs.

My phone dings and I tilt my head. I thought I left it upstairs. It comes again, and I look around.

Ben avoids my eyes, his lips twitching.

"Benny, what did you do?" I ask, and he grins.

He jumps up from the table and holds my phone in the air. "Oh, nothing, nothing at all. Tell me, does Lane always call you a fucking cock sucking witch bitch?"

He backs away as I narrow my eyes in warning.

"You're dead. Run, little Benny," I warn, getting up from the table as the others laugh.

He grins, blows me a kiss, and darts from the kitchen with me close on his heels.

He laughs as he races up the stairs, and I chase after him.

"Come get me, little witch!" he yells, and I giggle as I burst into the bedroom to find him standing on my bed holding the phone in the air.

"Come get it," he teases, and I jump onto the bed, reaching to grab it, but I'm too small.

I jump and end up falling forward into him. He laughs as we tumble backward. I land on his chest with our legs entwined.

Eyes dancing with laughter, he grins down at me, the phone forgotten. My eyes drop to his lips. My hair falls to the side, creating a curtain from us and the rest of the room. I can't help it. I lick my lips to ease their sudden dryness, and he follows the movement, a groan vibrating his chest.

"Sunshine?" He sounds pained.

"What did you do, Benny?" I lean forward, running my hand up his chest and around his neck to his face.

He pants and leans into me, his pupils dilating as his hands land on my ass and pull me in tighter to feel his hard length against me. "Nothing."

I lean down, running my hands higher to his hair and gripping tight as I lower my lips to his. "Tutut, what did you do?" I whisper, my lips brushing his with the words.

He swallows audibly as I let go of his hair and run my left hand up his arm until I reach his hand. Only then do I drop my lips to his. He groans and kisses me back, chasing me as I keep the pace slow.

Grinning, I slip the phone from his grasp, as he's distracted, and pull away.

He follows me, his eyes dazed, and I laugh, sitting up with the phone in my hand. It has blown up with messages from Lane and I scroll through the last few, keeping him between my legs with my hand on his chest.

I get to his message and groan. He sent her some coupons for sex toys and escort dates, and he signed her up for 'services,' claiming to be me during the whole thing. Dropping my phone to the bed, I arch my eyebrow at him as he watches me. I figured he would be laughing, but his face is serious, and his teeth pull at his lips.

"Kiss me properly," he asks. Not demands or teases, but asks.

I lay down again, our faces inches apart. "What sort of punishment would that be?"

I run my lips along his cheek.

"The best kind, having you on top of me, tasting you but unable to have you. Torture," he whispers, and I stop above his lips.

"Kiss him," a hard voice says from behind me.

I feel the bed dip, and then hands frame my hips, rough and hard, bruising in their pressure. I moan, breathless, loving the contrast between Ben's soft lips and Jason's hard hands.

I do as I'm told, loving Jason's dominant streak. I cover Ben's lips, tugging at the bottom one, and he opens for me. I sweep my tongue in and he follows, allowing me to do whatever I want. Jason's hand moves up, sweeping across my hip and back until he moves my hair to the other side.

Lips meet my neck, soft and wet. "Good girl," Jason murmurs, kissing up the side of my face and then back down my neck.

I groan into Ben's mouth when Jason nips the sensitive flesh on the back of my neck, wiggling on top of Ben to try and relieve some pressure.

When I pull away to pant, Ben grins over my shoulder to Jason, mighty pleased with himself. "Oh, she liked whatever you just did."

"Is he right?" Jason bites me again when I don't answer fast enough for him.

"Yes," I pant and lean down to kiss Ben again.

"Good." He bites again, then licks away the sting and I writhe, caught between Ben's softness and Jason's hardness.

Finish up, will you? You need to get ready.

I ignore Darius's grim as fuck voice in my head and rub myself on Ben until his voice comes again.

I will *come in there. Either fuck them or get dressed.*

He sounds pissed, so I ignore him again.

You want to play, fine.

Uh-oh, no nickname. This can't be good. I scream out loud, falling from the bed and curling up on the floor and breathe through the pain of him ripping away from my mind. Tears run down my face, but the moment passes, more shock than anything.

Darius slides back in, gently this time.

I warned you. Now, get dressed. His voice is soft now, regret in his tone.

Sighing, I sit up, knowing he didn't mean to hurt me.

I really didn't. I thought it would make you freeze. Sorry, princess. His whisper slips away.

I zone back in to find Ben and Jason crouched in

front of me, both panicking, their hands fluttering over me.

"I'm okay." I cough and wince.

"What did we do?" Ben asks, panicking more than I've ever seen him.

Unable to help it, I laugh, and once I start, I can't stop.

They glance at each other, their worry growing.

"Something's wrong," Jason says.

"Do you think we should get Alex?" Ben adds, and I roar louder with laughter, tears dripping down my face as I try to wave them away with my hand.

"Okay. I'm okay." I snort out another laugh. Blowing out a breath, I try to calm myself.

Them panicking more sobers me up enough to talk.

"Okay, I'm fine. Sorry about that, but you can thank Darius for the mental cock block," I finish, a giggle slipping out before I clamp my lips shut.

Their eyebrows raise and they look at each other with various degrees of perplexity.

"Do you know what that means?" Ben asks, and Jason shakes his head.

Grinning, I stand and they shoot to their feet, their hands held out to catch me. "Seriously, I'm okay. Just took me by surprise. Now you better let me get ready or Darius is going to throw a B.F."

"B.F?" Jason asks slowly, staring at me like I lost my mind.

"Bitch fit. Duh." I trot over to my wardrobe as Nev comes pounding in, a shoe in his mouth.

I grin, and he drops it at my feet, sitting back.

Crouching down, I examine it and laugh. "That Darius's, baby?"

He nods.

Biting my lip, I rub his head and lean closer to whisper, "Good boy."

They hear me anyway and laugh, obviously realizing I'm okay, and lay back on the bed to watch me.

I stand back up and turn with an arched eyebrow. "Can I help you?"

"Nope." Ben pops the p.

"Shouldn't you be getting ready?" I ask.

"Nah, we don't take as long as you. Come on, hot thing, show us what ya got." Ben wolf whistles, and I roll my eyes, although the smile doesn't leave my face.

I can barely remember the feeling before I met them, of constant loneliness when I hardly ever smiled. Now it splits my cheeks all the time.

Shaking my head, I open my closet door and look inside. I might not always be a girly girl, I like my punny shirts and big biker boots and leather jackets, but I drag Lane partying a lot and I do love dressing up. There's something about a nice dress and heels that can make any girl feel like they rule the world. Plus, I want to see their jaws drop, they never got to see me in the one from Perses, and I bet they would have loved it.

274

Rooting through the hanging clothes, I giggle at the dress I pick out. Hiding it in front of my body, not for modesty, more so they get the full effect, I slip into the bathroom. I shut the door, hang up the dress, and check myself out in the mirror.

I do my makeup, taking more time than normal by lining my eyes and matching the color of my eyeshadow with my dress. I even own matching lipstick. The dark plum looks amazing against my pale skin. The blush highlights my cheekbones. I lean back and play with my hair. It dried in a big, curly mess thanks to hands in it and me not drying it probably.

Grabbing a shit ton of bobby pins, I tackle the Hagrid beast and manage to twist it up with pieces falling around my face so I don't resemble a potato.

Satisfied I look all right, I slip off my clothes and grab the dress. It's beautiful: a designer piece Lane bought me for my birthday and I never wanted to wear because it's so nice. A deep plum, it has a low-cut vee neck, so low I can't wear a bra. A sparkly belt cinches in the waist and then it puffs out in hanging sections to just before my knees, showing skin as I walk. The back also plunges in a deep vee, and it's sexy as hell.

I pull off my bra and slip into the dress, readjusting my nips so they don't fall out and give anyone a free show, though I bet the guys would love it. They might fireball anyone's ass who sees them, though, so the nips need to stay contained.

Twisting in the mirror, I check myself out. Damn, I look good. I would totally fuck myself.

"Hurry up!" Ben yells.

"Calm ya man tits!" I shout back and lean forward to check my makeup one last time.

"Is everything okay?" The door opens, and Jason appears in the mirror.

His face darkens as he looks me over from head to toe, not missing a detail. Footsteps come from behind him, no doubt Ben. Jason slips in and slams the door shut, hitting the lock before he strides toward me.

I freeze. Staring at him as he stops behind me, my ass pushes to his jean-clad cock. He leans in over my back and breathes me in, making me shiver. His eyes meet mine in the mirror as he drops a kiss on my neck, making me lick my lips.

"Damn it, guys, let me in! I want to see." Ben knocks on the door, but we ignore him.

"You look good enough to eat. Maybe I will later," Jason says softly, laying another kiss then stepping back.

He leaves me gawking as he unlocks the door and slips out, letting Ben fill the doorway.

Ben whistles and I grin, dragging in a deep breath and turning to him. "Damn, you look beautiful. Ezra is definitely going to kill someone."

"Want to bet?" I tease, and he nods, his eyes still running over me, trailing witch fire in their wake.

"Loser has to do a practical joke on Darius," he offers, and I grin.

"Deal." I stretch out my hand and he grabs it, but instead of shaking, he uses it to reel me in until I'm plastered to his chest.

He grins down at me and drops a chaste kiss on my lips; then, as if he can't help himself, drops another. "You'll be lucky if I don't kill someone as well with how good you look."

He pulls away, and for a second time that evening, I'm left gawking after a man leaves my bathroom.

Witches.

44

AURORA

When I come out of the bathroom, Ben and Jason have left my room, and I spot Nev fast asleep on my bed. I walk over and drop a kiss on his head. "Be good, baby. We won't be long."

He snores and I laugh.

Grabbing some heels, I quickly slip into them and pluck my forgotten phone from the bedsheets.

My clutch bag already waits on the side, and I add my lipstick and compact to it before making sure I have everything. I can't wait to see the guys' faces.

Opening the door, I flick off the light and head down the stairs. I can hear them and when I lean over the banister, I grumble to find them all ready.

That shit isn't far. Men have it so easy.

I step down carefully, not wanting to face-plant in front of them. That would be bad. Concentrating on not falling, I don't notice the hush that falls until Darius's voice in my head drags my head up.

Holy shit, princess. I look around as his voice comes again. *I mean, you look nice.*

He mumbles it but appreciation and lust hum through our bond. Alex meets my eyes and the burning in them forces me to look away. Ezra's no better. They both promise things that have me clenching my thighs together.

Ben winks and Jason grins. Darius leans against the wall, his eyes pulled away, but he keeps flicking me peeks.

Mikael stands with his back to me but turns when everyone goes quiet.

He gulps and turns pleading eyes to the guys. "No killing any humans."

We all laugh.

The club is massive. The line stretches around the block in the industrial side of town. I can't say I've been here before. Music pounds and the lights in the warehouse span this darkened area of the city. Two massive bouncers stand at the door, dressed from head to toe in black.

Something about them puts me on edge.

We get weird looks as we walk to the door. A man

in line even gasps and points. I glance at him as he turns to his friends and they all stare back at us. Or, more specifically, at the men fanning out behind me.

Before I can ask, a warm hand meets the bottom of my back and pushes me forward gently. I glance over as Alex steps up next to me, and keeping his hand on me, stares at the bouncers. They run their eyes over us, stopping on me before Ezra moves in front of me.

They reluctantly let us in, and when I step through, I swear one of them sniffs me.

The door leads into a cloakroom area, and I pass over my leather jacket, step through the double doors, and gape.

I knew it was big, but this is seriously impressive. A huge dance floor takes up the middle, raised to be seen from anywhere in the club. A VIP section sits to the left with doors opening onto what looks like a patio and private bar. To the right is a long bar, covered from side-to-side in a throng of people. The whole club is packed; the smell of sweat and alcohol permeates through the air.

The music's base runs through the floor and up my legs. My heart pounds in time to it and all I want to do is dance. The guys lead me over to the VIP section, and without even sparing the bouncer a look, they stride through and to an empty table in the back corner, away from everyone.

My phone dings as I slide into the booth. I grab it

from my purse and grin. I guess I should have mentioned to the guys I invited Lane. I didn't see the harm, and she's feeling neglected right now.

"You invited the sheep?" Darius snorts, sprawling in the darkest corner.

The others turn to me, and I smile guiltily. "Sure as shit did. Anyone got a problem?"

They all shake their heads, but they exchange glances.

Alex sighs and leans back opposite me. "She can't be present for the talks with Henry, though, kitten."

I nod and smile sweetly. "Of course, cutie."

He groans and Ezra snorts from his seat next to me, his hand twining with mine under the table.

Alex winks at me. "Then I guess it's okay."

"Good, 'cause she's here." I scramble up before they can say anything. Backing away, I grin. "Grab me a drink, will ya? I'll go meet her."

"Kitten," Alex warns, his eyes narrowing, but he laughs.

I spin and leave the VIP area to slip through the crowd, back through the cloakroom, and to the entrance. I open the door and stick my head out to find Lane standing near the curb, glancing around as she fidgets.

Stepping out with my hand still on the door, I whistle. "Hey, hot momma, you looking for a good time?"

Heads turn, but Lane grins and strides my way. She looks amazing with her blonde hair down and wavy, her makeup minimal, and her dress a short black number. She slips past me inside.

"No more add-ons, witch," the bouncer to the left murmurs, and I turn to find him gawking.

A hand drops on my shoulder. I whirl to see Darius's grim face. He nods at the bouncer and draws me back inside, shutting the door.

"He knows what I am?" I ask, and Darius glares down at me, his face hard.

"Of course. They're shifters, after all." As he turns and walks away, I scramble to jump in front of him.

Lane glances between us.

"Like werewolves?" I ask, excited.

"Yes, princess. Now, can we get the fuck out of the cloakroom?" he grumbles, and I nod.

I let him past and link my arm with Lane's.

"You look good. Did you drive the boys mad?" Lane whispers, and I laugh.

"Yep." We share a grin before the music makes talking impossible unless we want to scream.

Lane gazes around in wide-eyed wonder as I pull her after Darius and back to the VIP area.

I drop back down at the table, and Lane hesitates, looking around at the guys who take up the rest of the booth. With a groan, I move over to sit on Ezra's lap and pat my vacated seat. She sits next to me, her eyes still locked on the dance floor. The girl has an obsession with dancing. She might be shy sometimes, but once she gets on a dance floor, she turns into a completely different person.

I snuggle back against Ezra, and Alex pushes a glass across the table, then another to Lane.

I grin at him and look around. "Where's Darius?"

Then I freeze when my eyes land on the witch in question.

Fucking asshole. Jealousy like I've never experienced surges through me, eclipsing everything else until my whole body vibrates with it, and my magic rises with it.

My eyes narrow on Darius and the girl as everything else falls away.

45

DARIUS

*T*he red-haired girl smiles at me all flirty, her eyes locked on me and filled with interest. She flutters her fake lashes, pouts her red-lined lips, and leans in, her hand landing on my forearm.

With my other hand, I take a sip of my drink and run my eyes around the club before I look back at the girl. She told me her name, but I can't remember it. Amber? Britany? Some stupid shit, no doubt.

She strokes my arm, licking her bottom lip, and I roll my eyes. I don't even know why I let her stop me, apart from the fact that, when I glance at our table, princess was laughing and cuddling on Ezra's lap and I saw red.

Maybe this redhead is exactly what I need to fuck all this obsession out of my bloodstream, but even as I think that, my mind whispers that I'm a liar. Even her touch on my arm makes me itch and want to pull away. She doesn't feel right.

I find myself wanting a certain little black-haired witch to be her, but she doesn't want to be. That much is clear, so I let the woman touch me as she prattles on about something, and I nod in the expected places.

I feel someone's eyes on me and glance up only to lock eyes with the witch in question. They're narrowed on me and her nostrils flare. Her hair floats around her, and her powers rise as she glares at me.

Hell, I can see her eyes shining and turning purple from here.

I smirk and lean into the girl, watching the jealousy and anger cross princess's face before she hides it and turns to the table, ignoring me.

Interesting.

"What do you think, baby?" the woman purrs, leaning closer and grinning at me.

"Huh?" My eyes dart from her to Aurora, hoping she's still looking.

"About dancing?" The woman pulls back with a frown, which she quickly wipes away and covers with a fake smile. The fucker looks painful, too, nothing like when Aurora does it. Like if she doesn't smile, she'll explode. It's a beautiful smile.

"Sure, whatever," I reply, already forgetting what she asked me.

"Good, let's go." Red stands, giving me a good view

of her tits and the junction between her thighs. "Oops," she says and tugs down her dress, winking at me to make sure I saw.

This time, I do roll my eyes. Downing my drink, I let her pull me to the dance floor. She winds her hips dancing against me, and her arms wrap around my neck.

I let her, standing stock still until I notice Aurora on the dance floor with her head thrown back in laughter as she dances between Alex and Ben. They have their hands all over her, watching her like she's the fucking moon.

Gritting my teeth, anger burns in me along with crippling jealousy as I watch Ezra palm her ass through her dress. Turning away before I do something stupid, like attack my brothers, I wrap my arms around Red and dance, trying to let the music carry everything away.

It's no use, and when Red runs her lips down my neck, I want to vomit.

Red runs her lips higher, and I suck in a breath, gripping her hips to push her away. This was a stupid idea. Did I really think some stupid hussy would make me forget about Aurora? *For fuck's sake, Darius.*

I freeze when Red's lips cover mine. I don't even know what to do, but when a gasp sounds, I push the girl away and wipe the back of my hand across my mouth, disgust coursing through me. Spinning, I watch

Aurora's retreating back. I push my way through the crowd, needing to make her understand. I don't want to look too closely at why it's so important she understand I didn't kiss the girl, but my chest burns, and my heart pounds.

Ben steps into my path, his face locked in disappointment and anger.

"Move, man," I demand, stepping around him, but he blocks me again.

"Not a fucking chance." He steps into my chest, pushing me back, his eyes flashing with his magic, and I square off, letting mine rise, too. "You listen up, you fucking bastard. You can be cruel to us all you like. We can take it. We have to, but that fucking woman has done nothing but defend you to us and protect you. You've done enough tonight. Go sit the fuck down."

Wow, I've never heard him swear so much. If it wasn't for the need to get through him and to my princess, I might even laugh. Seems Ben finally found something to be serious for.

"Move," I growl out.

"No. Fuck you. If you only came back to mess everything up, maybe you should have stayed dead," he spits, and I freeze.

Regret instantly covers his face, but it's too late. I let my fist fly.

He sees it coming, but he doesn't even move to

defend himself. It hits him square in the face, and he stumbles back, cursing.

"You have no idea what you're talking about. You think I want to be this way? This fucking hate coursing through me all the time? I can't stand it. I can't stand not being myself, but whatever the hell they did to me, it still has hold and the only way I can shake it is with that fucking, annoying, beautiful, loyal witch. She makes it all disappear. I can see through the vile and hate, like a goddamn witch light guiding me back to being human." The words spill out, and Ben's eyes soften.

His shoulders slump. "Darry, I didn't know."

Looking away, I grit my teeth. How the hell was he to know I'm drowning?

"I don't want to be this way," I choke out and slam my lips shut again.

His hands land on my shoulder. "Then let her heal you."

I look to him, searching his eyes. Why doesn't he hate me?

"She can. She healed us. Let her bring back Darry, 'cause I fucking miss him. I don't like this asshole version so much." He grins, and I can't help but laugh. "I love you, man, even if that means I have to let you punch me in the face sometimes."

He drags me in and wraps me in his arms.

I hesitate but wrap mine around him, too. It's so

familiar that it softens me, stopping the darkness that always swells inside of me.

"I love you, too," I whisper, but I know he hears.

He pulls back and slaps my back. "Go get her, brother."

With a grin, he blends back into the crowd.

Standing tall, I search for signs of Aurora, but when I don't spot her, I get worried. She shouldn't have gone off alone. It isn't safe. Supes pack the club, and not all are friendly to witches.

Blowing out a breath, I barge my way through the crowd and spot a hallway. I let my bond guide me and cover distance before stopping outside the door to the women's room.

Not wasting a moment, I push it open. A woman turns to me and starts cursing.

I glare at her until she leaves.

When I don't spot anyone else, I lock the door and stride to the stalls. One is locked, and I know it's her.

Leaning against it, I debate what I need to say. My tongue feels fumbly; I've never had this issue before. Usually, I can always say the right thing, but something about her always puts me on edge, and this moment is important.

"Princess?" I knock on the door.

She ignores me.

"Open the fucking door, your highness," I growl, then wince.

What the fuck, dude? That's how you make it better? Fuck, I'm so messed up.

"No," she mutters, but I hear it.

"Open the fucking door or I'll kick it down," I growl.

Okay, seems I'm going to roll with it. Every time I open my mouth to say something sweet, this... shit spills out.

When she doesn't, I step back and lift my leg, kicking it open. The lock clatters to the floor as the door swings wildly. I step in and see a startled Aurora slumped on the toilet before I slam the stall door shut behind me.

"You fucking prick," she fumes, standing to go toe-to-toe with me.

She barely reaches my chest, and I smirk as she pokes me, her eyes spitting purple and black, her magic wrapping around her.

The sight turns my cock into a steel rod and gives me the insane urge to push her harder. I love her anger. She's beautiful when she's sweet and laughing, but like this? She's fucking unstoppable. Power itself is addictive. I wonder what she would look like with that magic riding her as she rode me.

Not bothering with fumbling words, I let her see the regret and self-hate in my eyes. I'm drowning, and I need her to save me.

Her voice floats in my head. *What?*

I must have projected my last thought. Fuck it. Darting forward, I capture her hands and bring them to my face as I lower my head. She doesn't move away as I cover her lips.

Darius, she warns, but she pulls me closer, and I go willingly.

Look, you want to know us so badly. Look. I'm lost without you. Save me, princess.

I open my mind, letting her look if she wants to. She gasps into my mouth and something wet drops onto our joined lips. Pulling away, I see her eyes unfocused as tears drip steadily.

I close my eyes and lay my forehead on hers. I let her have everything; I let her see how I feel because I'll never be able to tell her—not with this inside of me.

Darius, she cries in my head, and my heart stutters.

It's like her voice is a bright, blinding light chasing the shadows away until I can see clearly for a moment. But I know it will overtake me again, the hate only held at bay for now, and it terrifies me.

Then I will be your light, always, she vows, and I choke on a laugh.

You can't.

She snorts. You *want to fucking bet?*

Her lips cover mine again, and my eyes shoot open to focus on her.

Shut your eyes. That's creepy. She laughs in my head.

I grunt before dragging her close and closing my eyes, sweeping into her mouth to taste her.

Her hands stay on my face where I drew them, and I wrap her up in my arms, finding solace there as she storms through my mind, fighting away the darkness as she twines with me.

I don't try to take it any further. I'm happy to have her in my arms and her lips on me.

She pulls back and lays her forehead back on mine, our eyes locked on each other and filled with lust and unspoken things. I can still feel her in my mind; not as strong as before, but more like she left open the link between us. I catch whispers of her thoughts every now and again—a buzz unless I want to hear them. But the best thing? I can think clearly. Like she flicked on the light and chased off the darkness.

It's still there, but not consuming me.

"What did you do?" I gasp, and I don't know whether it's in my head and hers or out loud.

"Saved you, princess. You can thank me now." She laughs, and I join in, the sound choked and harsh but still there.

"Thank you, princess. I can think of other ways to make it up to you," I snark.

"I bet you can, but you forget: I'm in your head. I've seen your... thoughts about me."

I grin, not the least bit ashamed, but it dims and I look at the floor. "Will this last?"

I hate the quiver in my voice.

"Yes. I won't shut you out, not again. We'll need to set some rules, but I think with the connection open, you can drain some of my… light and stop it from growing. It won't reverse what's already there, and you might have moments, but essentially, yes."

"You won't shut me out?" I need the reassurance even as mocking laughter sounds from the darkness in my head.

She wipes it all away with a soft kiss on my lips. "Never."

I let out the breath I held. "Let's get back. I bet that prick is here already."

She nods and follows after me, her hand wound through mine.

His ass looks really good in those pants.

Smirking, I don't tease her, even if I want to.

46

AURORA

*D*arius leads me through the mass of people on the dance floor with a new skip in his step. When I saw inside his mind… Gods. I don't know how he's been functioning.

No wonder he's been such a prick.

It was like darkness covered everything, sucking out any hint of light, love, or laughter until all that remained was hate, jealousy, and greed. It must be the leftover Perses warned me about. It twisted Darius's mind and heart, but behind it I sensed him. The real him. The man he was before he died. He's still the same man but with more fear and pain. The darkness remains inside him, and no doubt it will suck him in again, but I'll be there to fight it by his side this time.

He looks over his shoulder and smiles softly at me, obviously reading my thoughts.

Strangely enough, I don't mind. I love this connection we share even when he's a massive twat. His voice in my head, even the constant nicknames.

Looks like your little human found some friends. Guess you two are more alike than you thought.

Following Darius's eyes, I spot Lane dancing with three men. They're all tall and well-built from what I can see, but I can't make out many details; the lights blind me and the people between us block a good view.

What I can make out is her smile. She looks happy, so I grin and follow after Darius. Let's hope she finally gets some. It might keep her occupied while we meet with this man of Alex's, anyway.

When we reach the table, everyone else is already there. I slip in next to Darius and it doesn't go unnoticed.

I ignore the looks and stare at Alex. "Is he not here yet?"

"No, but we need to cover some ground rules first. Don't tell him who or what you are. Leave him guessing. Let us do the talking and try not to draw too much attention to yourself. I'm serious, Aurora; this man is dangerous. He sells people out faster than you can blink. You need to be unmemorable." Alex stares me down, worry in his eyes.

Not wanting to show how much he freaked me out, I nod and swallow hard. I'll do what he says.

Alex pushes a new drink across to me, and I accept it gratefully, spinning the glass with my hands.

They all sit up straighter.

"He's here," Ezra growls, and I follow all their eyes to a man striding our way.

He grabs a chair from the table next to us, swings it around, and sits backward on it, his head propped on the back of it as he takes us all in.

His eyes linger on me for a bit too long, but when he looks at Darius, he freezes. "Well, holy fuck. The prodigal witch returns."

Darius nods and Alex draws his attention by clearing his throat. "You wanted to meet?"

"Yes. Let me get a drink, won't you, my boy?" He waves over a waitress.

Alex grits his teeth, his fingers squeezing around his drink. He really doesn't like this guy.

Once the waitress walks away, the man turns back to us, his face falling from his shark-like smile to serious.

The change makes me sit back further against Darius, whose eyes look dead.

"I found the dream walker as requested, and now I need repayment." He watches me until Alex draws his attention back to him.

"We no longer need the dream walker," Ezra growls.

"Tough shit, hunter. You asked, I found. You're fucking paying. That's how it works." The man smashes his fist onto the table, and I jump. "Now, I'm betting the sudden need for a dream walker has something to do with the woman next to your dead man? I won't pass along this information, of course, but you'll pay."

He leaves the *or else* implied, and I almost hear the cogs in Alex's head turning. Wait, what did he mean hunter?

I ask Darius in my head, but he ignores it.

"What do you want?" Mikael pipes up, and the shark smile appears back on the man's face.

He sits back as the waitress returns and places a drink in front of him. He waits until she disappears before he replies. "There are a few human men I need you to… locate for me. I know they're in London; I just don't know where. So, do what you do best and hunt them."

I feel all the guys throwing looks at me, and when I go to open my mouth to ask what the man means, Darius snaps his hand over my mouth.

Turning, I glare at him, but he ignores me.

"What makes these humans so special?" Jason sits still under the man's probing gaze.

"None of your fucking business. You'll know them instantly. We've put a calling mark on them."

A few breaths suck in as I swivel my gaze around, trying to figure what the fuck's going on.

"We find them and bring them to you, I'm guessing?" Alex drawls, leaning back in his chair.

"Yep. Message me when you have them, and we'll meet." The man winks at me, and I narrow my eyes. He throws back his drink. "Do we have a deal?"

Alex glances at me and sighs. "Yes."

"Good. Once you have the men, I'll give you the dream walker." He starts to stand and Ezra shoots to his feet.

"That wasn't the fucking deal, snake," he growls, and the man freezes.

As he turns back to the table, I gasp into Darius's hand. The man's eyes have gone yellow, slitted and with a tiny pupil.

Something shifts beneath his skin, almost shining under the lights before he hisses out, "That is the deal, hunter. Accept or I will find out why you're so keen to keep the little witch hidden."

Alex stands, pushing Ezra down. "I said deal. Now, get the fuck out of here."

The man's eyes turn back to normal and he tips his hat before grinning over at me. "Nice to meet you, witch. Strange group you've taken up with. If you ever get bored, you can find me. You know how."

With a wink, he disappears into the crowd.

Slowly, everyone relaxes, but a bit of tension still rolls off them. Something that man said shook them. I just don't know what.

If you don't remove your hand, I'm going to bite it and then fireball your penis.

Darius laughs in my head and drops his hand.

Licking my lips, I throw him a glare before looking back at Alex. "What did he mean hunter? And how does he know you?"

Alex sighs, rubbing his head. I instantly feel bad.

"I'll tell you, kitten, I promise. But can we enjoy the rest of our night?" He looks so forlorn I find myself nodding.

Some life comes back into Alex's eyes. "Want to dance, kitten?"

Downing the drink, I nod.

He slips out and wraps an arm about my waist, steering me from the table, but my mind runs a hundred miles a minute. I guess I've been trying to ignore everything else Perses told me, and the fact they're witches. With it pushed into my face tonight, I realize I know nothing of how their world works and I need to—fast.

I can't forget my promise to Perses. It's been nice taking a break and recovering after everything, but after tonight, I need to get serious. We need to talk, and we need to come up with a plan for what we know about my future.

"Tonight, kitten. Keep your head focused on just tonight, not tomorrow, not a week from now. Tonight," Alex murmurs and pulls my body to his.

Standing on the edge of the dance floor, he gazes down at me, and I lose myself in his amber eyes.

"Tonight," I promise, but silently I add that tomorrow they will have to face what they so clearly don't want to.

Why were they here in the first place? Why was Mikael hunting me? Why are they a coven? Why do they exist outside of the secretive world of witches?

Who are they?

47
_____

ALEXANDER

*Q*uestions swirl in Aurora's eyes as she looks at me and silently worries at her bottom lip. I push down everything and concentrate on her. I knew the day would come when we would have to tell her everything, but I've held back. I've witnessed her anger firsthand, and she finds it hard enough to trust— only now just letting us in.

This might break that, and it terrifies me. Not for me, but I see the way my brothers watch her. They're gone. If she leaves, she'll break their hearts, and that will be on my shoulders.

They pleaded with me to tell her, but I worried about her past and her motives, not wanting to trust a rogue witch. Then, we were in too deep. With every day and every minute I didn't tell her, the weight grew in my stomach. I can't bear the thought of her hating me, of that softness and smile she gives me turning into a scowl. Of not being able to touch her ever again... Maybe that was why I held myself back, knowing then, at least, I might be able to protect myself a little.

Groaning, I push it all away. It's all tomorrow's problems. Tonight, tonight I will let myself indulge in case this is the last time she lets me hold her. My hand lifts to grab her bottom lip, and she lets it go from between her teeth. As my finger runs over it, I watch her eyes flare.

Dropping my hand before I do something stupid like throw her over my shoulder and carry her out of here, I drop my hands to her ass and pull her tight until no space exists between our bodies.

Her hands land on my chest as we dance, and the music guides us as she winds her hips. I watched her dance earlier and it had me harder than a rock as I imaged her touching me, moving against me like that.

Usually, I control my need and don't push, but I'm throwing everything out the window tonight, so why not?

Ezra moves through the crowd, the throng parting for the big bastard, his eyes already on her.

He grabs her hips and pulls until she falls back into him. Watching me, he bends down and licks her neck before dipping her.

I push back against her front and grab her waist, winding with them. All of us move in sync, the beating of our hearts as loud as the music. With each press of her tits to my chest, it drives my need wilder until I can barely breathe or see.

My eyes drop to her lips again. I know they've all kissed her. Even Darius. It seems only right I'm the last one, but I promised her I wouldn't until she admitted how she felt about it.

She must see the hesitation in my face because she spins, pushing that perky ass up to my cock and leaning on her toes toward Ezra. He dips his head and kisses her. His hand tunnels into her hair, and he holds her to him as he licks and nips at her lips before pushing inside.

I shouldn't be able to over the music, but I hear her quiet gasps and moans as her ass pushing back into my hard cock. Grinding my jaw, I wind my hand in her hair and pull her away from Ezra. He lets go as I twist her head to face me.

Triumph enters Ezra's eyes. He knew I would cave.

Her eyes are unfocused and filled with need. Her lipstick is smudged and her breasts heave as she rubs against us both. She's never looked so beautiful. My head drips to touch my lips to hers, and I'm lost.

Muttering, I tighten my grip, yank her closer, and she gasps in pain. I swallow the sound, pushing my tongue in and dominating her mouth, setting a punishing pace until our lips fight and our teeth clash with the force of the kiss.

She moans into my mouth, and when I lift my head, I see Ezra kissing down her neck and chest. He locks eyes with me and grins. We're both clearly thinking the same thing.

We don't share, not really, but with her…

But first, she's mine.

He must read that because he nods, dropping a kiss on her chest, over her heart, before he steps back. She turns her head to watch him go, but using her hair and waist, I spin her back to me, kissing her hard.

She grips me, her hand diving into my shirt to try and find skin, and when she makes contact and strokes, I shiver. If I don't get her out of here soon, I'm going to bend her over right here and now.

"Can you stop tonguing each other to death for one second?" comes a shout.

I roll my eyes, and pulling away, I drop a kiss on her lips before looking at Lane.

"What happened to your… friends?" I grin, and her face flames.

"Nothing. Look, I need to head home. I have an early meeting." She shuffles, and I sigh.

We aren't letting her go home alone.

Entwining my hand with kitten's, I smile at her. "Come on, kitten, time to go."

Her eyes flare and I smirk.

Leaning down, I whisper in the shell of her ear, "Then you're mine for the night."

She grips onto my hand tighter and grins, then reaches down to right her dress. She rubs my cock, and I narrow my eyes, knowing she did it on purpose.

With a wink, she follows Lane, pulling me from the dance floor as I laugh.

When we get back to the table, I almost groan.

Oh, this should be good. Stupid bastards.

A woman sticks to Jason's side as he tries to shuffle away, his eyes focused anywhere but on the obvious nipples through her see-through shirt. Another leans on Mikael, and yet another woman on Ben. He actually has an arm across the table, blocking her from being on his lap. One sits near Darius, but he glares at her and she looks like she doesn't know what to do. Ezra stands there growling, but to be fair, all the men appear uncomfortable, like the girls came over, sat down, and started flirting on their own.

Women complain about men being handsy and forward, but women can be just as bad.

I storm up there, ready to make them take a hike so Aurora doesn't get upset, but she lets go of my hand and struts to the table like she owns the joint. I watch her ass move as she walks and bite my knuckle to hold back.

This should be interesting.

Stepping up next to her, I watch as she leans over the table between Mikael and Jason, whose shoulders press together at this point to avoid the handsy women. Aurora locks eyes with the woman near Mikael and drops a kiss on his lips before turning her head. Glaring at the other woman, she kisses Jason, too. His eyes widen in shock as he watches her, and I laugh.

Her hands spread on the table, and with every eye on her, she throws back her hair and runs her eyes up and down the girls. "Now, I don't blame you. I really don't, but I am a possessive mother fucker. My daddy always said I didn't know how to share, so you better get your hands off my men before I decide to break them off and shove them through your enhanced lips. Understood?" She purrs, and the women gulp while glancing at each other.

The one next to Ben pipes up. "You can't have all of them, you greedy slut."

She didn't just fucking—

All the guys bristle, but Aurora holds her hand up, stopping us. "Now listen here, cupcake. I can have them all, and I do, but your green monster isn't fucking attractive, and we both know I'm not the slut. I mean really, your legs are spread so wide I can see your pussy hanging out. Desperate isn't a good look, sweetie."

I choke back my laugh.

"Now, get the fuck away from my men. Last warning," Aurora growls, her power running through her and touching all of us until we gasp and shudder. It feels like she stroked the whole way down the front of my body.

With a huff, the women slide from the booth, and

Aurora straightens and turns back to us.

"Fucking cheap slut," one of them spits, and before Aurora can spin around, Lane steps up and throws her drink in the girl's face.

We all stare at the human as the girl screams and rubs at her now ruined dress.

"Don't fuck with my best friend, cunt," Lane snaps, and the girls quickly walk away, still moaning about Lane and Aurora.

Lane turns back to us and Aurora laughs. My girl holds her hand up and Lane smacks it. Pulling away, they both do some weird handshake before turning to the side and bumping hips.

Darius snorts. "You two have a secret handshake?"

"Yep, got a problem with that?" Aurora arches an eyebrow at him.

We all tense, waiting for him to say some mean shit and piss everyone off. It's the only thing he seems to know how to do these days.

"Not a problem at all, princess. Maybe me and you need one." He winks at her.

Well, that's new, but she doesn't look surprised.

Grabbing her hand again, I pull her under my shoulder. She smiles up at me.

"Come on. Let's go home before you get in a fight with someone, kitten," I tease and she laughs.

The sound makes all the guys stare at her with soft expressions.

48

AURORA

We drop Lane off at home, and as I watch her open her door, I shift on Alex's lap and lean my head out the window.

"I'll get the dirty deets of your foursome later!" I shout and wave.

She drops her keys and swears, and we drive off, me laughing like a maniac.

Alex laughs under me, his arms tightening around me as I lean back against his chest. He drops a kiss on my head, and I grin, remembering the taste of him on my lips. Stretching my legs out, I lay them on Mikael's lap, and he grins at me, massaging them as he leans back in the middle seat. Jason sits next to him with Ben up front and Ezra driving. Darius crammed into the back as well. It's a tight squeeze.

Alex's hand lands on my thigh and strokes upward,

my dress lifting for his hand to run along my skin. He leans down and pushes the hair away from my ear. "I'm curious. I know you aren't wearing a bra, but if I run my hand higher, will I meet panties or skin?"

I bite my lip. Fucking tease.

"Panties," I whisper back.

"Too bad." He kisses my ear as his hand inches higher.

My eyes lock with Jason's and he winks, not the least bit bothered that his brother's feeling me up. Weird people, and now that I think about it, I haven't seen much jealousy between them.

Alex gets closer and closer, and my legs open a tad, needing him too much to care if I flash the whole car. He laughs quietly into my hair, and I narrow my eyes. Two can play that game. Shifting, I make sure my ass brushes right over his hard cock. He sucks in a breath and grabs me, stopping me from moving.

"You don't want to play, kitten. Trust me," he whispers again, his tongue darting out to lick my ear.

"What if I do?" I whisper back, winking at Jason.

His cheeks heat, but he turns his head and stares out of the window.

Alex's hand tightens on my thigh, bruising in its grip, and I grin, rubbing myself back on him.

"Kitten, I'm warning you," he growls out.

The hair on my arms sticks up on end at the magic in his words. It seems Alex is close to breaking. Can I push him a little bit further? I don't know why I want to break his control, other than to see if I can.

Shuffling back, I sit up and turn around, so I'm spread over his lap, facing him. His hands automatically drop to my ass to hold me still. I grin down at him as someone else chokes out a breath. No doubt, my dress has ridden up with his hands. I don't mind.

In fact, knowing they're watching makes me moan, and I dart in, kissing Alex. Biting his bottom lip, I pull until it pops away from me.

His eyes shine with his power, almost too bright to look at.

"I warned you," he says slowly, his arms coming around me.

"Alex, don—" I hear before someone swears.

Everything seems to slow down and liquify, like the car we're in is spinning. I gulp down my scream as my body pulls and stretches. It doesn't hurt, but it doesn't feel comfortable.

With a snap, I land on my feet and stumble into Alex's chest.

My head snaps up as I take in my living room.

"What the fuck?" I spin around.

Yep, definitely my living room.

Turning back to Alex with my eyes wide, I see him grinning. "Protector, remember? Now, where were we?"

He prowls toward me, and I step back. "The others—"

"Know you will be okay with me," he finishes as my back meets the wall.

"Alex—"

He smashes our lips together, teeth clashing, and I groan.

He pulls away too fast and bends down, hoisting me over his shoulder. I yelp, and he smacks my ass before he walks out of the living room.

Hanging upside down, I smack his ass back. "Put me down!"

"Nope." He laughs, making his way upstairs.

I hear Nev downstairs, making his way out the back door, as Alex kicks my bedroom door open, shutting it behind him.

He throws me on the bed, and I bounce.

Pushing my hair out of my face, I lean up on my elbows as he stares down at me.

"Well, are you just going to stare?" I tease, and he narrows his eyes.

Not speaking, he strips, and I watch as more golden skin is revealed. He looks like he was carved from stone. He's leaner than Ezra but with defined muscles. Popping the button on his trousers, he pushes them down, and I groan. He's going commando.

His cock springs free, long and hard. He's thinner than Ezra but definitely fucking longer. Holy shit. My eyes run back up his body as he lets me look my fill.

When I reach his face, he smirks. "Strip."

Shit, he doesn't have to tell me twice. This is going to be better than cookies.

Slipping from the bed, I unzip my dress and push it down until it puddles at my feet. Stepping out, I leave my heels and red panties on.

The others return home, the car pulling up outside, and we stare at each other. They laugh and talk as they crunch to the front door. Ben yells something. Footsteps sound downstairs, obviously searching for us, before they come up the stairs.

I swallow hard as the door starts to open.

Alex strides over, eating the distance, and slams it shut. A muttered curse comes from the other side.

Ezra's worried voice follows. "Just checking you traveled okay?"

"Fine" The muscles in Alex's back clench as he frames the door.

"Okay, okay. We're going to watch a movie…" Ezra trails off as he hesitates. "Shout if you need me, baby."

With that, he walks away.

Alex growls and rips himself away from the door. Taking two steps, he covers the distance between us and slams our lips together. Pent-up lust and frustration fuel our kiss as we fight for control.

We fall back onto the bed, my legs winding around his waist as the sound of the television flicks on downstairs. My heels dig into his ass and he groans, thrusting forward and rubbing against my wet pussy.

Groaning, I arch my neck as he kisses down it. He follows a trail down my body, avoiding my pussy to go down each leg until I tremble. I knew being with him would be like this: all-consuming.

He kisses his way back up, throwing both my legs over his shoulders as he settles with his face in my pussy.

"Alex, please," I moan, arching my body into the air.

He rips away my panties, which is more painful than sexy, to be honest.

"Ouch, dude. You could have totally pulled them— Oh, fuck," I gasp as he spears me with his tongue.

He eats me, alternating between thrusting his tongue in and licking around my nub. He sucks it into his mouth as he thrusts a finger into me with no warning. He adds two more, stretching me, and sets a hard pace of sucking and licking as he finger fucks me.

It's too much. When his other hand squeezes my breast hard, I scream, the orgasm rushing over me.

Arching into his hand, I tremble with aftershocks. He slows his thrusts and pulls away from me, but not without another lick.

Panting, I laugh when the TV gets turned up from downstairs.

Alex grins, lifting his head, and I instantly sober. His chin glistens from me and he looks fucking feral.

Crawling up my body, he kisses me, letting me taste myself on him. He pulls away and reaches down to the floor. Frowning, I stare in confusion as he brings up his belt and tie.

Oh, fuck yes.

I must say it out loud because he smirks down at me. "I take that as a yes, kitten?"

He slams the belt lightly on my nipple, and I groan and arch into it, loving the bite of pain.

"Yes," I moan, and he drops the belt and holds up the tie.

I nod, not caring what he does with it.

He covers my eyes and ties it around the back of my head. "Now, all you can do is feel. You're going to take everything I give you."

When I don't speak, he slaps the belt onto my thigh, making me yelp. He rubs the sting away, and I bite my lip.

"Yesss," I beg, and he licks up my stomach, making me arch into his touch.

He circles my nipple before pulling it into his mouth, sucking hard as I writhe beneath him. He pops it out of his mouth and blows over the wet tip before giving the same treatment to the other.

"Alex," I moan as he runs the belt along one nipple, catching the rough, cold buckle against it.

I collapse back onto the bed and let him do what he wants with me. The cold buckle and belt run down the middle of my breasts, down my stomach, and circles my belly button before stopping over my pussy.

He flicks the end lightly against my clit, and I bite my lip, loving the pain. He leans down and flicks his tongue over the nub, kissing it better as the belt makes its way down my wet cunt. He moves over to my thighs and gives me a slap on each, then rubs the sting away.

"Fuck me already," I moan, and he pulls away.

Yelping, my face smashes into the bed. He fucking flipped me like I'm a goddamn feather. Turning my face to the side to breathe, I strain against the dark material covering my eyes, but it's no good. The barrier only enhances my lust. I don't know what he'll do next or what he's doing now, and that is a huge fucking turn on.

He's so in control, dominating me completely.

The belt lands on my ass with a slap, making me let out a squeal of pain. His hand rubs away the sting, mixing the pain with pleasure. "I knew you would look fucking hot with my marks on your ass."

Oh shit. My fingers dig into the bedding. He gives two more quick whips, rubbing the pain, then massaging with his hands. I push my ass back, needing more.

He lifts my ass with one hand. "Stay like that."

I nod into the covers. He circles my clit again as he lands another hit on my ass, the pain of the hit and pleasure as he flicks my clit are so different. I shake from the intensity of it, my body fighting in each direction.

"Alexander, please," I beg, and he groans.

The belt hits the floor with a clunk, and he flips me

again. I feel him line up at my entrance, and he drives into me in one hard fucking thrust. He doesn't give me time to accept him or grow accustomed before he pulls out and hammers back in, pushing me up the bed until my head smacks into the headboard.

Little noises escape my mouth as he fucks me hard.

"Alex," I moan long.

He grunts before he rips the blindfold away.

I stare into his eyes, unable to look away as he pulls out and thrusts back in. Bracing my hands above me on the headboard, I arch into the thrust, using the leverage to push down on his cock, making him tighten his hands on me.

He grips a thigh and tosses it over his shoulder before gripping me under my ass and tilting me. The angle, so much deeper, hits that spot inside of me every time he pulls out and fucks back in.

I repeat his name like a mantra as he slams into me. Shit, another orgasm already builds. I want to see him break, too. I push down as he thrusts up and tense my pussy. He moans long and loud as the sound of our skin slapping together fills the room.

Sweat drips down my body and his, too, and I reach down again, flicking my clit on the way before circling his cock and cupping his balls. Looking back into his eyes I squeeze gently. He shouts as he loses his punishing rhythm and hammers into me. I have no choice but to hang on.

He reaches between our bodies and rubs my clit as he thrusts into me harder, bottoming out. I clench around him, milking him as I come. My hands scramble on the bedding, writhing because it's that bloody intense. He yells and stutters, his hips smashing into mine as he comes, too.

He slumps down on me, sliding down and out of me so not to crush me. His head pillows on my breasts as we both gasp for breath.

"Holy witches' balls," I pant, and he laughs, shaking against me, and I groan again.

He lifts his head, a soft smile on his lips as his eyes twinkle.

I reach up and run my hands through his hair.

"Witches balls?" he asks, and I giggle, actually fucking giggle.

I sigh and he drops his head back down again. I hear running footsteps, but I can't be bothered to cover up.

The door opens and a grinning Ben pokes his head in. "If you two are finished, we ordered pizza, though I think the teenager who delivered it thought we were killing someone up here."

He ducks his head back as Alex waves his hand and the door slams shut. He laughs as he races back down the stairs.

I should be embarrassed the whole house heard us,

but I'm not. You only live once, right? Oh god, I did not think that. Witch me now.

"Come on, kitten. We better feed you." Alex rolls off the bed and lands gracefully on his feet.

Reaching down, he lifts me up like I weigh nothing, and I wrap myself around him as he walks into the bathroom.

He turns on the shower, drops me in, and follows. I grin and duck my head under the spray. Winking, he grabs my shampoo and squirts some in his hands.

"Turn around," he commands, and I do.

I let him massage it into my hair, closing my eyes and relaxing as he takes care of me.

When we exit the shower, Alex insists on putting lotion on my stinging ass before we dress. By the time we make it downstairs, most of the pizza is eaten, but Ezra pulls a box from behind him on the sofa and passes it over to me.

Alex reclines on the sofa. "Where's mine?"

Ezra scoffs. "Get your own."

I laugh and plop down next to Darius and Ben on the floor.

"Work up an appetite, did you?" Darius snides.

I grin at him, way too happy from pizza and

orgasms to care. "Yup. Now shush so I can enjoy my cheese."

The others laugh as we watch a movie. It's like before the whole almost dying thing, except for the wild sex interlude. Looking around, my grin dims. I have a feeling tomorrow will come crashing down on us, and I don't even know why.

I finish my pizza in, like, five minutes and stretch out, a yawn splitting my face. Cuddling into Ben, I lay my head on his shoulder and watch the movie.

I only get halfway through before I call it a night. I wave a tired goodbye and trot upstairs to find Nev already passed out on my bed.

Smiling, I drop a kiss on his head. "Night, baby. Sorry I've been so busy."

He snores louder.

Shaking my head, I drop the joggers so I only wear a cami and slide into bed, my eyes shutting straight away. What a bloody night.

I must fall asleep pretty fast because my eyes shoot open in disorientation when the door clicks shut.

Alex comes into view, and when he spots me watching him, he smiles. "Go back to sleep, kitten."

He drops his pants, leaving him in boxers, and crawls into bed in front of me.

I close my eyes and cuddle against his chest. His arms wrap around me and our legs entwine. A smile coats my lips even as exhaustion crashes over me.

49

AURORA

I wake up warm—really freakin' warm. I groan and kick the covers off, but realize I can't lift my legs, at all. Popping one eye open, I come face to face with a sleepy Ezra, his eyes at half-mast as he watches me. Alex still lays at my back, his groin pressed against my ass and his arm wrapped around my middle.

Ezra must know I've been with Alex. I mean, they heard us, but he still holds me close, one thigh pressed between my legs and his arm wrapped around me, hand on my ass. He drags me closer and covers my lips in a gentle kiss.

Pulling back, I try to question him with my eyes, but he leans in again.

"Shh, or you'll wake him," he whispers, and I nod.

He kisses me again, rubbing my ass in circles, and I

moan at the friction on my already tender cheeks. I fully wake up as he sweeps in. Rubbing against his thigh, I tangle my hand on his chest and slide it down. My eyes pop open when I meet nothing but skin, and he grins against my lips.

Wrapping my hand around his already hard cock, I coat my fingers in his pre-cum and lift them to my lips, watching him as I lick them clean.

He groans, his mouth parting as I squeeze his cock and pump him. His heavy breathing fills the silent room as I work him.

"Baby," he groans and leans in to kiss me softly.

As I squeeze hard, he thrusts into my hands, working himself as I rub against the sheets, already needy again despite my and Alex's fuck-fest earlier.

Ezra's hands roam my body, pushing up the cami as he cups my breasts and flicks my nipples. It takes me an embarrassingly long time to realize there's more than one pair of hands.

My eyes snap open, and I pull away from Ezra's kiss to look over my shoulder.

Alex is awake, his amber eyes locked on me as he runs his hands between my thighs, pushing them open and stroking over my panty covered pussy.

Ezra doesn't seem bothered. In fact, his dick jerks in my hand and he tightens his hold on my breasts, making me gasp as they both caress me.

"Let us look after you," Ezra says softly, dropping his hand to stop my motion on his cock.

I swallow hard but nod. As I let go, he grins.

"Lean back, baby," he coos, and I do.

Alex moves to make room and leans over my right side. With Ezra to my left, they run their eyes down me.

As one, they push up my cami. I lift my back and let them pull it off. My panties go next. I'm left naked between them, their eyes eating up every inch of skin and making me shiver before they even touch me.

I'm still a bit sore from Alex earlier, but they're gentle.

Alex leans down and kisses my throat and chest, circling one of my nipples and sucking. Ezra runs his lips down my stomach, kisses my thigh and foot, then works his way back up again. They kiss and lick, tasting me all over, working me up slowly to a fever pitch. Every caress of their hands makes me arch beneath them as they worship me.

Alex brings his head up and kisses me gently, almost leisurely, exploring my mouth without any of the earlier frenzy in his touch, and I follow his lead, kissing him almost lazily.

Ezra runs his nose along my pelvis and dives lower, parting my lips and licking a long line up to my clit and circling it. Reaching down, I grip his hair, holding his head to me as I push my pussy to his face. It's almost too much. My clit is still sore after the pounding it took earlier. He seems to sense it because he goes slower, teasing me with his fingers as his tongue laps me up, making me gasp into Alex's mouth. My eyes nearly roll back into my head when his finger presses to my other hole, just pressing there until I relax and then he slowly pushes it inside making me jerk up from the bed. It's not my first time with someone playing with my ass so when he adds another finger I groan and grind down onto his face and fingers.

The pace isn't rushed, and the orgasm builds within me slowly, every kiss, every caress another drop in the bucket. I explode against them, moaning into Alex's mouth.

Ezra works his way back up my body, kissing here and there as I catch my breath. Pulling away from Alex, I watch them both as they shift around me. Even after my orgasm, all I can think about is having them. Having them both.

"I need you," I grab them both, making sure my meaning is clear.

"Are you sure?" Alex asks, always the protector.

Leaning forward, I kiss him gently, letting him feel my answer. Pulling away, I watch as his pupils dilate, the dominant Alex coming out to play.

"On your side," he orders, and I turn to face Ezra who lays down next to me and grins.

Ezra's big hand lands on my thigh, and he pulls it

over his leg until we're lined up. I drop a kiss on his chest as he rubs the head of his cock along my pussy.

Fucking tease.

Reaching down, I grab his cock and line him up again. He groans, gripping my thigh harshly as he slips the tip of his cock in.

Staring into my eyes, he pushes in slowly, fighting through my tight channel until he bottoms out. We breathe hard as Alex settles behind me.

I hear him fumbling around in my side drawer before a bottle clicks open, the sound loud in the quiet room. Then his cock, covered in something cold, rubs on my ass.

"You ever had anal sex?" he whispers.

Still looking into Ezra's eyes as he lays with his hard cock in me, I swallow. "Yes."

They don't speak. Ezra's eyes glint, and he twists his hips, making me gasp as Alex parts my cheeks and begins pushing into my clenching hole, past the tight muscle.

He stops part way and pulls out before pushing back in again until he's balls deep. All of us breathe deep. I lay between them trying not to scream. I'm so fucking full. Every shift sends a pang of pleasure through me, and I need them to move.

As if they hear me, they do, slowly. Ezra in, Alex out. They work together, pushing and pulling as they make love to me. Because that's what this is.

Alex leaves branding kisses along my shoulder as Ezra captures my lips and swallows my moans. All it takes is for Ezra to twist his hips and Alex to thrust in, and I come, screaming into Ezra's mouth.

They follow me. Ezra yells into my mouth as Alex bites my neck to hold in his yell.

Their cum spurts into me, and I lay shaking between them.

Holy shit.

Running my hands across Ezra's chest, I decide to ask them some questions. We still lay in pretty much in the same position. Alex got up and cleaned us both, and Ezra slipped into the bathroom before we all curled back up together.

They know a bit about my past, but I know close to nothing about theirs.

"How did you meet everyone?" I ask as Alex rubs the sore muscles in my back, making me groan.

Ezra hesitates. I can feel him tensing under me slightly. "Baby, I want to tell you. I do. But—"

Pain fills his voice, and I open my mouth to tell him it doesn't matter, but Alex speaks first. "I have this, brother."

Ezra nods and wraps his arms around me as much as he can, as if for comfort, and my heart pounds. I know this isn't going to be good, but it warms my heart that Alex is protecting him.

Alex's hands move down to my ass and legs, massaging as he goes. "We met Ezra when he was eight-years-old. Our families, they were all part of the higher-ups, the ruling families. Well, most of them. There aren't a lot of children in the covens, so we tended to get pushed together, but Ezra always kept to himself. He was quiet and often looked scared. Something in me, even as a kid, recognized him. I'm guessing that would be our bond, but back then, it seemed only natural to try and befriend him. I spent every day walking across the forest three miles to and from his house. We would sit outside in the back garden. He wouldn't talk, would barely look at me, but every day I went. I spoke about everything and anything, showing him my favorite toys, something new I'd learned. Books from Jason, games from Ben. Jokes from Darius."

Ezra shakes beneath me, and I wrap myself around him tighter as he buries his head in the top of my hair. In my head, all I see is a tiny kid version of Alex, looking so determined as he sits next to a smaller Ezra.

"One day, he started talking back to me. We brought him out of his shell, and he started actively seeking us out, coming to play with us. At lessons, all of us became best friends, but it wasn't until Ezra turned eleven that we became inseparable brothers through a secret we've buried so deep between us, one that not even the council knows the full truth."

Alex's hands run lower as he spins the story and my heart aches for Ezra. What happened?

"It was Ezra's birthday. His dad reluctantly threw him a party, and we were all there. Just being stupid kids. Ben and Darius were joking around. We were all playing hide and seek. Ezra warned us not to go into his dad's office because he would get mad, but we did anyway. Luckily, Ezra found us all hiding in there, but we could all hear his dad coming. It's the only time apart from when we thought we'd lost you, that I've ever seen him panic. He hid us again and told us not to come out, no matter what."

"I had to protect you," Ezra whispers, his voice catching, and I drop a kiss on his chest again, letting him know I'm there.

"You did. His father came in and found Ezra. He was so mad, I could feel his magic pressing on us all as he screamed and shouted. He said... well, some horrible things, and then he hit Ezra. He went down, but from the look in his eyes, I knew this wasn't the first time. We had our suspicions, that something was going on, but never did I guess that—" Alex blows out a breath, his hands stilling on me.

Ezra reaches over me and touches Alex. "You couldn't have known, bother."

"Anyway, his dad started using his magic on Ezra,

throwing him around. Hurting him. But not once did he scream. I couldn't let it happen, so I burst from my hiding spot and told him to stop."

Of course he did, because that's who Alex is.

"He didn't, of course; he turned his attention to me, but the others wouldn't have that. They all came out and we stood in front of Ezra. I can still remember his dad's sneer now. He would have killed us all and not batted an eye. This was a man we were brought up to respect, but he should have known better than to mess with us."

"Why?" I interrupt for the first time.

"Our families, our legacy, our gifts. They made us all special. We were… chosen, if you will. The council's prodigies." I nod, and Alex continues. "So, we did something we'd never done before. We drew on our magic. We weren't supposed to. Our magic was too wild and young to control, but it was the only way."

He stops and I feel them both reliving it. It pains me so much, but I know they won't stop now.

"What happened?" I whisper.

"We killed him," Alex says plainly, as he begins massaging me again. "Then, I went before the council. I told them they should have known what was happening. I blamed them and I warned them that none of us would stand punishment for killing the witch, or their precious little prodigies would disappear. We were so young, but I meant every word. They had let us down and I would take my brothers and leave if it meant protecting them. It was the first time I saw the greed and taint within our own kind."

"Not me. I had grown up seeing it my whole life," Ezra rumbles, some of the life returning to him.

"Yes, you did, brother, and I regret every day not getting to you sooner," Alex replies, his voice pained.

"You were both children. Don't blame yourselves," I demand, and Alex drops a kiss on my shoulder.

"It's my burden to bear, kitten. Anyway, they agreed to our terms and buried Ezra's father's death."

"What happened to you all after?" I ask, and for the first time since they bared their souls, they hesitate.

"That's a different story altogether, kitten, and one no less painful," Alex says softly.

I nod. They told me more than I expected, so I drop it, for now.

Rolling off Ezra, I turn on my side and face them both. "Thank you for telling me. I know that wasn't easy. I can't believe how strong you both—all—are."

They smile at me, and I snuggle back into the covers.

50

EZRA

She closes her eyes with a soft, sleepy smile on her face, and I can't stop from lifting my hand and tracing her face. Who knew such a small witch could change everything? I sense Alex looking at me, but for some reason, it feels important I commit this moment to my mind.

"Come," Alex whispers, slipping from the bed before leaning over and dropping a soft kiss on Aurora's forehead, his face softening as he watches her.

Telling her about my past was therapeutic, even if I didn't get to tell her the full truth about who we are now. One day, we will. We'll tell her everything and hope she doesn't hate us for it.

Dropping a lingering kiss on her lips, I slide from the bed and grab my clothes.

Meeting Alex at the door, I give her one last look.

She moved over to the spot where I laid and cuddles up there.

"We need a meeting." Alex clasps my shoulder, and I nod before slipping from the room.

Nev trots in and jumps on the bed, cuddling up behind her as I softly shut the door.

51

BENJAMIN

*S*ipping my cup of tea, I lean back in my chair, closing my eyes at the silence in the house finally. I thought they would never finish up there. Jealously surges through me, but I know Aurora and I will happen. There's no rushing what's between us, but it doesn't make my blue balls easier.

Jason's sigh from the cooker, obviously thinking the same thing. Mikael and Darius come in from the living room and take seats at the table. I eye my brother. Whatever Aurora said to him seemed to work.

He looks happier than before, and I can see my brother again.

The door swings open and a satisfied Ezra walks in with Alex on his heels.

Bastards.

Kicking my leg up, I smirk at them. "Have a good night?"

"Better than yours." Ezra grins, sliding into an open chair.

"Lucky prick," Mikael mutters.

Well, well, well. Seems she's getting to all of us. Doesn't help when she keeps walking around in those fucking skimpy pajamas.

"Enough. We need to talk." Alex's voice cuts through the kitchen, and we sit up straight, the mood shifting.

Jason turns off the cooker and sets food and drinks in front of us all before him and Alex sit.

"What's wrong?" Darius asks, all of us silently urging Alex to tell us.

Alex sits back and eyes us all. "I didn't want to tell you, but we were sent a job."

"What?" I burst, out, banging my mug on the table.

"When?" Ezra rumbles.

Alex takes a sip of his tea and sighs. "When Aurora was saving Darius."

"That fucking long ago?" Ezra shouts, and we all freeze as we glance at the ceiling.

When Aurora doesn't come running downstairs, we all sit back and talk quieter.

"I didn't answer them. I couldn't. But that means they'll be searching for us soon. Wondering why their hunters have gone silent," Alex finished, dropping the bombshell.

"We can't lead them here," Mikael says, his voice hard, and it's obvious he's pissed at Alex, too.

"Indeed. We also can't let them see Darius or they'll ask questions, questions we can't answer. That's why the meeting. We need to vote on what to do. We can't avoid the council forever, but we need to protect Aurora."

"What if we contact them and say we're still searching for Mikael? That buys us some time to come up with a plan. We then move to a safe house before we slowly start letting little truths drop to them. Go on jobs, leaving Darius with her, until the council is ready to understand. When we have them on our side, only then do we introduce them to Aurora and Darius again," Jason states and everyone nods.

"That's a good idea, apart from one thing," I grumble. "We need to tell Aurora who we are, and your plan hinges on the fact she'll stay after she finds out. Also, we know the council. We know what they're like. Do you really think they'll be happy about us lying to them for so long and sheltering a rogue witch? It's our fucking job to hunt them and bring them in for sentencing."

Ezra growls. "So, what the fuck are you saying we do?"

Alex leans forward, getting between the argument brewing. "I like Jason's plan. We buy ourselves some time, say we're searching for Mikael. We move to a safe house and hope Aurora understands why we kept this from her. We earn her trust back if we have to. We have enough on the council and connections on our side to get them to understand. It will take time, time we use wisely to make sure we can protect her. As for Darius, we do not out her on that. It will only make them more intrigued. We tell them it was one of us, one of our powers growing. They'll like that. Is everyone in agreement?"

We all nod. It's not perfect, but it's the only choice we have. We knew this day was coming, but we've been moving from one thing to the next since we met Aurora. I pray to the gods she forgives us and doesn't hate us.

"When do we tell her?" Jason asks.

He sounds as worried as I feel.

"Soon. Let her enjoy today. Tomorrow we'll tell her everything," Alex orders, making sure we all understand.

That means I have today to make sure she loves us enough to stay.

"She's awake," Darius announces, his head tilting as his eyes get a faraway look, a smile dancing on his lips.

Fucking bond, I wish I had one.

52

AURORA

*S*tretching, I roll over with a groan as my muscles remind me of everything that happened last night and this morning. A yip brings my eyes open, and I grin at Nev.

"Hey, my boy, you been looking after me?" I coo, and he nods, shifting closer and nudging me with his nose.

Scratching his head, I let myself enjoy the cuddling and relaxing. That ball in the bottom of my stomach is still there, warning me of something, but for now, I ignore it.

"Where did you go all night, hmm?" I ask, and Nev's tongue lolls out at me.

A pop sounds, and I groan. Turning over, I clutch the sheet to my naked chest and eye Bob as he wanders

around my room, picking up things and putting them
back down again.

"Whatcha' doing?" I ask

He jumps, puffing up.

"Woah there, puffa!" I shout, and he relaxes back to
his normal size, his thin lips twisting into a scowl.

"Silly witch, thought you were sleeping! Don't
scare me!"

I roll my eyes as he rants. "Bob, what's up?"

He huffs before jumping onto the bed and sitting
cross-legged to face me. Grumbling, I scoot back to the
headboard and relax as Nev places his muzzle on my lap.

"Perses sent me to help, silly witch." He nods, still
looking miffed.

I stroke Nev's head. "Uh, uh. Help with what?"

"Destinies, of course. I am to tells you there's a book
by mistress Hekate left for you."

Sitting up straighter, I concentrate on Bob. "Hekate
left a book for me?"

"For her descendants, the blessed ones. Three books
to be exact; her lost journals split up and left for you.
You must find them. They will help you."

Slumping back, I run my hands through Nev's fur
as I think. "How do I find them?"

"Easy peasy witches sleazy," he spouts, and I
chuckle. "Silly witch must look into her past. You have
dream walker for reason, witch. Find one who can help

you locate the book." With that, he pops out of existence.

Brilliant.

Okay, find a dream walker who can help. Didn't the guys already find one?

I'll have to ask them to get his information from Henry. My door bursts open, and Ben and Jason come in. I grin.

I'll ask them later.

I eat breakfast in bed with Jason and Ben. They keep me entertained with stories from their childhood until I kick them out so I can dress.

Slipping on socks, I grin as Lane's voice floats up from downstairs.

I rush down the steps and wrap my arms around her waist from behind.

She giggles.

"Guess who?" I demand in a lower voice.

"Erm, an annoying bitch? Brad Pitt?" She squeals, and I giggle as I pull away.

"Damn, I wish. That boy is fine," I say, and we both sigh.

A cough sounds from in the living room, and I smile innocently over at the guys. "What's the plan for the day?"

I drag Lane over to the sofa and sit next to Darius. He stretches his arm over my shoulder and goes back to watching TV.

"We thought we could do whatever you wanted, maybe work on some magic. Show you some fun stuff," Ben gushes. "Make you understand," he finishes quietly, so quietly I pretend I didn't hear him.

"Sounds good!" I clap, excited I get to play with them again.

I love pushing myself now that power constantly runs through my veins, and watching the boys gape at me is fun, too.

"Can you grow wings?" Lane bursts out, then covers her mouth, embarrassed.

"Huh, I grew some wicked looking smoke wings twice. I wonder if I can grow actual ones?" I hope my failure at Perses's was a fluke.

"Why don't we find out?" Alex suggests.

Lane and I share a look before jumping up and racing outside, the guys laughing as they follow us.

When I reach the grass, I let go of Lane and blow out a breath.

Okay, wings.

Reaching deep, I grasp the darkness in me. It still hovers there, as if uncertain with my magic racing around my body. It comes willingly, but rather than rushing, it slowly crawls, covering my magic until it dots it out like a cloud in front of the moon.

Gasps come from behind me. Whirling, I open my eyes to see every eye on me.

Glancing over my shoulder, I frown. Fucking smoke wings again.

Alex must see my disappointment because he steps closer. "Maybe with you being half reaper, you can't conjure full wings? Have you tried to use any other reaper powers? Time or place hopping?"

When he steps closer, I turn to face him. His eyes keep going back to the wings.

"Place hopping? Like you did?" I guess I don't know much about what I am.

"Similar. Mine takes magic and drains me, but yours should come naturally. It's how reapers get around so fast. They exist in the in-between. I've even heard stories of them being ghost-like. Being present but nobody but the dead can see them."

Biting my lip, I touch my power, whispering what I want. Eyes closed, I imagine the spot behind Alex. A yell sounds, and when I open my eyes, I face his back.

He whirls, his eyes widening when he spots me, then he grins. "Good, let's try again. Test how far you can go."

I nod and close my eyes again, building the image in my head, but at the last minute it changes, and I scream as I reappear atop the house.

Scrambling for a grip on the tiles, they cut my hands as I slide down the roof, the ground coming up fast. Everyone yells from the ground, but I concentrate hard, not wanting them to save me again. As I fall away from the roof, my body plummeting to the ground, I build the picture in my head.

When I don't feel the impact to the earth, I crack open my eyes and blow out a relieved breath.

"Aurora!" Ezra yells, searching wildly.

"I'm here, big guy," I reply, laughing as I look around at the grass.

Shit, that was a close call.

"Aurora, answer me this fucking second!" Ezra yells again.

Puzzled, I step forward, almost touching his heaving chest, but his eyes go right through me.

"I can feel her, she's here. She's confused," Darius says, searching around.

I wave, and when no one responds, I gulp. *Err, maybe tell Alex… I think the whole invisibility thing is real.*

Darius laughs. All eyes swing to him as he repeats my words.

Their shoulders drop as they peer around, calmer now that they know I'm okay.

I poke Ezra's chest, and his eyes widen as he steps back. Oh, this could be really fun.

Don't do it, princess.

Darius's laughter floats in my head as I race over to Ben and trip him up.

He squeals as he falls, pouting when he sits up on the grass.

"Babe, that's not nice. Now, kiss it better," he demands, looking around, but I'm already moving away.

I brush a kiss over Jason's cheek, and they tint even as he smiles. I stroke Alex's arm, and he smirks. Stopping in front of Mikael, my eyes zero in on those lips I've been thinking about since I first met him in that cell.

Using the confidence of my ghost form, I lean forward, not touching him as I stand on my toes and brush a soft kiss along his lips. He gasps, his eyes shooting wide before he grins. He tries to chase me and ends up kissing my eyelid, making me laugh.

Obviously feeling my breath, he finds my lips and kisses me. I gasp, leaning into him as he kisses me softly. I bet it looks super weird, but I let him until someone laughs.

I pull back and glance at the others.

"It seems when you, erm, get distracted, you lose your ghost form." Jason coughs, grinning at me.

Oops. Laughing, I pull away as Lane hollers, "That was amazing!"

"Okay, let's try some more magic!" I shout, bouncing on my toes as they all grin.

53

JASON

*A*urora avoids the magic with a twirl, faster than normal humans. It seems not only does her reaper half allow her to access the in-between and the dead, but she possesses their strength and speed. While she's still upset about the wings, I'm impressed with how much power her body holds.

She darts around me, hiding as magic shoots her way. I block it effortlessly, this game one we've played since we were children. It's similar to paintball the humans play, but instead of little paint bullets, we dodge magic attacks. One hit and you're not out, but you're usually frozen, singed, or hurt.

Alex was reluctant to play, but when she turned those eyes on him, he gave in.

Besides, none of us would ever let her get hurt.

She fires back, dodging again as she races through the trees. We started on the grass, but it soon turned into a forest game. We split into teams, with Darius, Ben, and me on Aurora's team and the others against us. The team with the most players standing at the end of ten minutes wins.

Lane is our unofficial ref. We keep her well out of the way, and Nev protects her from any stray magic.

Aurora tosses a fireball at Ezra, and he manages to block it, but he doesn't block her next hit, which lifts him from the ground and sends him flying into the trees.

She hesitates, obviously scared she hurt him.

"Brother, you better let our girl know you're okay!" Ben shouts, darting it and blocking a hit from Alex.

"Ugh, I'm good, baby," comes a muffled yell, and she relaxes, getting back into the game.

We all trade blows.

Aurora slips into our groups easily and decimates the other team.

Even Alex goes down just as Lane shouts from the tree line. "Time! Aurora's Power Rangers win!"

I laugh. She gave us a name? Out of breath and sweating, I get dragged into a group hug by Ben.

Aurora grins at us, her eyes sparkling as her power rides her. She's so fucking beautiful it takes my breath away.

Sweaty and laughing, she snuggles into us.

Darius stands behind her and wraps his arms around her. It's nice to see him happy, too.

It finally feels like we're catching a break.

54

AURORA

*A*fter Magic Ball, we all slump on the grass as Jason and Lane go inside and grab us snacks and drinks. The sun shines down on us as I lean back into Alex's side. Ben curls up on my other.

"I wonder what happened to her?" I murmur and feel them all look at me.

Alex runs his hands through my hair. "Happened to who, kitten?"

"Hekate. She loved her life so much. Perses said she died. How do you kill a goddess?"

"I don't know. Maybe we can find out?" Jason suggests, rejoining us.

He passes me a bag of cookies with a smile, and I sit up and rip it open.

"That's a good idea, but first I need a shower," I say with a cookie stuffed in my mouth.

"Cute, real sexy, babe." Lane, sitting opposite me, laughs.

Opening my mouth, I stick my tongue out with half-chewed cookie, and she shakes her head in disgust.

"So, tell me about the hotties at the club," I say after swallowing, and all the guys groan.

"Don't like girl talk, head inside now," I warn.

I swear, they've never moved so fast, and soon Lane and I are left giggling to each other.

We spend hours catching up, talking boys and anything that comes to mind.

It's nice not to hold back, anymore. She knows every part of my life and sticks around anyway. If my dad saw me now, with a human for a best friend, he would die, or whatever reapers do.

55

EZRA

*W*hile Aurora and Lane have their girl talk, we all clean up, and Alex and Ben nip to the shop to buy supplies for tea.

They make sure to buy our girl more cookies.

Sitting back on the sofa, I listen to Jason and Darius laugh as they brew tea, Ben no doubt joining in as Mikael and Alex sit in the living room debating what to watch.

A girly giggle reaches my ears, and I tilt my head as Aurora and Lane come in. She gives me a soft smile before walking Lane to the front door.

After she says goodbye, she joins me on the sofa, curling up at my side.

Kissing her head, I lean back and listen to my brothers. I can't remember a time when we were this happy.

"Food will be ready in thirty. You pick what we're watching yet?" Jason shouts.

Alex rolls his eyes as he starts to yell back, but I sit up straight and he falls quiet, his eyes narrowing. "Ezra?"

Holding my hand up, I close my eyes. Something's wrong; a disturbance. The air practically vibrates with it.

"Magic," I growl as five forms appear in the room.

Aurora jumps to her feet, her magic already forming as I push her behind me.

Alex stands slowly, his face pained before he clears it.

The others must feel it too because they all crowd into the living room, Aurora between us.

Fuck. I thought we'd have more time.

"Alexander, what a surprise. And Mikael, it seems they have found you," William sneers, stepping forward from his little guards.

"Yes, we found him today," Alex replies.

Aurora stares at us all, but I make sure to block her view.

"Indeed, why don't you tell me why I had to track our best witch hunters to the corner of fucking nowhere?" he sneers, and his guards laugh.

Aurora gasps, her hand falling away from my back. The sound cuts straight through, but I need to concentrate on the now, to make sure I'm ready in case they attack.

Alex looks at me, his face resigned. Fuck, no. I shake my head, but he turns anyway, straightening his shoulders as he faces the council elder. "We found a witch. We were gathering information before we reported back."

While not a lie, it's not the whole truth. It's unheard of to lie to the council. We've been doing this hunting gig since we were seventeen and not once has Alex disobeyed them. Until now. Until Aurora.

"I see. Bring her forward." William waves his hand as we reluctantly part.

"Hide your reaper power," I whisper, turning my face away from the council member so he can't read my lips.

Eyes hard, she doesn't look at me as she steps forward, her head held high.

We brought the monsters she ran from right to her door, and the worst part is, I can't even explain why to her.

56

AURORA

Swallowing hard, I lift my chin and face the man who spoke.

I don't look at my men, shock and horror coursing through me.

The signs were all there. I should have pushed harder. Should have guessed. But I didn't. The men chosen to be mine are hunters. Not just any hunters. Witch hunters. All this time. The reason they probably got close to me was to turn me over to their precious fucking council, one of who no doubt stands before me. They make no move to protect me.

Instead, they let the man take me in from head to toe. "Her magic is strong, but I sense something else. Tell me the truth, Alexander, *now*."

The last word booms around the room, making me swallow a scream as it seems to rip through my soul.

The power behind that one word is unimaginable, but it also leaves a bad taste in my mouth.

"Councilman, if you would allow us to—" Alex begins, and he cuts him off.

"The truth, or I shall rip it from the girl." He doesn't even look at me as he talks, already dismissing me.

"She's half witch," Alex says, his voice tired.

Every fucking word cuts to my core. He works for them; they all do. The men who tried to kill my family, the people who rejected and terrified my mother. The very same people Hekate wants me to end.

"Interesting. A halfling? It's unheard of. Human, I presume?" the man says, looking back at me with fresh light, but I can see the disgust in his eye. "Pity. She's strong, but to sully the bloodline like that? Never mind. You will, of course, be rewarded for your find. Guards."

The men at his side step forward, and I let my magic fill my palms.

It only makes the man throw back his head and laugh. "Oh, she thinks she can fight us? How cute."

Alex steps forward as fury washes through me. "Sir, we shall bring her in."

"No need. I'm here now. Head back to debrief. We'll take the sullied."

Alex hesitates, and the man's head swings as he offers Alex a look. Without glancing at me, Alex steps back, and the guards surround me.

There are too many. I know I can't fight them. Even

now, their magic pushing on me, wrapping around me to extinguish mine. How fucking stupid of me, to think I was powerful. To think I could trust…

I stare at Alex's profile, but he refuses to look at me.

"Alex—" Ezra begins, but Alex turns to him and cuts him off with a glare.

"This is our job. Now, shut up and do as you're told," he speaks clearly, his tone threatening, and I almost stumble back.

Who's this man? He isn't the man who held me the other night, who touched me and kissed me like I was his light. This man is a hunter, and I'm nothing but prey.

My heart shatters when no one else voices a protest. Not one of my men tries to stop the guards surrounding me.

Princess—

My heart shattering drowns out Darius's words, not that I want to hear them. Gasping, I draw everything inside, throwing up walls once again, but at the last second, I build a bubble around my bond with Darius. Even though he betrayed me, I can't stand to break my promise to him.

Tears fill my eyes, but I push them back. I refuse to shed them. They might have taken my heart and stomped on it, but they don't get to see me weak. Not ever again.

The room begins to spin as the guards join hands. A glow emanates from the circle and fills me.

Looking up, I meet Alex's stricken eyes. They implore me, but I turn away.

Fuck them. Fuck all of them.

Perses was wrong. Hekate was wrong.

I was wrong.

57

AURORA

*A*bomination. Sullied. Monster.

Just some of the names they've called me. I let each one bounce off me harmlessly. They can't hurt me more than what's already been done today.

Once I woke up from whatever magic they pulled from me, they dragged me to a cell where they chained me to a stone wall. The chain, they helpfully told me, stops all forms of magic.

Basically, it makes me human and weak.

I know; I tried to attack them. It didn't go well. My ribs still hurt from their beating, but I refuse to lay back and wait for someone to rescue me, especially when the people I thought would protect me betrayed me.

When the guards finally leave, losing interest in their councils' new toy, I tug on the chain and manage to get enough slack to walk around the cell.

Nothing but three stone walls and magically electrified bars. Not even a fucking bed or a pot to piss in. Darkness shrouds my cell, but instead of being scared like they hoped, I hide in it, letting it surround and comfort me.

"Where's the freak? Did you hear she's part human?" a voice laughs from outside my cell.

I lean back into the wall, closing my eyes, but when Alex's last expression flashes through my mind, I quickly open them. I'm trying to ignore my heart, but whenever I think about the guys, it sends a stab of agony through my body so strong it nearly doubles me over.

"I heard they played her; grew her trust so they could find out who her parents were," another voice says, and I breathe through the anger and hurt.

"It doesn't matter. The council will execute her like the others," a deeper voice replies as they walk away from my cell.

The others? More half breeds like me? And my men —no, not my men anymore—brought them here to their deaths?

Leaning over, I heave. Tears fall from my straining eyes before I drop to the floor and wrap my arms around myself. How could they? I trusted them. I touched them for fuck's sake.

Time passes slowly as I replay every word they ever uttered to me, but when all that does is make me angrier, I try to think of other things.

I hope Lane looks after Nev. I hope she forgives me for disappearing again. Tom, God, he'll be so mad. It's better than grieving for me, at least.

Princess? Hold on, okay?

Screaming, I push his voice from my head. I don't block him out even though that's what they deserve. But I push him so far back I can't feel him anymore.

Laughing bitterly, I lean back on the cold stone. I thought the darkness inside his head was bad. Fuck, I should have looked more closely, because now it's inside me, too. The hate and anger burn through me for what they've done.

People walk closer again. Why won't they leave me be? Or kill me already, if that's what they have planned. This waiting and wondering is torture.

"Come out, little sheep. We need to talk," a cruel voice says from my cell door.

Lifting my head, I look into the dead eyes of the man who appeared at my house.

"About what?" My voice is steady if not a bit rough, but shit, at least it doesn't sound like I've been crying.

"The hunters who brought you in for one, and who you are for another."

The magic running over the door dies and it swings open. He steps inside, and I gasp. It's like all the air is sucked from the room and the blackness surrounding him is thick and moving.

The taint, just like Perses said, but how do I stop it when I'm in chains?

"Will you talk, or do I need to make you?" he asks almost gleefully; his eyes dance, making his preference clear.

Clambering to my feet, I lean back on the wall, knowing what my choice will be. "You'll have to make me."

An evil grin stretches across his face. "I was hoping you'd say that."

58

MIKAEL

"*H*ow could we let them take her like that?" I seethe.

Alex looks from the closed council door to me, a warning clear in his gaze.

"Did you see her face?" Jason whispers, his eyes red and sad.

I nod as Ezra growls. Even Ben looks devastated, and Darius and Ezra haven't spoken a word since we were pulled into the council.

"She wouldn't even look at us. God, I bet she hates us," Ben whispers, his voice cracking. "I had it all planned, how we would make her forgive us..."

"Enough. We don't have time for this. She needs us now more than ever, even if she doesn't know it. First, we need to come up with a story about Darius. Then, we protect the truth of what she is. Once we have the council on our side, we'll start to plan how to free her," Alex orders, but he starts to pace, his fists clenching at his sides.

I can't imagine how hard this is for him, to have to let the council take his woman and do nothing as it broke her heart. Fuck.

"They'll kill her!" Ezra booms, not even lowering his voice.

"We won't let them," Alex snaps back as we hear shuffling footsteps from inside the council chambers. "For now, we need to offer a united front. You can hate me all you want, but this is how we need to do it."

Ezra glares at him as the door swings open.

"The council will see you now."

Kneeling before the chairs of the council, I hang my head; not in shame but in an effort to hide my anger.

"Mikael, we are aware your coven was searching for you, and you come back with a new scar. You ran into some trouble, I take it?" Methyos, council member and head of house Athena, sits back in her chair and watches us coldly.

She's not someone to mess with. In fact, I've been on the receiving end of her punishments, and it's not something I wish to experience again. I guess I never really thought about how corrupt our council is, or about the darkness that seems to cling to them. Only Aurora opened my eyes to something I clearly never wanted to see.

Now, all I find is the corruption of their magic, greed as they taint what was given to them.

"Nothing I couldn't handle," I reply, my eyes still on the floor.

I know the rules well and all of my coven know how to play them. They see what they want to see: the good little slave witches. We need to play the part.

"Hmm, the scar around your neck says otherwise," cackles Yilo, the head of House Kratos.

I ignore him and count the tiles on the cold floor. My knees hurt, but I won't shift. I'll only draw their attention back to me again. They're toying with us, and we know it.

"What about the dead witch? I remember him dying clearly. Yet here he kneels. Explain," Yilo booms.

When none of us answer, Trew, Ben's brother and head of House Asclepius, speaks up, "Benjamin, the council asked you a question."

He's young for the council, but what he lacks in age he makes up for in malice. I never liked the prick, the way he treated Ben and still treats him, chafes on me.

"It seems our powers are expanding. We managed to draw Darius back; he wasn't quite dead. The power of his magic and, of course, the council's magic, kept him tied to this world. All we needed to do was tug. We will be exploring these new developments and the council will be pleased to have more firepower in their hunters," Alex says dryly, playing them perfectly.

I almost snort at how thick he lays it on. If anyone can play the council, it's Alexander Derol.

"Of course, we will be discussing this later. For now, we are here to discuss your latest capture." William's voice comes from the end of the chairs. He's the meanest bastard of them all and head of House Themis and the council.

Lifting my head slightly, I scan the room we're in. Their thrones—because that's what they fucking are—line a dais in front of where we kneel on the marble steps leading up. The rest of the room is a long rectangle with chairs for observes. A red carpet runs down the center, leading to the magically enchanted double doors at the end of the room. Stained glass windows set high into the chamber's ornate ceiling, refracts the light through them, creating a myriad of colors on the plain marble floor.

Guards are stationed around the room for our protection, of course; not because the council fears the monsters they created. That would be treason to admit.

"Yes, let's discuss the half breed," Methyos simpers.

"I have spoken to the female in question. She was forthcoming with some pressure," William says, making the council members laugh even as my blood turns cold and my body hardens.

They hurt her? Rage and hate pour from my coven, and the only thing keeping us from snapping is the power swirling in the room from the council. It would be suicide and who would be left to help our girl then? But they will pay. For every fucking hair they touched, I will take it from their flesh. If they notice the influx of our power, they ignore it.

"It seems she's not half human after all, but half reaper," William finishes, sounding smug.

Fuck!

"Interesting," Methyos adds.

"Does that mean she's who we suspect?" Yilo yells.

"I would say so." William's fingers tap on the arm of his chair, his eyes taking us in. He sees too much, so I drop my eyes again. "But I believe the only reason she told me was to distract me from something else. She's protecting something."

Us. She's protecting us. Even now, when she thinks we've betrayed her, she protects us. We don't deserve her, but in Hekate's name, we will not let her go.

Wait, they know who she is? That means they knew her parents.

"I say we call a trial," Trew suggests.

"Seconded," Methyos calls.

"Agreed," Yilo answers loudly.

"Carried. Trial for the hybrid will take place tomorrow evening when the moon reaches its highest point."

Murmurs of approval come from the others, then I feel all eyes back on us.

"After that, we'll discuss with the hunters their part in this and test this new magic of theirs," William mocks, his voice telling us he doesn't believe us.

Not only do we need to save Aurora, but it looks like their cruel gaze has turned to us, and if we aren't careful, they'll kill us, too.

59

AURORA

*A*gony, pure fucking agony.

Every time I shift, another wave of it bursts through my abused body, yet not one wound shows across my pale skin. No, the witch was too smart for that. Instead, he turned his black magic on me and unleashed it. I still feel the whip of it slicing through my insides, boiling my blood and heating my brain until I screamed wordlessly.

The torture seemed to go on for hours, but it could have been minutes as he asked me question after question.

The pain loosened my tongue, but even then, I told him only half-truths, enough for him to be satisfied to leave me alone. I wanted to taunt him about his famous fucking hunters, but something in me wouldn't allow it.

It seems my stupid heart still loves them, and with the bonds between us, I wasn't able to.

Instead, I gave him what he craved, power over me.

Laying back on the cold stone, with my face pushed to the floor as I struggle to keep my eyes open, I let the tears fall. How could such a happy day turn into this? It seems years ago since I played with them in the woods.

Sighing, I watch the dust dancing in the air.

Before he left, William told me I would face death tomorrow. It means I have until then to escape. I need to concentrate on that, not wondering where my guys are or if they miss me like I miss them.

Escape, heal, then figure out a plan.

I need to get my hands on Hekate's book, and it's obvious I need to train more with my magic before I face the council again. Fuck, I even need to find the other men destined for me. I hoped to have time, to ignore all of this, but fate has different plans. I can't ignore it any longer, or people will suffer.

So, how to escape?

Something shifts in the darkness against the far wall, and I suck in a breath, straining my eyes to see through the shadows.

"Who's there?" I croak, my voice sounding like sandpaper.

"You don't recognize me?"

The voice makes me freeze and sends me back to being a scared child again, hiding in her room from the monster under her roof. He steps out, letting the shadows that cling to his form fade enough to reveal his face.

My father.

Swallowing, I refuse to let him see me weak or afraid. So, even though it feels like torture all over again, I push myself swaying to my feet and lean back against the wall to place us eye-to-eye.

"What are you doing here?" Anger flashes through me.

I've been running from this man for years. Hiding, hoping it would all go away. It seems my past and my blood caught up with me today.

"I felt your power. How could I not when it's so similar to mine?" He steps closer, and the moon from outside the cell hits half of his body.

He doesn't even hide his wings or anything that makes him a reaper, like he did when I was a child. The last time I saw my father, he was a broken, damaged thing filled with anger and hate. The reaper who attacked us told me he was stripped of his charges, and it makes me feel sorry for him. Look what it did to that other man? No wonder my own father hates the sight of me.

Because of me, he lost everything.

"Why are you here?" I ask, my voice gaining some of its usual strength.

"I figured I should see how my daughter turned

out." He prowls around the cell. "When you ran, I gave you a couple of months before they found you." He jerks his head toward the cell, and I know he means the witches. "Your mother was always so careful to protect you from this side of yourself and from them, but you can't seem to stay away from trouble."

He stops suddenly, inches away from me.

I have his eyes, and in him I see myself.

"You look like her," he admits softly, and sanity flashes in his eyes before it's blotted out again.

It reminds me of why I ran in the first place. In his drunken stupors, he threatened to throw me to the council, hell, even to the reapers. He told me in great detail how they would kill me, that I couldn't be left to live not being the abomination that I am. He's a bastard and my mother's death warped his mind. Maybe he never loved me. I don't know, but this isn't my father in front of me. It's a twisted hate-filled reaper; one who blames me for the death of the love of his life.

"I wonder how they will kill you?" He strokes my face.

I snap my head back, not wanting him to touch me. Calling on my magic, I try to blast his ass, but it fizzles out like every time I've tried, thanks to the chain around me.

He laughs, stepping back into the shadows. "I'll be there watching. I have nothing better to do these days, and maybe with your fucking death, I can reclaim my job."

The cell falls silent, and I shift nervously, searching the shadows for signs of him.

Stepping forward hesitantly, I push my hand out in front of me and keep walking until I meet stone. He's gone.

Thank fuck. My shoulders slump, and I lean against the wall again, exhaustion running through my body. Being cut off from all my power leaves me weaker than ever. Who knew this was what I was doing to myself when I tried to hide from them? And now, what I wouldn't do to have them again.

I guess I should be sad. My own father wants me dead. But it's a fact I've known for a long time. Plus, I don't have time to have a breakdown.

I need a plan, and I need one fast.

60

ALEXANDER

*A*fter the council dismisses us, I lead my coven to a safe meeting place. Careful of the eyes and ears on us, we remain silent until we enter the warded, secluded library which my father built.

As soon as the door shuts, everyone talks at once, and I rub my head, trying to dismiss the headache building there.

Do they not understand I feel the same way? That I'm worried for Aurora, too? But she's strong. She'll have survived whatever William threw at her.

That doesn't mean I'm not going to kill the bastard for touching her, though.

"Enough!" I shout, and they grow quiet, looking at me in shock.

I let them see my worry, my anger, and my heartbreak because it's breaking with every minute I spend away from her. Regrets cloud my judgment. What if I told her sooner? What if I let her bond us all like she needed? What ifs will get us all killed. I can't afford that. As much as it pains me, I push all those thoughts aside to be the leader they need.

"Enough. We don't have time to fight. We need to come up with a plan and fast. We're getting her out tonight." They nod, and I sit at the table, waiting for those standing in the middle of the room.

Reluctantly, they all sit.

"So, what's the plan?" Ben fidgets in his seat, his eyes sad and filled with worry.

Even Jason isn't distracted by the books in here today. An anger and seriousness not a lot of people know him for are plastered across his face.

"We do what we have to do to get our girl back. Darius and Ezra, I need you to check your bond with her. See how she's doing and get her to tell us exactly where she is. Jason, I need you to figure out a spell to break the spells holding her. Ben, I need you to go and play nice with the guards and council. Figure out the rotations so we can get her. Mikael, you're with me."

They all nod, a new determination hardening their shoulders, all apart from Darius who stares at the table.

"I've tried, but she's pushed me out," he admits quietly, trying to mask the pain in his voice.

Blowing out a breath, I lean over the table and clasp

his arm. Ben does the same as every member of our coven leans over to offer him support.

"She's hurt, that's all," I say. "We'll make her understand. We'll tell her the whole truth and earn her forgiveness. For now, we need to get her out, so I need you to use whatever fucking charm got you in her heart and get us a location."

Darius laughs. "Fucking charm. I was an asshole to her."

I can't help the smirk pulling at the corner of my lips. "Then be an asshole again and get me that location."

61

DARIUS

The others split off to do their jobs, with Jason tearing through books faster than a book-whore on a new release.

Leaving him to it, I find a quiet spot behind a shelf of books and slide down to sit cross-legged. I don't know where Ezra went. I think he believes she won't answer him, although I haven't heard of them talking mind to mind. Maybe he's tracking her another way.

With Alex's words ringing through my head, I close my eyes.

I find our link instantly, her mind linked to mine. Pushing through the partial block she threw up, I linger in her thoughts.

Gasping, I hold back my cry of pain. Her whole body is alight with agony, and I know William's responsible for that. I tuck that away for later, to make sure I remember how much suffering I need to put him through.

Princess?

She ignores me. Her thoughts rub in my head, but I refuse to push inside them. It will only make her hate us more.

Well, come on, your highness, don't ignore me. It's not like you to be quiet.

A burst of anger hits me, and I smile. Good. I'm getting somewhere.

Aww, is little Aurora upset? Did I hurt your delicate sensibilities, baby?

Fuck off, Darius, you momentous cuntholio, she sneers.

I laugh. *There she is. Now play nice, princess. Are you hurt?*

She hesitates, and I hold my breath.

Not physically.

Her curt response makes me wince. I guess I deserve that. *Okay. I need you to show me exactly where you are. We're going to get you out.*

Why?

Her suspicion is like a knife twisting in my gut. *Because we care about you.*

She shuts down so fast I'm flung back into my own head, but not before I feel the pain of her heartbreak.

Opening my eyes, I stare at the books in front of me, tears swimming in my vision as Jason mutters to himself nearby.

Blowing out a breath and sucking down her pain, I close my eyes, ready to try again.

62

JASON

Slamming the book shut, I grab another, searching for a way to bring down the barrier the council will have added to Aurora's prison and no doubt the magically infused chain. It's standard procedure, and I've never thought to research a way to break it before.

The obvious way is to kill the witch who cast the spells, but that won't go down well, though I do contemplate it for a moment, if for nothing but its simplicity.

I don't know how long I've been at this now. I seem to have worked through half the bloody shelf. I can still see Darius, well, the back of his head, as he tries to get through to Aurora.

If the grunts are anything to go by, he isn't doing any better than I am.

Grabbing the next stack of books, I open the first one and start scanning. Nothing. Fucking nothing. Swiping the pile from the table, I drop my head into my hands.

Come on, Jason, think. They're relying on you. She's relying on you.

Racking my brain, I come up with a stupid idea; one that might work. I can't kill the spell caster, but maybe I can seek him out on grounds of knowledge.

I'm almost certain who they'll have used to do the spells: my old tutor.

With fresh determination, I leave the library, making sure to lock the door behind me. It won't keep people out, but it will give Darius a warning if someone comes.

We can't be too careful here.

63

EZRA

Four fucking hours... that's how long I've walked around this never-ending, over the top mansion the council calls home, praying and concentrating on my bond with Aurora. I can't feel her in my mind. Odds are she blocked me out.

Instead of trying to do something I've never done before, like push into her mind, I thought I'd follow the bond between us and let it lead me to her. But so far, nothing.

It's like she doesn't even exist anymore.

The chains and magic could be blocking her, but I keep going anyway. I need to figure out where she is, and there are lots of places the council could be hiding her. I get some odd looks from guards, but one snarl from me and they soon fuck off.

Stopping suddenly, I tilt my head when a low thrum

runs through my body. I turn in the direction it came from and follow it as it pulses through me softly, so soft that if I wasn't looking so hard, I wouldn't catch it.

Three turns and four flights of stairs later, I step into the basement of the mansion, a place not even us hunters are allowed into. Spotting two guards standing in front of a door, I square my shoulders.

Marching right up to them, I arch my eyebrow.

They shift nervously but don't back down.

"We can't let you down there, sir," says the one on the right.

"Why not?" I growl.

"Council's orders. No one in or out. I really am sorry, sir." The kid sounds scared.

Gritting my teeth, I nod and walk away, knowing if I push, it will look strange and be reported back to the council. At least we know where they're keeping her. Now we need to figure out how to get down there.

Hang on, baby, we're coming.

64

BENJAMIN

*L*aughing at the joke the guard made, I down my drink, trying to numb my anger. Playing nice is the last thing I want to do right now, but it's not like any of the others could. Jason would just stare at them. Ezra would probably kill them. They're all terrified of Alex.

So, me it is.

Ignoring the chatter around me, I nod and laugh at appropriate times, earning their respect and trust as I project myself as one of them. Oh, they all know who I am, but they also know I'm the easy going one.

"I heard you guys have been asked to work double," I slip into a lull in the conversation, sipping my drink casually.

"Yeah. It fucking sucks, man. All because of that

piece of ass you brought in." The guy nudges me, and I laugh even I as tighten my hold on the glass.

"Yeah, even got us working all night now. With partners, no less! Me and Terry here are due to swap out guard duty on the woman tonight," another says, leaning back in his chair as he studies the cards in his hand.

"That sucks, guys. You're working eight-eight?" I ask, sounding sympathetic.

He nods and throws a card on the table.

I make sure to stay a bit longer and join in the conversations so they don't grow suspicious. Letting them know I have to get back to work, I ignore their ribbing and head to the one place I despise above everything else: my brother's office.

Striding through the packed hallways, I nod and smile as people greet me.

When I reach the open door, I slip through.

His secretary sits behind her little desk, but I ignore her as she hurries toward me.

Pushing through the doors into his office, I close them in her startled face.

"I'm busy, Benjamin, make an appointment," Trew says without even looking up from the papers he reads intently.

Striding closer, I throw myself in a leather chair opposite his desk and cross my ankles, staring at him.

After five minutes, he sighs and leans back,

glowering at me in exasperation. He might only be five years older, but he acts like my father. He's a rat bastard, too.

Where I look more like my mum, Trew looks like dear old daddy. Short cropped black hair and dark brown eyes. The only thing he got from our mother is her good looks. The shitty attitude and snake-like backstabbing he inherited from dad.

He steeples his hands under his chin as he observes me. "What do you want, Benjamin?"

"Names Ben, asswad," I murmur.

To get back at him, I pull the hair tie from my hair and let it fall around my shoulders. His eyes narrow. He hates that, as he's told me often by saying, and I quote, 'I keep my hair like a girl'. It's the little things in life that keep a person happy, like rubbing this in his face every time I see him.

"Can't I want to catch up with my brother?" I almost spit the last word.

He isn't my brother, but I need to get on his good side.

He eyes me harshly, clearly losing his temper. "What do you want?"

Well, two can play that game. Sitting up, I narrow my eyes at him. "I heard you've upped the guards on the sheep we brought in." Even saying that word makes me sick, but I know he won't hesitate to go to the council if he thinks I sympathize with Aurora. "I'm curious why.

Alex wants to know if we need to expect trouble. To protect the council, of course."

"Of course," he mimics, sitting back in his chair, acting like the lord of the fucking manner. "We've upped security as a precaution. We don't like the unknown, and the girl is the unknown. You'll all be safe here; the council will see to that, and once the execution is held, you can go back to hunting down rogue witches, and I can go back to my paperwork. In peace."

Gritting my teeth, I stand. I know I won't get anything out of him when he's in this mood. I nod and turn to leave. At least I know when the guards change shift.

"Oh, and Benjamin, don't think I haven't noticed the little rebellions and lies your group are shrouded in. I'll be sure to mention it to the council once this business is concluded." He laughs.

I don't give him the pleasure of an answer and storm out of his office.

Once a snake, always a snake. Brother or not.

65

MIKAEL

Striding down the hallway with Alex at my side, I ignore the looks of worship and lust thrown our way. We're legends in our own right among the witches, with over fifty confirmed captures in the last year alone. But it all seems pale and unimportant in the face of our hardest mission yet: rescuing Aurora.

Two girls' step into our paths, young and filled with uncontrolled magic, yet they bat their lashes at us and plaster themselves to our fronts.

"I heard you brought in a hybrid," one coos.

"That's so cool," the other one finishes.

I push her away gently. We don't have time for this.

Alex does the same but gives them a fake smile as we move around them.

"We'll be at the trial tonight. Maybe afterward you

could come and show us a thing or two," one of them calls, the other giggling.

I spin on my heel and march right up to her.

Alex places a warning hand on my shoulder, but I glare at the girl.

"What do you mean tonight? The trial is tomorrow," I snarl, bored of the games and pretenses.

She gulps, her eyes wide as she quivers in front of me. "No, the council moved it to tonight. In an hour, to be exact. Everyone's going."

No.

Shaking my head, I stumble back from her and the girls take the chance to escape. I face Alex, and he looks as stricken as me.

We can't rescue her in an hour, we just can't. It's not possible. The whole plan relies on the trial being tomorrow. We won't even get close to her now.

We can't save her.

66

AURORA

They leave me alone for the rest of the day.

The only thing to break up the quiet and pain of waiting for them to decide my fate is Darius. He tries to talk to me, push into my mind. When being sweet doesn't work, he becomes an asshole. When that doesn't work, he tries sweet again until I get bored of his game and stop answering him.

I won't be his fucking entertainment.

Footsteps head my way, and I stand. My ass is numb from the cold stone, but at least the after-effects of the torture left me and I'm once again stronger. Not as strong as when I have my magic, though.

The magic at the door drops, and I brace myself to sprint, but four men pour into my cell, three with magic already formed in their hands.

Not wanting to risk it, I relax my stance.

The only man not holding magic heads my way. He shackles my hands and feet together with more of the numbing magic shit and unclips me from the wall like a bloody pet.

None of them speak as they pull me from my cell, and I find my mouth opening and shit pouring out, because hey why the hell not.

Can it really get any worse?

Yes, yes it can get worse.

Snapping my mouth shut to the happiness of the guards, I gawk at the people in the room.

They all turn as I'm dragged inside, some gasping. Some women even pretend to faint. Murmuring rises between themselves, snatches of conversation drifting to me as the guards drag me down the center aisle toward the waiting steel cage in the middle of the room.

It looks like a bloody courtroom with chairs lined up behind the cage of the crowd and a huge, curved desk sitting on a dais filled with chairs. Only four chairs are filled, with who I guess are the council members.

William sits in the center seat.

The cage locks behind me and the bars instantly turn blue with the same magic from my cell. Brilliant. I was too busy gawking to try to escape. Not that I would have made it far. There has to be over two hundred people in this room. All witches.

They look at me like I'm dirt, like I'm disgusting. It kinda knocks a girl's confidence.

Running my eyes over the crowd, I meet six familiar sets of eyes, all hard and filled with concern. Ignoring the men I once considered friends and lovers, I turn back to face the waiting council.

"I do love Judge Judy, don't get me wrong, but do I get a lawyer? I know this dude who went to law school. I mean, he practices from home now, but his mom makes amazing cookies." The words blurt from my mouth and the crowd falls silent.

I refuse to be paraded around and laughed at. They already all hate me. Why not give them something to really talk about. I hear a muted laugh, and I know it came from one of my ex-guys.

"No? Nobody here speaks? We all sit around looking ominous? Do you guys practice those facial expression in the mirror? I bet you do."

"Silence!" William glares at me.

"Sure, no problemo." I fake a salute and a stick shoves through my cage and rams into my side.

An electric current races through my body, making me drop to my knees as my teeth clash together. I stay locked like that for minutes before it passes enough for me to stand again.

I refuse to be on my knees before them.

"Well, damn boys, I didn't realize you were into the kinky shit. Give a girl a warning, though, will you?" I run my eyes over the council until I meet the cold blue ones of a woman. "I bet you love the freaky shit, am I right? Wax play and daddy complex?"

I don't finish as another current strike me.

"Hekate damn. I feel like a fucking plug socket," I moan, spitting through the cage to clear the burned taste from my mouth.

Princess, stop baiting them.

I ignore Darius's plea.

"So, what are we thinking? Burned at the stake, electric chair, fireball to the face? I got to admit, I'm not a fan of burning to death, but it does seem oddly fitting, am I right? Wait, did the humans really burn witches at the stake? I never asked."

The council stares at me, lost for words.

William finally stands, leaning over the table. "I said silence, half breed."

"Yeah, see, I struggle with that. My dad once called me a television with no off button. Perses himself even tried to mute me once, which worked because, you know, he's a god and everything."

William stares at me, flabbergasted. I bet the people usually in this cage cry and beg for their lives. "Let's talk about your parents. I shall ignore your blasphemous use of one of our gods."

"Silly me, of course you want to get to know me.

Well, let's see. I enjoy cookies and walks in the forest. I don't like guac, but I do like sour cream—mother fucking ass toad!" I yell when I get hit with the stick again. Looking at the witch who keeps poking me, I narrow my eyes. "You poke me with your little stick, which is clearly making up for your small cock, again and I will snap it in two and stick it up your ass and let you fry to death."

The witches in the crowd gasp again, screaming and shouting as I hold a staring contest with the man. He cowers back away from the cage.

"Smart man," I coo and turn back to William as he silences the crowd with one look.

"Where was I? Oh, right, family. Mother is dead. Father is an asshole who I wish was dead. By the way, you two should share torture techniques. I think he would really love to know that one with the blood boiling," I joke, and Wiliam's face turns so red I fear he might explode.

Lane would be laughing right now, feeling sorry for the man. Sadness cuts through me knowing I won't see that little smile of hers again, but I push it away.

"You should take your trial more seriously, child," the woman snaps.

"Sure thing. Do we get breaks? I'm a little hungry. Now, I'm not trying to say your hosting skills are bad but—fuck me in the face!" I shout as the stick hits me again.

Snapping my hand out, I grab the stick as he tries to pull it back through the cage, snap it over my knee, and throw both ends at his face. He screams and tries to bat them away as he falls away from the cage.

William barely spares him a glance. "Your mother, what is her full name?"

He studies some papers in front of him. Either that or he's pushing out a fart and doesn't want anyone to see.

My eyes widen as a familiar little gremlin winks at me from behind William before disappearing.

"Answer him, half breed!" another man yells, his meaty fits banging on the table.

"Uh, sorry, what was the question again? I zoned out," I tease.

"Council leader, if I may. The half breed is clearly not taking this seriously. I say we move straight to the sentencing," a young man on the left says, throwing me a narrowed eye glare.

He looks familiar, but I don't know why.

"What? Skip the foreplay and straight to the shaft? Really? No wonder you all look like you need a good shag," I laugh.

"I vote execution on terms of the creature being too volatile and uncontrollable to live. All council who agrees, say aye," William booms, ignoring me completely, but I know he heard my barb from the tightening of his eyes.

"Aye," comes a chorus of replies.

Wow, harsh.

Don't worry princess, we're coming up with a plan. Hold tight.

"I'm afraid that can't happen," a lyrical woman's voice says.

At that sound, my whole body stands on attention and love unfurls in my chest.

"And why is that?" William laughs, searching the room for the owner of the voice.

"She is important. You are not."

A woman appears before me, her face familiar from the paintings and fountain at Perses's house. My blood sings as she gives me a loving look, one similar to how a mother would look at a child, but in her, I also sense sadness and acceptance. What could upset a goddess? Why is she here? I thought Hekate was dead, but here she stands looking at me with her back to the council like they're nothing more than an annoyance.

She reaches through the cage, the magic dropping automatically for her. "I'm sorry, my child. I wish I could have helped you more, given you the world of magic and love I dreamed of. I had hoped we would have more time, but it seems I was wrong. Forgive me for that. Find the books I left you. They will help guide you on the journey. Aurora, please trust in your bonds. And, my child? Tell my father I'm sorry, that I love him, and that I finally learned what true, world-destroying love looks like."

A single tear drops from one of her eyes as she gazes at four men I never noticed before. They're blurry, like they aren't really here, and as I watch, they seem to dissolve more.

"They're too old for this world. My world kept them alive and sucked the darkness from them, but to come back meant their deaths," she explains, watching as they fade more in front of our eyes. "My loves, I will join you soon. Wait for me," she cries, and they nod.

The one on the left raises his hand, and she copies the move before they fade into nothing.

I don't know whether it's because I'm from her line or because of how close she stands, but I feel her heartbreak. Longing and regret pile through her before she looks back at me. "Love is never easy, Aurora. I made mistakes and it cost them. Even in the darkest of times, even when I believed the things I could see with my own two eyes, I was wrong. Not everything is as it seems, and those we love take the biggest risks to protect us." She leans through the bars and lays a kiss on my forehead. It burns and seems to settle into my skin. "Watch them when you're ready."

She turns once again into the goddess of the stories. Her power whips through the room, finding the unrighteous and damned. The Mother of Witches.

"You sully our gift, then try to harm the one I send

to save you?" She floats across the room, walking even as her feet don't touch the ground, still addressing the council who pale and shake before her.

I gasp when the cage opens, and I turn to see Nev and Bob side-by-side.

"Hurry up, silly witch, we don't have all day."

Nodding, I hurry from the cage. My eyes keep drawing back to her form in the middle of the council room. She's breathtaking. Through the power she wields and the beauty she holds from stories, I can still see the sadness and weary look in her eyes.

Bob takes my hand, but I can't look away from her. I hear my name being called, but I gasp as William stands before Hekate.

"We're not your worshippers any longer. We're stronger than the gods. We're free!" William flings his hand out toward her.

Black magic hits her square in the chest. She could protect herself, though. I know she could.

I'm drained from releasing you, my child. I had only so much left after the blessings, I'm sorry. It's the only way. Her voice whispers through my head, and I scream as black veins crawl along her skin.

She throws me a soft smile as she lifts both hands. Walking unhurriedly toward William, he tries to back away, but he can't move. She wraps her arms around him and sings as fire bursts from his feet and eclipses first his body, then hers.

And still her song goes on even over his screams of pain and dying.

"Aurora! Wait!" Alex's voice penetrates the haze, and I swing my head to see them fighting through the fleeing witches to reach me.

A tingle starts in the hand Bob holds, and when I look at my feet, they're disappearing.

"No, please!" Alex screams.

"Aurora!" Ezra shouts, his voice heartbroken.

Looking back at the flaming column that was Hekate and William, I fade from the room with Bob and Nev, her heartbreaking song following me into the other.

Love you my whole life. Watch over you I will. Dead or alive, here or there. I'm yours.

EPILOGUE

LANE

*E*yeing up the seedy bar I found online, I square my shoulders and channel my inner Aurora. Even her name sends a pang of pain through my chest, but I know she's okay. She has to be.

It's been two weeks since she disappeared in the middle of the night. Two weeks with no word, and I know something is wrong.

The boys' house is cleared out and hers hasn't been touched. I can't get through to any of them, and I woke up in the middle of the night two weeks ago in a cold sweat with a bad feeling forming in my chest, stopping my breathing.

No, I know something happened to my best friend, and I plan to save her. Just like she would for me. I went to Tom first, but he was as freaked as me. He told me he would put out some feelers to the 'community' and let me know.

Like I'll sit back on my ass while she's out there, probably hurt and definitely in trouble.

Flipping my hair over my shoulder, I stride toward the door of the club named 'Fangers'. I managed to get such information from someone I did a job for online. This is the third club I've hit tonight in search of supernatural.

Who knew it would be so hard to find them.

The bouncer eyes me strangely and stops me from entering by placing a pale, tattooed arm across the door. He's a big man; long black receding hair pulled away in a ponytail, muscles on muscles, and taller than the door frame itself. I guess you have to be strong for a supernatural club. I wonder what he is. Fudge, I really didn't think this through, but it's too late to back out now.

"Ya know the rules?" he rumbles.

Faking confidence I don't feel, I smile sweetly at him and pop my hip out. In my short golden, sparkly dress, mixed with my thigh-high black heels, I look killer I just need to act like it.

"Of course, sweetie," I purr, stroking down his arm.

He watches me, a strange smile on his lips, almost like he's holding them still. He jerks his head at the door without a word and steps back. Swinging my hips, I force myself inside. The door shuts with a bang, making me jump and shiver.

Directly in front of me is a set of steps. The walls are painted black and the ceiling red, but that's all there is. Okay, then. Guess down I go. I sound like that Alice chick.

Holding onto the railing, I walk down slowly, the light from the top of the stairs dimming until I have to squint.

The bottom is in near complete darkness. Blowing out a breath, I trail my fingers along the wall until I meet the wood of a door in front of me. Searching it, I find the handle and yank.

As I stumble through, my mouth drops open. It's not liked any nightclub I've been in before, that's for sure.

Large chandeliers with what looks like floating candles inside hang across the ceilings and scatter throughout the room. Hell, they probably are floating. The walls are a deep, dark red, almost the color of blood.

To the left, booths line the walls, pin-spiked cushions inviting you to take a seat. To the right, people waiting to be served at a short bar with stools. In front of me, steps lead down into the thriving dance floor as some sexy bass music plays so loud my heart races in time to it. I find myself swaying automatically but force myself to stop.

I'm not here to have fun. I'm here to find a supe.

Trying to look casual, I wander over to the bar and lean on the wood. Not a minute later, a man pops up in front of me, making me jump. Gripping my chest, I throw him a glare, and he grins.

I freeze when I spot shark-like sharp teeth, but when I blink, they're back to normal human ones.

Shaking my head, I drop my hand and give him a nervous smile.

"Whatcha having, lamb?" he calls, his voice rich and earthy.

Blond spiked hair stands up in all directions and one green and one blue eye locks on me. His hands don't stop moving from wiping the bar to grab a glass.

"Vodka, straight," I reply.

He nods, still grinning like the Cheshire cat.

Turning to the side, I stare at his ears, which poke through his hair. Are they pointy? Well, either I'm on drugs or it looks like I'm in the right place.

He pops up again not a minute later and slides a drink over to me. I sniff before taking a sip. The alcohol explodes on my tongue, making me groan.

"What is that?" I ask, an orange flavor filling my mouth now.

"Special home brand." He laughs, and I'm not sure why.

Well, no time like the present.

Keeping the drink in hand, I lean on the bar, and he

leans in closer so I don't have to scream over the music. "I'm looking for someone."

"Uh, uh. Course you are, lamb. The guys you want are in the back." He leans away.

I start to get annoyed. "Erm, I don't know what you mean. And why do you keep calling me that?"

"Like a lamb to the slaughter." He laughs and disappears down the bar before I can chew him out.

What the actual chips?

I wait for another five minutes, but he becomes busier and busier and I don't get a chance to grab him. Sighing, I take my drink and slip away from the bar, walking around the room, watching everyone.

Aurora said there are all sorts of supernaturals in this world. I wonder what's in this club. Surely there must be a witch in here somewhere.

Staying back from the fray near the edge of the dance floor, I bite my lip and sip my drink, trying to think of a way to find what I'm searching for.

Holding my drink to my chest, I search the area. I can't go around asking everyone, but I need to start with someone. I freeze when I spot two familiar men.

Aren't they the hotties I danced with when we went clubbing last? I lean closer when a hard chest blocks my gaze.

Running my eyes up it, I meet the cold blue ones of an attractive man. His short brown hair is styled in waves and his face is all perfect angles.

"Lost something?" he purrs, stepping closer until I step back.

"Maybe. Are you going to help me find it?" I ask, enthralled by his eyes. They're bright and pull me in until I can't look away.

"Oh, I plan to." He reaches out and grabs my drink, putting it down on the table next to us. "Join me."

Yes, why don't I? I'm here to have a good time after all, and he's handsome, so of course I'll join him.

I drop my hand in his and blink. Pain forms in my head. Wait, was I looking—

"Now," he demands, his voice harsher, and the thought slips away as I smile dreamily.

"Yes," I say, breathless as he walks me around the bar.

I catch the bartender's eyes. He nods and smiles knowingly. He mouths the word *lamb*, but then I'm being dragged through a black door at the back of the club that I never noticed.

My head whirrs, and I'm slammed back into a wall. The stranger kisses up my chest, laying open mouthed bites along my neck before covering my lips.

As fast as the kiss started, it ends.

"You taste divine." He grabs my hand and pulls me after him down a corridor.

Lots of doors span each side, but I don't get a chance to investigate, because he opens the last on the left and pulls me through. Shutting it behind him, I stumble into the middle of the room.

Three more men wait in here, sitting on the sofa.

A curved black sofa is right in front of me with a bed to the left, and to the right, a rack holds what looks like sex toys. My mind screams at me, and I turn to leave only to find the stranger blocking the door.

"Sit," he orders.

With a gasp, I try to fight it, but my body walks over to the sofa and sits. The men move away slightly as if to watch, and the stranger follows after me, sitting close enough for me to smell the alcohol and copper tang on his breath.

He kisses along my face again and down my neck, his tongue darting out to moisten the skin there. My body shakes even as I beg it to move, but it's like I'm locked in place; his command ringing through my head.

No.

No, I need to move.

I manage to make my fingers twitch as he reaches my chest.

Move. *Now!* I scream at myself, and with a ragged breath, I tumble from the sofa and stand on unsteady legs in the middle of the room facing them.

He leans back on the sofa, crossing one black trousered leg over the other.

"Interesting. It seems the lamb has a little fight in her." His mouth opens wide to reveal massive fangs hanging over his lower lip. I stare at him dumbly as he watches me. "I can't wait to break that and drink you dry."

This can't be happening, but it makes sense; the fangs, the smell of blood, hell, even why I find myself back here. He's a friggin' vampire. The others laugh and watch us like we're tonight's entertainment.

"I've watched all the seasons of CSI and binge-watched all How to Make a Murderer. I know how to make your death look like an accident. Vampire or not. Don't mess with me," I threaten, my hands shaking slightly as I face off with them.

For all my bravado, I scream when they move. One second, he sits on the sofa, and the next, I'm bent over. I howl as he bites me, his fangs ripping through my neck non-too gently. Warm blood trails down my neck as I start to feel dizzy. I'm losing too much blood. It even streams into my one good gold dress.

One second, I'm held in my murderer's arms, and the next, I'm grabbed and pushed behind three extremely tall and wide bodies. The room blurs around them, allowing me to make out little detail.

"The human is ours," comes a deep voice from the guy to the left.

There's an accent there I can't place.

I stumble forward, my heels and blood loss mixing until I collapse. My hand meets the back of one of the guys, and he spins to me with his fangs bared. The face of the guy I danced with the other night stares at me.

"Oh, for fuck's sake, not another vampire," I groan before falling into his arms.

A ringing fills my head, my body cold and numb. I can't seem to move. Even opening my mouth feels like too much effort.

"Fuck, he drained her. She's dying!" comes a shout, and the words register numbly.

Huh, so that's what's wrong. Fudge. Aurora's going to be so mad.

"Shit, he's right. She's cold to the touch and has lost too much blood. He must have hit an artery. I don't think even a hospital can save her now." It's the accented man speaking now as my eyes slip shut, and I start to float away.

"*Fuck!*" comes a screech and crash. "She can't fucking die. We just found her!" a different man yells.

Hopelessness and desperation fill his voice until all I want to do is wake up and comfort him, but it's so cold and dark.

I'm sorry, I whisper, hoping it leaves my lips as everything fades.

TRANSLATIONS

ύπνος, απόγονος μου - sleep, my descendant.

με βοηθήστε, απόγονος μου - help me, my descendant.

oOι μάγισσες είναι ήδη δικές σου, ο απόγονος μου - The witches are already yours, my descendant

Έτσι θα είναι, ο απόγονος μου - So it will be, my descendant

Ήρθε η ώρα, έλα σε μένα - The time has come, come to me

ABOUT THE AUTHOR

K.A Knight is an indie author trying to get all of the stories and characters out of her head. She loves reading and devours every book she can get her hands on, she also has a worrying caffeine addiction.

She leads her double life in a sleepy English town, where she spends her days at the evil day job and comes home to her fur babies and other half.